# FALLING
# FOR HER

# FALLING FOR HER

A K2 Team Novel

## Sandra Owens

Montlake
Romance

Published by Montlake Romance, Seattle

www.apub.com

Amazon, the Amazon logo, and Montlake Romance are trademarks of Amazon.com, Inc., or its affiliates.

ISBN-13: 9781503947818
ISBN-10: 1503947815

Cover design by Eileen Carey

Printed in the United States of America

*My books—now and forever—are dedicated to my husband, Jim, who supports me in every way possible. I also want to dedicate this one to all the fans of my men at K2 Special Services who have eagerly been waiting for Saint's story. Y'all rock—your e-mails, your support, and the fun times we have on social media mean so much to me. Enjoy!*

# CHAPTER ONE

Jamie Turner came to a dead stop when he spied the beautiful woman waiting for him on the other side of the security barrier. The passengers behind him grumbled as they swerved around him, their wheeled carry-ons bumping his legs.

If he were a cussing man like his teammates, he'd be muttering some very bad words about now. The flight from Somalia had been miserable, and even though he'd felt sorry for the woman sitting behind him trying to calm a crying baby, he'd resented not being able to catch up on some much-needed sleep. He'd come close to getting shot on his mission, was dead tired, and was not in the mood for Sugar Darling. No way. Nohow.

"Move it, asshole," snarled a man with a shaved head and tattoos on his arms and neck, elbowing Jamie as he passed.

Jamie, ex-SEAL and still in the business of black ops, narrowed his eyes at the back of the jerk's neck, right at the point where he could press his thumb and put the man out cold.

"Jamie! Over here."

He squeezed his eyes shut, hoping when he opened them he wouldn't see the blonde beauty currently bouncing up and down as she waved her hand in the air—that she had just been a figment of his frazzled brain. Nope. When he looked again, she was still there.

The woman had been a thorn in his side since he'd met her, and he rued the day he crossed her path. Mostly because he hadn't been able to get her out of his mind, and that was unacceptable. As she had been his teammate's neighbor at the time, he supposed meeting Sugar Darling had been inevitable. It wasn't the first time in his life he'd wished he could go back and do some things over. If he'd known Sugar was Jake's neighbor . . . what was done was done, though, and, blowing out a sigh, he headed toward her.

Tattoo Man zeroed in on her and changed direction. He stepped in front of Sugar and said something, but Jamie was too far away to hear. She shook her head and backed up. Tattoo closed the gap, crowding her. Her eyes widened, and Jamie could see the panic in them.

Granny's panties. He was going to have to intervene. As if he needed that after the week he'd had. Why was she at the airport anyway? Jake Buchanan was supposed to pick him up, not Little Miss Southern Belle.

"Hey, buddy, find someone else to annoy," Jamie said, tapping the dude on the shoulder.

"Get lost, asshole, I'm busy here." Tattoo sidestepped, putting himself between Jamie and Sugar.

Jamie saw the elbow coming at his stomach before the guy moved it an inch. He grabbed Tattoo's pinky and twisted it back, while at the same time, he locked a leg around the other man's, putting him facedown on the floor. He lowered his mouth to Tattoo's ear. "What part of *find someone else to annoy* didn't you understand?" When the man tried to pull away, Jamie pushed harder on his finger, just to the breaking point.

"The minute you let go of me, asshole, you're a dead man," Tattoo snarled, then spit on Jamie's boot.

"You really need to work on your language skills, Tattoo." They were drawing a crowd, and any minute security would show up. Jamie glanced at Sugar. "Start walking. I'll catch up with you. Now," he growled when she continued her impersonation of a wide-eyed statue.

She jumped like a startled cat and backed away a few steps before turning and running toward the exit. At the sound of an authoritative voice ordering people out of the way, Jamie bent Tattoo's finger just enough to cause the man to hiss air out of his lungs. It would take him a few seconds to get his breath back, giving Jamie enough time to slip through the crowd.

While Jamie tuned his ears to the noise behind him, his eyes scanned the people walking ahead until he found his target, a man the size of a bruising linebacker. As the sound of running feet grew louder, more than one airport security guard's voice joined in the shouting.

Timing was everything in an operation, something Jamie was very good at. Just as he sensed the air behind him change, he stepped in front of his target.

"What the hell?" Linebacker grunted when Tattoo tackled him. Jamie's last sight of the two as he slipped away was that of a wrestling match with three guards trying to pull them off each other. Setting up the diversion had been the easy part.

Standing outside the door, waiting for him, was Sugar Darling. Trouble with a capital T. "Where's Buchanan?" he said in greeting.

"Hi, Saint," she responded, somehow managing to infuse her Charleston accent into two short words.

"That wasn't the right answer." He sighed for emphasis.

She gazed up at him the way a thirteen-year-old would eye Justin Bieber. "What you did back there was so freakin' amazing."

He really wished she wouldn't eyeball him as if she'd like to devour him. "Where. Is. Buchanan?"

"Oh, the boss wanted him to do something. I'm not sure what." *The boss?* "What boss?"

"Mr. Kincaid, silly. We gonna stand here all morning, or are ya ready to go? The boss said to bring you straight to K2."

And he'd thought the day couldn't get worse. "Lead on, Macduff."

"Who's Macduff?"

"A character from . . . Never mind, it's not important." As he followed Sugar to her car, he tried to keep his gaze off her bottom, but his eyes refused to cooperate. It would help if the black jeans she wore didn't appear to be painted on.

She stopped at an orange, older model Ford Focus and unlocked the door. Jamie eyed it with misgiving. "I don't think there's any way I'm going to fit in there." Slipping off his backpack, he tossed it on the backseat, then scrunched himself inside the thing.

The problem revealed itself as soon as Sugar Darling slid behind the wheel. Their proximity was entirely too close. Her arm brushed his, and he couldn't help noticing the warm softness of her skin. When he caught himself leaning toward her, inhaling her scent, something that reminded him of summer and beaches, he jerked away, smashing his right side against the door.

"Blue butter," he muttered.

She laughed, low and kind of sexy sounding. "Sometimes you say the funniest things."

When he'd decided to turn his life around at the age of twenty, he'd quit drinking, doing drugs, cursing, and sleeping with women at every opportunity. Strangely, the cussing had been the hardest habit to break, and he'd taken to substituting stupid words. After a while, it had become a game, the sillier the words, the better. He wasn't about to share all that with Sugar Darling, however.

And who named their child Sugar Darling anyway? It was a stupid name. When he'd first met her, he'd laughed and said her name couldn't be real. She'd sworn it was, offering to show him her birth certificate.

"Why do ya do that?"

"Do what?" Couldn't she just chauffeur him and not talk? Although he did like to listen to her. Her southern accent made him think of warm summer days, sweet iced tea, and porch swings. Of a time when he hadn't carried pain around in his heart that felt like a two-ton boulder had taken up residence.

"Say things like *blue butter*."

"It's a game, that's all."

"No shit. What's the rules?"

Jamie angled his head just enough to look at her without seeming to. As much as it irritated him to admit it, she was one of the most beautiful women he'd ever seen. Hair the color of golden honey, eyes that were sometimes blue and sometimes violet—depending on the color of her clothes—and a peaches-and-cream complexion. That she even had him thinking in terms of peaches and cream annoyed him. Then there was her knockout body . . . he shut that thought down.

All that was true, as was the fact she drank like a fish, cussed like a sailor, and was just too cheerful. No one could be that happy all the time.

"So why are you running errands for Kincaid?" If she said the boss had hired her, he was job hunting, starting tomorrow.

"The boss hired me."

Terrible turtles, he was going to really miss his job. It also occurred to him that he only "Saint cursed"—as the team called it—that much when he was around her. She grinned, her eyes sparkling in amusement as if she knew what he was thinking. It was disturbing.

"It's just temporary until Barbie returns from vacation."

"Good," Jamie grunted. He could surely handle two weeks. Maybe. "I thought you had a job." She was the bookkeeper, or had been, at the Booby Palace, a popular strip joint. Another strike against her, although he supposed it was only fair to give her points for not actually stripping.

"Oh, I still do, but I had paid vacation time coming. Killed two birds with one rock."

"Stone."

"Huh?"

Today her eyes were violet. Even angry, he was noticing how pretty they were. He gritted his teeth. "The word is *stone*, not *rock*. Killed two birds with one stone."

She shrugged. "Don't really see the difference. Anyway, it gave me a chance to do Mr. Kincaid a favor and make some extra money at the same time."

"Watch out!" He grabbed the wheel and jerked them back into their lane seconds before she would have sideswiped another car. Muttering monkeys, the girl was a walking time bomb. "Keep your eyes on the road, not me. And slow down. You're ten miles over the speed limit."

Heat crept up Sugar's neck, and she was sure her cheeks were flaming bright red. That was the trouble with a fair complexion, there was no hiding one's embarrassment. It was too bad she was fascinated by the blue-eyed devil sitting next to her. Although she didn't understand why, he'd taken an instant dislike to her the moment they met.

The way Jamie had tackled that man to the ground . . . just, wow. It had been like having an honest-to-God hero champion her. The tattooed guy had scared her, the look in his eyes one she knew too well. It said he had a right to her, and he would do with her as he pleased. For a moment, she'd forgotten she was Sugar Darling and not that other woman, the one she had banished. It had been the gleam of possession in the man's eyes—one that was way too familiar—that had frozen her in place. Then Jamie had been there, telling her to go. So she did what she knew how to do best: run.

Jamie made her nervous as hell, and around him, she found herself acting like a brainless twit one minute and a perky cheerleader the next. Not that she'd ever been a cheerleader or even been friends with one to know how they behaved. Girls from the wrong side of Charleston's Calhoun Street didn't stand a chance of landing a spot on the squad.

The thing of it was: she knew perfectly well who Macduff was and that birds were killed with stones. For some strange reason, she took perverse pleasure in fostering his misimpression of her. Plus, it helped her deal with the fluttery nerves that always appeared when he was within smelling range. And oh mama, did he ever smell good. If she started drooling, it would be entirely his fault.

Sadly, Mr. High and Mighty couldn't see past her act to the real woman. She had an IQ of over a hundred and forty, and someday, when she was free of bad cop and bad cop, she would get her MBA.

"So there."

"You say something?"

Had she spoken aloud? "Nope, not a thing." Sugar kept her eyes on the road. Wouldn't want to upset the touchy man by so much as glancing at him. She could feel him looking at her, though, and she stiffened her neck to keep from turning her face the slightest degree toward him. Her driving skills were questionable as it was, and having him in her car sent them to the wrong side of poor.

"Why do you work there?" He tried to stretch his legs, grunting when his kneecaps got stuck under the dash.

Although she knew where he meant, she continued her dopey-girl impersonation. "I told you, I'm just doing a favor and filling in for Barbie." A very male sigh filled her little car, and she swallowed a grin. He really was fun to aggravate.

"No, why do you work at the Booby Palace?"

Because it was an excellent place to hide out while making a living.

"Why not? They pay me decent money, and the drinks are free." That last bit should put a scowl on Saint's face, and she couldn't stop a smirk when out of the corner of her eye, she caught the downward turn of that beautiful mouth of his.

He squirmed in his seat as he tried to maneuver his long legs into a more comfortable position. The boss had offered one of the company cars for this little errand, but she'd declined. Her dang luck, she'd take down a fire hydrant or a telephone pole driving one of those big things. She'd bought the little orange car because not only was it cheap, but she figured the less automobile she had to work with, the easier to keep it out of places it shouldn't be.

For someone who could calculate in her head the fuel mileage a race car used on any given track, she'd yet to grasp the art of driving. Of course, only having limited experience behind the wheel of a car could have something to do with her lack of skill. Another thing she blamed on Rodney. Not allowing her to learn to drive was just another way to keep her under his thumb. After landing in Pensacola, she'd depended on buses or cabs to get her to places she needed to be. After over a year of public transportation, she'd tired of it, and had bought the little Ford the previous month and taught herself to drive. Sorta.

"You do know this isn't a real car," he grumbled, his knees now pressed hard against the glove compartment door.

"Magic mushrooms, but you're a grouch today," she said, forgetting she was supposed to keep her gaze pointed straight ahead, and laughing when he narrowed his eyes. She wasn't sure what the word game was or the rules, but she'd puzzle it out eventually.

"Stop sign!" he yelled, scaring the shit out of her.

Miraculously, she managed to get them back to K2 all in one piece. "You're welcome," she called to his retreating back just before he disappeared into the building. The only thing he'd said after she narrowly missed not only the sign itself but also the oncoming beer truck was, "I've come to the conclusion, Ms. Darling, that you are more dangerous than an enemy sniper."

"Well, on the bright side, there mighta been free beer," she'd quipped, as a nervous giggle spilled out of her. She hoped he hadn't noticed the quiver in her voice or how white her knuckles were as they held a death grip on the steering wheel. She was sorta used to tense moments when she was behind the wheel, but that had terrified even her.

He had actually growled at her flip remark. Funny, she'd been excited when the boss had asked her to pick up Saint, but now she wished Jake Buchanan had been available to do it as originally planned. Instead of moving down on Jamie's scale of *how much I dislike Sugar Darling*, she figured she'd just blown the top off.

Not only had he ended up having to deal with the creep at the airport, but she'd almost sent Saint to heaven via a beer truck. Maybe it was time to accept he'd never like her. Sighing, she locked her car and returned to the receptionist's desk.

K2 Special Services rarely had visitors—it was not the kind of place anyone living in Pensacola even knew existed—and the only thing she had to do for the next two weeks was answer the phones. At least they rang constantly, keeping her busy. The scenery was a definite plus if one liked big, hot, alpha dudes, all ex-SEALs. She wouldn't have thought she would, considering why she was in hiding, but they made her feel safe.

They were mum on just what they did, but she had answered calls from phone numbers with a DC area code, most of them asking for the boss. Not being as dumb as a *certain* person believed, she'd put two and two together and concluded K2 had government ties of the sort one didn't talk about.

Although she wasn't totally bored, her job at the Booby Palace was more interesting. Numbers were her thing, and she'd reached a point with her employer where he trusted her, giving her complete control of all the Palace's finances and payroll.

Admittedly, the work environment left a lot to be desired, and she never ventured out of her office once the Palace opened for business. As for the free drinks she'd boasted of, that was true if she wanted them. But one, she didn't drink on the job, and two, she wasn't about to hang out at Booby's bar in her off hours.

What she'd really like would be a permanent position at K2, and she hoped if she did a good job answering the phones and anything else they asked her to do, they might offer her such a position. Maria Buchanan, the boss's sister and Jake's wife, had mentioned several weeks ago that she was planning to hire an accounting manager. When the opportunity to cover for their receptionist for two weeks had arisen, Sugar immediately volunteered.

Maybe, just maybe, something would come of it and she could work someplace where every time she went to the bathroom, she didn't have to see titties or listen to the girls bitch about some dude not slipping enough dollar bills into their G-strings.

The really big plus—and it was a biggie—if she worked at K2: she'd be surrounded by a bunch of badass former SEALs should Rodney Vanders finally track her down.

# CHAPTER TWO

Saint dropped heavily onto the chair across from Logan Kincaid's desk. "That woman's a menace to society."

The boss sat back, flipping a pen through his fingers. "Who? Sugar?"

"Who else? I had to discourage one of her admirers at the airport, and in thanks, she almost plowed us right through the middle of a beer truck. Instead of apologizing about scaring the beanie weenies out of me, her only comment was that we might've gotten free beer."

The boss rarely smiled unless he was with his wife, but there was a wide grin on his face. In his current mood, Jamie longed to wipe it off. The grin morphed into laughter.

Jamie fast-tapped his fingers against the arm of the chair. "I'd really like to smash my fist into your face about now. It's not funny."

"Actually, it is. I've never seen a woman twist your boxers into a knot like that one does. Fess up. She fascinates you."

"No. She. Doesn't." And even if she did, he'd never admit it. But she didn't. No way. Nohow.

"Methinks someone protests too much." Kincaid pushed a button that closed the door to his office. "Let's get down to business. Fill me in on the details you couldn't put in your message."

Jamie pulled his sunglasses from his pocket as Kincaid took a miniature screwdriver from his desk drawer and handed it over. After removing the screws, Jamie slipped out a thin tube from the left temple and gave it to the boss, knowing it would soon be on its way to the CIA. What was on the microfilm, he didn't know and didn't care.

"It got dicey," he said. "Our contact apparently had trouble keeping his mouth shut and bragged to the wrong people that he was about to come into some money. They got suspicious and put a tail on him." He'd followed the Somalian government official for two days prior to their scheduled meet, discovering that the man's tongue got loose when he drank.

"After I realized he was being followed, I had to make a few changes to the plan," Jamie continued. "I got away with the film and a bullet whizzing past my ear. Our friend wasn't so lucky."

The boss shrugged. "If he'd kept his mouth shut, he'd still be alive with some money in his pocket. Good job, Saint. Go home and get some rest. Take tomorrow off."

That worked for him. One less day he'd have to see the woman out to kill him. He stopped at the door. "Don't ever send Sugar Darling to pick me up again. I stand a better chance of surviving in a river swarming with crocodiles."

"Don't be so hard on the woman. She's pretty nice once you get to know her."

"I never said she wasn't nice. She's just ditzy and a menace behind the wheel of that clown car of hers." She did have a great bottom and pretty eyes though.

"Maria said she's smart. Said she gave Sugar some . . . I don't remember exactly what, some accounting stuff to do and she whipped right through it."

"Just keep her away from me," Jamie tossed over his shoulder before heading for Maria's office. Time to do a little reconnoitering to make sure Kincaid's sister had no plans to continue Ms. Darling's time at K2. After getting Maria's assurance that Sugar was only there until Barbie returned to the receptionist desk, he headed home.

Jamie dropped his duffel bag on his bed, stripped, and then took his first shower in a week where there was enough hot water to last until he finished. He loved his job, was good at it, and took the hardships in stride when he was in a third-world country. More times than not though, there was never enough hot water in the places he stayed. If he was even lucky enough to have heated water. As he was something of a clean freak, he considered that his biggest sacrifice.

Following tradition, this being his first shower at home after a mission, he took twice as long as usual. Sometimes, two were necessary before he felt clean again. With a towel wrapped around his waist, he returned to his bedroom and flipped on the TV. His stomach growled, and he debated running to the grocery store, but decided to put it off until the next day and order pizza instead.

He picked up his phone and scrolled through his contacts for the delivery number. Just as he started to press Call, a commercial came on. With his finger frozen over the keypad, he watched a beer truck race down a road, past impossible obstacles, then up a bridge rising for a sailboat. The truck reached the top and flew through the air, landing on the other side, continuing on its way.

"Sugar Darling's probably driving the flipping truck," he muttered, turning off the TV before the end of the commercial.

An image of her turning those violet-blue eyes on him when she'd almost killed them flashed into his mind. She'd looked up at him and laughed. At the time, he'd wanted to yell at her for being so stupid, then laughing about it. With his heart back to its normal beats, he realized it had been dread he'd seen in her eyes, and apprehension had tinged her laughter.

Had she been afraid of his reaction? Maybe he should have been a little more understanding. It wasn't like she'd tried to take out a beer truck on purpose, but there was just something about the woman that brought out the worst in him—the parts of him he'd long ago left behind.

Why she called to the man he used to be was a puzzle he had no intention of solving, and because it irritated him to no end, he fought the attraction by doing his best to ignore her. He had spent too many years burying that man to allow a violet-eyed ditz to undo all his hard work.

"Pepper pie," he muttered. He'd just spent five minutes staring into space, thinking of Sugar Darling and her beautiful eyes. Scrolling past the pizza delivery number, he stopped on Jill's and dialed. Looked like he'd be going out to eat after all. Jill would take his mind off the very dangerous—to him, anyway—Ms. Darling.

Completing his call, he dressed for dinner. That was what he liked about Jill. She never asked for anything, but was always glad to hear from him and happy to see him on his terms. So Jill was a little boring. So was he. Perfect match.

Jamie smiled and tried to pretend interest as Jill told him about the couple who couldn't make up their minds about which house to buy. He blamed Ms. Darling for wondering why Jill's eyes didn't sparkle with excitement when talking about her day. Come to think of it, Jill rarely showed enthusiasm over anything, even a multimillion-dollar sale.

Although attractive, she was the kind of woman who would be lost in a crowd, one he would walk past on the street and not notice. The kind of woman he preferred these days, the kind that didn't appeal to the old Jamie. Brown eyed, short brown hair, and lips a little on the thin side, not at all like Sugar's lush mouth. Pickled pipers, he had to stop comparing Jill to a violet-eyed witch with lips made for kissing.

He'd been dating Jill for three months, and it was time to decide whether or not to move the relationship further than dinner dates and phone conversations. Would she meet his criteria for a wife? Would she not awaken the wildness in him in the bedroom? Would she be the perfect wife, like his mother had been?

The reel of an old movie, *The Stepford Wives*, suddenly flashed across his eyes. He glared at the glass of water on the table in front of him, willing his mind back to the peaceful existence it had lived in before a woman with a very fine bottom had almost split a beer truck in two.

From the time he'd made himself over, he had searched for a woman to love the way his dad had loved his mom as a way to honor their memory. Although he'd come close once or twice, in the end, it just hadn't happened. Since the wreck, he'd become good at soul-searching and understood he still hadn't buried the man deep enough who thrived on living on the edge.

His choice of a job helped. Facing danger replaced the craving for a woman who pushed him to his limits. Or so he had thought until Sugar. She was exactly what the old him would have moved mountains to possess. Unless he missed his guess, she'd be up for anything once he got her in his bed.

Not that she would end up in his bed.

Just thinking of her aroused him. As hard as the wood of his chair, he shifted, trying to find more room in his pants. He was not that man anymore. He'd clamped down on his urges so hard that sex, when he did have it, was . . . well, forgettable.

*Damn you, Sugar.*

Turkey feathers—he'd just thought his first curse word in years. Why couldn't Jill have eyes the color of flowers? Why couldn't she have been the one to set his blood on fire with the fluttering of long, dark eyelashes?

*Did you notice, Saint? Eyelashes a different color from her hair.*

Was her honey-blonde hair fake then? If true, the revelation pleased him. If he could find enough things about her that weren't real, he could put her out of his mind.

He dragged his attention back to Jill when he realized she'd asked a question and he had no idea what. "Sorry. Did you ask me something?"

A slight frown creased her face. "Do you want to see *The Picture of Dorian Gray* with me tomorrow? I don't have any house show- ings in the afternoon or evening, and you said you'd like to see it."

"Sure." Not really. He was tired and hated film noir, liked his movies in full Technicolor, preferably heavy on the action. But he'd promised he would take her when he returned from his business trip. She didn't know what he did; she thought he was an analyst who helped struggling companies.

"If you don't want to go, I under—"

"No, I do. What time do I need to pick you up?" He blanked his face when she studied him, wishing she wasn't always so understand- ing. The irony didn't escape him that part of the reason he still con- tinued the relationship was because she didn't push him. She was safe.

"They're showing it at four, seven, and ten. Whatever time works best for you."

"I'm off tomorrow, so we'll catch the first one. I'll pick you up at three fifteen. I need to stop by the office on the way, if you don't mind."

After leaving K2 at the end of the day, Sugar scarfed down a ham- burger she'd ordered at the drive-thru, then hurried into the Booby Palace. If she could make it to the back office without Kyle seeing her, she'd consider it a good day.

"Hey, Sugar . . . *darling*."

Shit. No such luck. Why did he always seem to think it amusing to turn her last name into an endearment? She pivoted, fixing him with a get-away-from-me stare. "Shouldn't you be behind the bar? It looks busy out there."

Tall, with green eyes and black hair, he was a handsome man, but the way he'd watched her from the first day they met gave her the shivers. And not good ones. If she'd had a crystal ball and seen him in it, she would have picked a different name for herself. Something like Hortense Ratman. See what he could make of that one.

"Ah, darling," he drawled, dramatically clutching his heart. "Why won't you admit you want me and stop playing hard to get?"

The man scared her. Something shimmered in his eyes that just creeped her out. She'd tried to politely rebuke him, but that hadn't worked so maybe it was time to change tactics.

"You seem like a decent enough guy, but I'm seeing someone so here's the bottom line. I don't want you, Kyle, and I'm not playing hard to get. Good-bye." She turned to head for her office. A hand wrapped around her arm, fingers digging into her skin.

"You think you're too good for me? Well, I got news for you, Sugar. I *will* have you."

She jerked away, practically running to her office and slamming the door. Oh God, she had to get out of this place. Why did men look at her and see something they wanted to possess, no matter what she wanted? What was it about her that put a gleam in their eyes, reminding her of the way Rodney's gaze lingered on the parts of her she really, really wished he'd never noticed? Every time she'd been forced to sit with him in her father's living room, his gaze had roamed over her as if she already belonged to him.

Maybe that was why Jamie was the first man in her twenty-five years to spark her interest. He didn't want any part of her, and for some damn reason, she felt safe with him. There was more to it, though. When he'd been in her little car, so close she could feel his body heat, his arm had brushed hers, and something new had taken possession of her body. She had wanted him to kiss her, wanted to know if it could be different. That in itself was something she'd never thought to want from any man. Not after having Rodney Vanders's lips and hands on her.

*No thinking about Rodney. He's in your past and will never find you.* Although she didn't doubt he was searching for her with her father's help. She'd hidden her tracks as well as she knew how, and now all she could do was pray nothing showed up anywhere to give her away. When two cops were looking for you though . . .

No, she wouldn't even think it. So what if they had access to resources most others didn't? It wasn't like they were big-city cops, trained to find their quarry without doing much more than clicking on the Internet. Her father barely knew how to turn on a computer and Rodney, although more proficient, was no technical genius.

Sweat drenched the back of her neck at the thought of Rodney getting his hands on her again. Sometimes she could go days without thinking of him, then something would trigger the memories. It was usually when a man looked at her in a way that reminded her of the bastard.

Yet, the guys at K2 Special Services were different. Not only did she feel safe around them, but not one of them had leered at her in a way that creeped her out. One, Brad Stewart, flirted with her sometimes, and she thought if she gave him encouragement he would ask her out. He had honest eyes, though, and didn't scare her. Although he was cute, there'd been no chemistry, for her anyway.

No, she had to be attracted to a golden-haired hottie who couldn't stand the sight of her.

# CHAPTER THREE

Sugar glanced up from the Excel spreadsheet when K2's front door opened. A woman she'd never seen before walked in, followed closely by Jamie, his hand resting possessively on her lower back.

Sugar's heart did a stuttering dance in her chest, and it hurt. At the pain, she idly wondered if she was having a heart attack. Resisting the urge to press her hand over the ache, she mustered a smile. It should have occurred to her a man as hot as Saint had a girlfriend.

"Hello." That sounded cheerful enough, right?

The woman glanced at her, then turned her attention to the K2 lobby, scrutinizing it as if she was assessing it. Kind of weird, really, the way her gaze lit on each item as if calculating the value. Definitely not the type she'd ever have connected with Jamie.

"Wait here, love," he said, leading her to the leather sofa.

Sugar knew right away he'd never called her *love* before by the way the woman startled. What was going on? She slid her eyes to Jamie to see he was watching her. Was he waiting for her reaction? If so, she wouldn't disappoint.

She gave her perky cheerleader smile, the one she'd watched the popular girls give, and walked from behind the desk. "Welcome to K2, Miss . . . ?"

"Jill," Jamie said. "This is Jill. See that she's happy."

With that, he strode to the inner door, punched in his code, and put his thumb on the pad. The door slid open and he disappeared inside. All righty, then.

"Ya heard him," Sugar said, drawing out her southern accent. "What can I do to make you happy? Coffee? Tea? A back rub, maybe?" She probably shouldn't have said that.

"What is this place?" the must-be-made-happy Jill asked.

If Jamie hadn't shared K2's purpose, she wasn't about to, but it pleased her that Jill was clueless about what he did. "Honestly, I don't know. I'm only filling in for their regular receptionist for a few days." Apparently, the devil was at work, because she added, "My regular job's at the Booby Palace." Languid brown eyes looked her up and down, giving Sugar the impression she was found lacking. Go figure.

"Why am I not surprised? Jamie's taking me to see a black-and-white movie, a film noir."

So the gloves were off. Was that supposed to put her in her place? Was she supposed to ask what a film noir was as if she were some backwoods, ignorant idiot? And why was she supposed to care, anyway? "No kidding? Bet he's looking forward to that. You seem a little tense. Would ya like me to make you a cup of soothing tea, a ginseng or chamomile perhaps?"

"No thank you," the apparently-not-happy Jill said.

Well, she'd tried. What did Jamie see in her? In a million years, she'd never have put him with Jill. The woman was just too . . . beige. With her brown eyes and hair, she really should opt for colors in her clothing other than, well, brown. It wasn't her problem though, was it? When she heard the door behind her open, she grabbed the phone and pretended there was someone on the other end. At the last second, as Jamie escorted Beige Jill out, he glanced over his shoulder, their gazes colliding.

"Y'all have a great time," she called after them.

When he disappeared from view, Sugar exhaled, the air rushing out of her lungs. What had just happened? Some kind of strange spark had seemed to travel on a direct line from him to her, stealing her breath. She rubbed the goose bumps on her arms and tried to decipher exactly what she'd seen in his eyes when he'd looked at her. It hadn't been his usual dismissive expression, but something similar to what she'd seen in her cat's eyes when stalking a bug—intense focus and want.

But he didn't want her. He'd made that very clear. Shaking off her ridiculous notions, she gathered the billing statements she'd printed out from the spreadsheet and took them to Maria's office.

"I'm done with these," she said, standing in the doorway.

"Come on in." Maria rotated her shoulders, then sighed. "I could use a break."

Sugar pulled a chair over to the side of the desk. "Jamie's girlfriend seems nice." Well, hell, why'd she say that?

Maria's eyes lit with interest. "You met her? When? He's never brought this one around."

This one? How many were there? "Just now. He brought her here, parked her in the lobby with me. Guess he needed to see the boss or somethin'. They're on their way to the movies."

"What was she like?"

The conversation was turning a little uncomfortable. For some reason, she didn't want to talk about Jamie behind his back. "Like I said, nice. Kinda bland though."

"Hmm. Aren't they all?"

What did that mean? "Are you saying he has more than one girlfriend, and they're all bland?"

Maria shrugged. "Seems that way, although he only sees one at a time and never for more than four or five months."

Sugar wanted to ask more questions, but she was still uneasy talking about him. She handed Maria the statements. "I think you should take a look at two of these before they're mailed. Based on the work y'all did for them, I think the billing hours aren't enough." She handed over the two statements in question, watching as Maria pulled up the spreadsheet on her computer, narrowing her eyes as she scanned it.

"You're right. Good catch."

"Thanks." The praise warmed her and gave her hope that maybe Maria would consider her for the accounting manager's position.

After printing corrected statements, Maria handed them to Sugar. "My time's spread so thin, sometimes I get in too much of a hurry. I'm good at the financial side of the business, but my love is the law. As soon as I can get everything organized enough to bring in someone to take over this part, that's where I'll put my efforts."

Interesting. "In what way?"

Maria stood and went to a small refrigerator in the corner of her office. "Water? Or if you'd prefer, I have sodas."

"You got a root beer?"

"I do. Saint drinks them, so I keep them on hand."

They liked the same soft drink? Not that it meant anything, but at least they had one thing in common. She took the offered soda and sat back, listening to Maria's future plans for K2. Her friend must trust her if she was willing to share the information.

They'd met six months ago when Maria had come to Jake's condo, looking for him. To Maria's disappointment, Sugar hadn't known the whereabouts of her next-door neighbor. Nor did she know the full story on what had been going on between the two of them then, but the second time Maria came by, she'd had Saint with her. Having fully embraced her persona as Sugar Darling by then, she'd acted the quirky, flirty role she'd adopted for herself. The kind of woman Rodney would never think to look for.

Unfortunately, Jamie took an instant dislike to her, and his opinion hadn't changed in the times she'd been around him since. For a while, she'd thought maybe Maria was playing matchmaker, inviting her to cookouts and lunches where Jamie was present. Nothing had come of it, and if her friend once had intentions in that regard, she'd apparently given up.

Maria pulled out the bottom drawer and propped her feet on it. "Our plan is to branch out by offering consulting for corporations wishing to do business in foreign countries. We can ease their way by taking care of all the legalities. That's my specialty, international law."

Sugar didn't know what all K2 did. There was a lot of secret stuff going on, and unless she missed her guess, some of it involved dangerous missions. She was pretty sure Jamie had just returned from one. Hannah would have feared being anywhere near the place, but Hannah was dead. Sugar, on the other hand, thought it beyond exciting.

Although she'd planned to wait a few more days to bring up the subject, it seemed an opportune time to express her interest in the accounting manager's job.

Furtively crossing her fingers, she made a little wish as she took a deep breath. "If you're taking names, I'd like to throw mine in the hat."

Maria raised a brow, then picked up a band from the top of her desk. She swept her long, black hair back and deftly wrapped the band around the ponytail. Was she stalling for time to figure out how to say no? Sugar pressed her lips together to keep from jabbering on, which she would do if she tried to talk. To her ears, her heart sounded as loud as a jackhammer busy tearing up asphalt.

"You've certainly impressed me, Sugar, but I think the position requires someone with an accounting degree and experience in managing a company's finances."

"Both of which I have." During the days while Rodney was at work, she had secretly taken online classes from the University of Alabama, earning her bachelor's degree.

Not wanting to draw unwelcome attention to herself, she never shared details of her life. She'd never implied to anyone she did anything more than work as an accounting clerk for the Booby Palace. Her love of numbers was one of only two things she hadn't been able to bear giving up. The other, her eye color, was unique enough that people noticed it. Both of which her father and Rodney could use to eventually find her if they exercised what few brains they had.

The job at K2 would be higher profile, but she'd weighed the risks and decided being surrounded by a gang of badass ex-SEALs tipped the scale. Proof of how badly she wanted to get away from the Booby Palace.

It was time to take the plunge. "I have a Bachelor's of Accounting degree and plan to get an MBA. At the Booby Palace, I have full control of all their finances and payroll. I've worked there for almost two years, and my boss, the owner, has even turned over his personal investments to me. He won't be happy to lose me, but . . . but I hate working there, Maria."

"Why?"

Damn. She hadn't meant to say that last part. Maria might be a friend of sorts, but this was a job interview, and she shouldn't be saying she hated the place she worked. The door had been opened, however, so she trudged on.

"There's a guy, the bartender, and he creeps me out. He doesn't seem to want to take no for an answer. I just think it's time to move on."

"Would you like my brother to have a word with him?"

Oh, wow and holy mother moly. Maria's brother was scary as hell. Kyle would probably crap in his pants if Logan Kincaid cornered him. What if it turned into a fight and someone called the police? The last thing she needed was that kind of attention.

"Ah . . . although tempting, it's probably better if I just find a new job."

Maria stared at her long enough for Sugar to want to fidget.

"What aren't you telling me?"

*My life story.* "I'm not sure what you mean. If you don't think I'm qualified, I understand but reserve the right to disagree."

"You're hired."

What? What? "Pardon?"

Her friend smiled. "You have secrets, but don't we all? I know I do. Maybe someday I'll tell you mine. The job is yours if you want it after we talk salary and benefits."

It was a close call, but Sugar managed to resist slobber-kissing the hand Maria placed over hers. "Okay, so I make thirty-five thousand a year at the Booby Palace. I think I'm worth more than that."

"Have I ever told you how much I like you, Sugar? I know I asked you when we first met, but is that really your name?"

"No and no." Well, hell. Might be a good idea to slap some duct tape over her mouth. Much to her surprise, Sugar found herself telling Maria about Hannah Faith Conley. Not everything, but enough to explain why she'd changed her name.

Hannah crept out of the bed with practiced stealth. If the sleeping man caught her, there would be a punishment, but she couldn't bear to spend another second next to him. That had been happening more and more lately, her repulsion toward him causing her to take such a risk. It wasn't her; not really. She didn't have the courage to defy him. A stranger had taken up residence in her head, one who seemed to take control of Hannah's body and make her do things that she was too scared to do on her own.

She curled up in a dark corner of the room, and watched the man sleep. *You have to escape before he kills you,* the woman's voice said in her mind. "I don't know how," she whispered. Where would she go? How would she live? Those questions worried her, but the most frightening question of all; if she did run, what if he found her?

But God, she wanted to get away. She winced when she moved her legs, the pain in her groin worse than ever. Something was changing in him. He'd always liked hurting her, but if the new games he played went on much longer, she would end up damaged beyond repair. He was too mean and too powerful to fight; against him she had no chance.

*You have to run.* Yes, the voice was right. It was the only way unless she wanted to end up dead. She shifted, trying to get comfortable on the carpeted floor. Pain shot up into her stomach and down both legs. A moan escaped, and she slapped a hand over her mouth.

The bedside light snapped on, and she froze.

"What the hell are you doing on the floor, girl?"

There was no explanation that would satisfy him, so she stayed mute as he rose from the bed. From her position looking up at him, he seemed ten feet tall. A monster, a thing of nightmares, walked toward her. The eyes he had locked on her promised a punishment, one he would thoroughly enjoy.

"You have to run!" Sugar yelled at the girl cowering in a dark corner. In her desperation to get away from the monster, Sugar ended up on the floor next to her bed.

Gulping in huge breaths of air, she frantically searched the room. As she'd not been able to sleep in the dark since escaping, every outlet had a night-light plugged into it. She was in the bedroom of her condo, not in Rodney's house. He wasn't in her room.

Her cat perched on the edge of the bed and peered down at her. "Oh God, Junior, I was so scared." She hadn't had a nightmare in months, so why now? Perhaps sharing some of her secrets with Maria had brought it on.

"He's not here," she whispered, and reached up to pet Junior, needing to touch his warm, soft body. He purred his pleasure.

Normally, she didn't take a nap between her two jobs, but the long hours had caught up with her, and she'd thought to catch a few hours of sleep before having to leave for the Booby Palace. It was the last time she would do that no matter how tired she was.

"Time to get ready to go to work, sweetie," she said, giving her cat one last rub.

Bored, Jamie fell asleep halfway through the movie. Dorian Gray's eyes turned a violet-blue color, his face morphing into Sugar Darling's. She was running away from the cab of a beer truck as Jamie yelled at her to stop. Angry that she ignored him, he took off after her. Did the confounded woman think she could just leave the truck in the middle of the hotel lobby for the Somalian rebels to find? Did she not realize they would guzzle all the beer, and then the idiots would be so drunk he'd never get the information he needed?

He tried to catch her but she crossed a shimmering red line, dropping out of sight in a wasteland. When he reached the place she had disappeared, the only thing she'd left behind was her ugly orange car. He stared at the clown car, rage building that she'd escaped his grasp. "Dang it, Sugar!" He would find her and when he did . . .

"Jamie! What's wrong with you?"

Someone was shaking him. Her voice didn't have a southern accent, and he didn't want to listen. He needed to find Sugar.

"Jamie. Stop yelling. You're embarrassing me."

He jerked up, disoriented. A quick glance around brought him to his senses. Murky mermaids; he was in a theater, not in the middle of a wasteland in some Godforsaken, barren country.

"You were calling her name," Jill whispered.

"Whose?" he asked, although he knew. It occurred to him that if it had been Sugar sitting next to him when he called out another woman's name in his sleep, she'd probably bash him on the head and not be whispering.

*Bash me on the head, Jill. Show you care that much.*

"I would like to go home," she said, still whispering.

It appeared his plan to carry their relationship to the next level was off. That should probably disappoint him. It didn't. "I'm sorry," he said, and from her expression, he knew she understood he was apologizing for more than talking in his sleep.

When he walked her up to her door, he said it again. "I'm sorry."

"Me, too," she answered before disappearing into her house, the door lock clicking behind her.

Jamie stood on Jill's steps and examined how he felt knowing he'd never see her again. Nothing. It appeared Jill wasn't *the one.* He'd known she wasn't for a while; he just hadn't wanted to admit it. Not at all happy, he returned to his car. Halfway home—a place he really didn't want to go at the moment—he called Jake Buchanan.

"Up for company?" he asked when his friend answered the phone.

"Well," Jake drawled, "I was about to ravish my wife, but I suppose that can wait. See you soon."

A dial tone sounded and Jamie clicked off. The boss, Logan Kincaid—once his SEAL commander—and Jake Buchanan, a former

SEAL teammate, were now married and by all accounts deliriously happy. Jamie tried not to envy them, but ever since he'd lost his parents, he'd wanted a wife to love, and a family. Kids, white picket fence, the works. He'd bought his house with a future family in mind. It was a longing he'd never shared with anyone, not even Buchanan, his closest friend.

Two hours later, at the end of a friendly game of poker with Jake and Maria, he threw up his hands. "There's no way you can have a full house, Maria."

"She cheats," Jake said, cheerfully.

"I do not." She glared at each of them as if insulted.

Since both he and her husband knew she absolutely did, they rolled their eyes. What impressed Jamie though: he'd never been able to catch her at it. According to Jake, he hadn't figured out how she did it either.

"I have a favor to ask," Maria said as he stood to go.

"Sure, what?"

"It's about time for Sugar to get off work. I'd like you to see she arrives home safely."

Not happening. "No. I'm tired, and it's past my bedtime." He jiggled the keys in his pocket for emphasis.

"Please, Jamie. There's a guy she works with that's hassling her, and I'm worried."

"All right, but you owe me one." It was likely Sugar's active imagination, but the idea of a man sniffing after her set his teeth on edge.

# CHAPTER FOUR

The building really was silly. Sugar held up her phone and took a picture of the two domed structures placed side by side. There were even nipples poking up on the tops of both. Why she wanted a photo of the Booby Palace, she wasn't sure. No, she did know. In her later years, when she wondered if she really had worked at a place designed to look like a pair of titties, she would have the proof.

She needed to remember to take another shot in the daylight, but she wanted a picture of the place when all the shining spotlights lit it up in all its infamous glory. The owner, Robert, had told her when he'd first finished construction and the sign went up, churches had organized pickets, protesting it as obscene. That he'd even obtained approvals from the city to build the Booby Palace was amazing in itself.

Although he hadn't seemed surprised, Robert hadn't been happy when she'd given her notice earlier. He'd offered her more money and when that didn't work, he'd thrown in free insurance and a three-week vacation.

"I don't even take the one week I have now," she'd reminded him. She liked Robert and she liked the work, but the clientele she had no use for, nor the bitchy girls. Then there was Kyle. If she told Robert the bartender was hassling her, he would put a stop to it. Still, she'd never felt comfortable working at the place. No, she would be a lot safer at K2, especially now that Maria knew her real name and why she was hiding.

That had been a surprise; not only that she'd spilled some of her secrets, but Maria's reaction. Her friend had assured Sugar she'd be safe at K2. It had been a risk, but she was glad she had trusted Maria. She felt a lot better about not accepting the job under false pretenses.

"Hey, darling. You hanging around, waiting for me?"

As if. She dropped her phone in her purse and clicked her car door unlocked, opening it. "Nope. Just leaving."

Kyle pushed her door closed. "What's your hurry, babe? Come on, I'll buy you a drink. We can go to Annie's, have a few beers, dance a little." He edged closer, crowding her. "Maybe get to know each other better after that."

"No thanks." She tried to turn away, but he pressed himself against her. "I said no, Kyle." Panic welled inside her, and she fought down the bile rising in her throat.

"I heard you, darling, but your eyes say yes."

She pushed against his chest. "Get off me!" Suddenly, he jerked backwards like a puppet on a string.

"The lady said no."

Jamie? At hearing his voice, the panic receded, and an inappropriate giggle escaped. Feeling giddy with relief, she peered around Kyle and waved her fingers. "Hi, Jamie." How had he snuck up on them like that? "You gonna put him on the ground like you did that guy at the airport?"

"Who the fuck are you?" Kyle said.

"You want me to?" Jamie asked, ignoring the man he held by the back of the neck.

It would be satisfying to see Kyle dropped on his face, but she still had to work at the place for two more weeks, and Jamie wouldn't be around to keep an eye on the creep. She had a feeling the bartender wouldn't appreciate eating dirt and would blame her.

"No, I just want to go home."

"That's too bad. I was looking forward to it. Lucky for you, Kyle, the lady wants to go home. Apologize to her, then disappear."

When no apology came, Jamie tsked. "You have one more chance."

When Kyle's eyes bulged, she squinted at his neck, trying to see what Jamie was doing to the man with just his fingers. However he was doing it, it was a neat trick.

"I-I'm sorry."

"Now say, 'I'll never bother you again Ms. Darling.'"

"I won't bother you again."

It was kind of like watching a ventriloquist at work, and Sugar swallowed a giggle, certain Jamie wouldn't see the humor. Her reaction didn't match what had almost happened, but for some reason she felt like she'd just inhaled some kind of laughing gas.

"'Ms. Darling.' You forgot that part. And say it like you mean it."

A girlie squeal sounded from Kyle. "That hurts, man."

"I'm waiting," Jamie said, following it with an impatient sigh.

"I won't bother you again, Ms. Darling."

Jamie glanced at her. "Do you think he means it?"

She studied Kyle's face and almost felt sorry at the pain she saw in his eyes. But he'd refused to believe she meant no, so he had this little lesson coming. "I think he does, but if he bothers me again, I'll be sure to let ya know."

"I won't," Kyle croaked, sounding almost like a frog.

"What's his last name?"

"Baxter." *Don't laugh. Don't laugh. Don't laugh.* But he really had sounded like a frog, and she was feeling a little like she was drunk. Jamie had appeared like some kind of superhero, and that made her happy. Could happiness give one a high?

She put her finger in her mouth and bit down on it enough to hurt. This was even better than the airport dude. She'd missed most of that when Jamie had ordered her to leave.

"Here's the deal, Kyle Baxter. Ms. Darling so much as hints you're bothering her, you and I'll have another little chat. Understand?"

Kyle bobbed his head. Jamie let go of him, and Kyle about tripped over his feet in his haste to leave.

Jamie, hands on his hips, watched until Kyle's car disappeared from sight, then turned to her. He frowned. "Why are you eating your finger?"

She lost it then.

Of course, the woman would think it was funny. What had he expected, that she would understand men like Kyle Baxter took what they wanted? If he'd not come along when he had . . . Jamie shook off the thought, not even wanting to contemplate what might have happened.

"Is this to be our relationship then, Ms. Darling? You drawing men to you like bees to honey, and me riding in on my white horse and rescuing you?"

With her lips pressed tightly together, she gave a furious shake of her head. When he'd walked up behind them and heard her tell the man no, an unexpected pleasure that she wasn't a willing participant had invaded his heart. He was a warrior. Invasions were meant to be fought, and fight this one, he would.

"You were seconds away from being assaulted, and I fail to see the humor in it. Would you like to share why you found this situation funny?" Her eyes were a sexy dark blue, but it could be the artificial lighting from the spotlights shining around them, or so he told himself.

"Frogs . . . ventriloquist . . . you know," she gasped, her neck-length hair swirling around her like silk threads. She waved her fingers at him, then turned and covered her face with her hands. Her shoulders shook and little snorts emitted from her.

"No, I don't know." What did frogs have to do with anything? Nothing she just said made sense, but his lips twitched anyway. Being a serious type of man, he didn't see the humor in much of life, although he used to. Why was it that out of all the people he knew, this woman had him wanting to laugh?

Except when he wanted to strangle her. "When you're done, let me know." He moved to the front of her car and leaned against the grill, slid his phone out of his pocket and checked his messages, then his e-mail. Suppressing the part of him that longed to be included in the joke, he listened to her laughter until it trailed off.

"I'm sorry. My reaction was inappropriate, I know. I'm just happy, is all. You can't know what that means to me."

She stood before him, her hands clasped in front of her, reminding him of a disobedient child waiting to hear her punishment. There had been something implied by her last sentence, and the question was on the tip of his tongue to ask why she would say such a thing. He held back the words, though, because it was a stupid thought. The woman was always happy.

"No need to be sorry." He pushed away from the hood. "Get in your car and wait for me to come up behind you. I'll follow you home."

"You don't have to. I'm sure you have better things to do than playing nursemaid."

If the night had gone as planned, he certainly would have. Strangely, he wasn't all that disappointed he wasn't with Jill. "Go on, Sugar, get in your car."

He expected her to argue, but she only shrugged and turned away. Someday he might figure her out. Not that he particularly wanted to.

At the door to her car, she stopped. "Ya know, that's the nicest you've sounded when talking to me. Your tone of voice I mean." She slid behind the wheel and stared straight ahead.

Piddling puddles. Did he always come across as being mean to her? Maybe he'd try to be nicer, not that he'd be around her much longer. A little less than two weeks and Barbie would be back at the lobby desk, then Ms. Darling would return to her little hole in the Booby Palace. As he walked to his car, he eyed the breast-shaped building. Why in the world did she work there? It wasn't a safe place for a young woman. Any woman for that matter.

He pulled his car behind hers and blinked his lights. Her little orange car surged forward in spurts until it turned out of the parking lot. Jamie shook his head and chuckled. Someone needed to teach the woman how to drive. It wasn't until they were on the road and away from the illumination of the parking lot that he realized she hadn't turned on her car lights.

"Sugar, Sugar, Sugar," he muttered. "How in God's name do you manage to stay alive?" She didn't just need driving lessons, she needed a keeper—or at the very least, a chauffeur. A bodyguard wouldn't be amiss either. He clicked his brights and instead of turning on her lights, she pulled to the side of the road.

"Is something wrong?" she asked when he walked up to her door.

"Yes, your lights."

Her eyebrows scrunched together. "What about them?"

He sighed, something he should probably get used to doing when around her. "You don't have any."

"They're broke?"

"I really worry about you, Sugar." He leaned in, reached past her, and turned on her lights.

A mistake, he instantly realized when his arm brushed against her breasts, all soft and warm. Unable to help it, he breathed in, inhaling her scent. She smelled like a combination of coconuts and vanilla, making his mouth water. Jerking his head out of the car, he backed up a step, far enough away that he couldn't smell her.

"You worry about me?"

"I meant . . ." The pleasure shimmering in her eyes stopped him, and he couldn't bring himself to tell her the remark had been meant to imply he wasn't sure she had any brains in that beautiful head of hers. "Yeah, I guess I do." And he kind of did.

A brilliant smile lit her face. "Thank you."

Jamie considered bashing his head on the roof of his car when he reached it. The soft way she'd said it—as if she couldn't believe someone cared enough to worry—had him wanting to make promises he had no intention of keeping. He did not want her turning her beautiful smiles his way, nor did he want to be the one worrying about her. No way. Nohow.

Sugar Darling might have once been the type of woman he was drawn to, but no longer. He was not the same man. He'd put too much effort into locking down the wildness that had robbed him of his parents. No drugs, alcohol, cursing, or wickedly sexy women— his self-imposed punishment for his sins.

As he followed her home, he vowed that as soon as her time at K2 was over, he'd avoid her at all costs. Not being a stupid man, he could admit she was dangerous not only to herself, but to him. He brought his forearm up to his nose and sniffed, then popped a sour lemon candy into his mouth to combat the lingering scent of coconuts.

He would call Jill and apologize again, explain he'd been under a lot of pressure on his business trip and hadn't been himself the last few days. Jill was exactly the kind of woman he wanted in his life, one who didn't call to the beast in him that had stolen the lives of those he loved.

If she bored him at times, all the better. It kept him settled on the course he'd set for his life. He frowned, wondering exactly how that made any sense.

Sugar pulled into her condo parking space, and he stopped behind her little car, leaving his ignition on. *Just wave and go inside, Sugar. Don't come back here.* Apparently, she couldn't read minds.

"Thanks, Jamie." She leaned past the window and kissed his cheek. "See you tomorrow."

Blasted bleeping bunnies.

Just great. Now his "Saint curses" had expanded into three words. He stayed until she disappeared inside, trying not to think about how her lips had felt on his skin. A coconutty aroma wafted up and he groaned. Why did she always have to smell so damn good?

Just great. That was twice a cuss word had popped into his head when thinking of her. He touched the spot where she'd pressed her lips, where the skin still tingled from the kiss. If she could do that to his cheek, what would it feel like to have his mouth on hers?

He grew hard just thinking about kissing her. "Get a grip, Saint," he growled. *It's not ever gonna happen.* The last thing he wanted was a passionate love affair with a beautiful, violet-eyed woman who was trouble with a capital T.

# CHAPTER FIVE

Sugar stood in the dark and peeked through her blinds. Why was Jamie just sitting there? Should she have invited him in? She almost had, but settled on an impulsive kiss, afraid he'd reject her invitation with the disdain he normally showed toward her. Finally, he drove away, and she dropped the blind back into place.

God, why did she have to act so stupid around him? He'd just made her so nervous that she'd giggled like an idiot, then hadn't even remembered to turn on the car's lights. But he'd been nice to her, and he'd said he worried about her. How long had it been since anyone had cared enough about her to worry? She picked up the cat making figure eights around her legs and held him above her head. "He's worried about me, Junior. What do you have to say about that?"

Dale Junior meeped, his word for *feed me now*! Apparently, her cat didn't understand the importance of having someone concerned about her. Something had changed. Jamie had actually smiled at her. How pathetic that a few kind words and a brief smile had sent her heart racing.

Junior meeped again, louder and more insistent.

"Okay, okay. I'm fixin' to feed ya. Have some patience." She carried him into the kitchen and set him down. At the sound of the can opener, his figure eights took on the speed of his namesake behind the wheel of a race car.

Once Dale Junior was happily feeding his face, Sugar went into the living room and turned on her stereo before heading to her bedroom. She stripped off her clothes, dropping them in the hamper, then turned on the bathwater. After adding vanilla-and-coconut-scented bubble bath into the tub, she walked back to the kitchen to pour a glass of wine.

Hannah would have been mortified walking around nude, even alone in the privacy of her own home. It had been a coincidence that she'd read a novel not long before she put her plans to disappear into motion. In it, a government agent was teaching a man wanted by drug kingpins how to disappear.

One of the things he'd drilled into the man over and over was to do absolutely nothing the same. Don't watch the same TV shows, don't subscribe to the same magazines, don't have the same interests, no matter how much you might love something. "You must become a new man, a completely different man, if you want them to never find you," the agent had said. "Dangle one tiny thread of what they know about you, and they will find you."

Sugar had taken the advice to heart, figuring the author must have researched how to drop from sight when writing the story. If Hannah liked something, Sugar didn't. If Hannah didn't like something, Sugar did.

Sugar liked wine, NASCAR races, cats, and walking around her house nude. She tried not to miss mint green tea, the Discovery Channel, her dog, and her warm, comfy robe. At least she'd managed to find a good home for her schnauzer before running away. When Rodney had asked where Baby was, Hannah had lied to him for the first time in her life, telling him her dog had gotten out and run away. To support the lie, she'd posted flyers on light poles and cried for a week.

The tears had been real.

Two long years she'd been alone since then, afraid to make friends, fearing she would slip up. But she seldom felt a stir from Hannah these days—she wasn't sure she could go back to the person she had been no matter how hard she might try. Now that she had a taste of all she'd been missing, she had no desire to give up her new life.

Sugar set the wineglass on the edge of the tub and stepped in. Reaching over, she turned off the water and leaned back, sinking down. "Mmmm. Feels good." As she sipped her wine, she found herself thinking about her new friend, Maria. She'd never had a girlfriend after her mother died. Friends visited each other's houses, and never knowing what her father's mood might be, she hadn't dared to invite anyone over.

She was almost afraid to hope that someday she could consider Maria her best friend. To have a girlfriend she could call if she just needed to talk, maybe someone to shop with on occasion, wouldn't that be something?

Maybe a day would come when she would even have a boyfriend. She'd never had one of those before. Rodney didn't count. Not wanting to go there and spoil her good mood, she closed her eyes and brought Jamie's face to her mind. Wouldn't he make a fine boyfriend? So what if it was a dream that would never come true? Nothing wrong with wishing.

"Mowwl."

"When are you going to learn the word is *meow*?" Sitting on the rim of the tub, Junior blinked green eyes at her before turning his attention to swatting bubbles, one of his favorite things to do.

She'd found him a year ago behind the Booby Palace, a dirty, starving kitten. A cat was the perfect pet for her, and Junior had turned out to be a good listener. When he brought his paw up to his mouth and licked it, he wrinkled his nose and did a cute little tongue flick.

"Silly boy. No matter how many times you test them, they're still going to taste like soap." He wasn't a pretty cat, just a common orange tabby with a bent tail and the tip of one ear missing. She'd always wished he could talk so he could tell her what had happened. Pretty or not, she loved him dearly.

"The water's getting cold. Are you ready?" Apparently, watching the water drain was a fascinating event to a cat. To hers, anyway. She left him to his amusement, wrapped a towel around herself, and picked up her wine.

It was time for her nightly ritual of surfing the Internet to see if bad cop and bad cop were up to anything. An hour later, she sat back. Her greatest hope was to one day see that their dirty deeds had caught up with them. Nothing would please her more than to have a picture pop up of the two of them in handcuffs, doing the perp walk in front of cameras.

Although she watched for bad cop's and bad cop's crimes to catch up with them, if that ever happened, there was no doubt in her mind that Rodney would try to drag her down with him. Running away from an abusive situation was one thing, but there was much more to her disappearance than that.

She stared at the picture of Rodney at a ribbon cutting for a new beauty salon, her father standing close behind in his usual ass-kissing place. It saddened her that the man she'd once adored was no more. After her mother died, he'd started drinking. That was bad enough, but then he'd met Rodney Vanders, the chief of police of the small town of Vanders, South Carolina. The Vanders had ruled the town with an iron fist for four generations. Rumors abounded of the bribes and bullying by Rodney, his father before him, and so on. Unfortunately, everyone was too afraid to do anything about it.

Junior jumped onto the table and tried to catch the cursor. "Well, Junior, it appears nothing's changed."

She started to turn off the computer but paused. Should she? Probably not, but her curiosity got the best of her. She typed in Jamie Turner of Pensacola, Florida, then James Turner. Nothing. She'd lay odds the boss had a hand in keeping his men under the radar. To test her theory, she entered the names of the other men from K2.

"You really are scary, boss man," she murmured when her prediction proved true. It only made her want to work for K2 even more. After she started her new job, she'd talk to Maria about things she could do to stay hidden.

Taking a guess, she typed in James Turner and broadened her search. There were a lot of them, but she paused when she came to a James Sr. from Akron, Ohio. It was an obituary for a husband and wife killed in a car crash ten years ago. They were survived by their son, a James Jr., age twenty. She guessed Jamie to be about thirty, give or take a year. Right age.

After that, it was easy to find the article detailing the accident. "Oh, God, Junior. He was driving the car." Her cat lowered his body onto the desk, prepared to listen as he did each night when she ranted about bad cop and bad cop. "Says here he was speeding and hit black ice. His father was having a heart attack, and Jamie's mother was in the backseat with him. Neither one of them had on their seat belts, only Jamie. They were both killed, and Jamie walked away without a scratch."

If that had happened to her, she'd never get over the guilt. Was this her Jamie though? She keyed in a search for Jamie Turner of

Akron, Ohio, and was surprised at the number of hits. Jamie the quarterback, winning the homecoming game with his Hail Mary pass. Jamie the homecoming king, laughing as a crown was put on his head. Jamie smiling at the homecoming queen who looked back at him with adoring eyes. Then there was Jamie winning a gold medal at the state swimming finals. Jamie pitching a shutout against the school's rival.

"Holy freaking Batman, Junior. He's Superman." Or, he had been. After high school and the wreck, the only thing she could find about him was a follow-up article on the school's hero a few months after the accident, announcing he'd enlisted in the navy.

What she found interesting: there were no stories about him after he graduated until the accident. Wouldn't a kid that talented go to college? Surely, he'd had scholarship offers. There was a missing piece, though, and she was more determined than ever to solve the puzzle of Jamie Turner.

What she now understood, however, was why he never laughed.

Jamie intentionally arrived at K2 thirty minutes early for the sole purpose of getting into the inner sanctum before he'd have to acknowledge Sugar Darling. SNAFU. There she was, a cheery smile on her face.

"Good morning, Jamie. Thanks again for seeing me safely home."

It would be rude to ignore her, so he stopped at the receptionist's desk. "No problem. Are you working there tonight?" *Shut up, mouth.* Not his concern. The purple blouse turned her eyes the violet color he liked best. They were almost as pretty when they were blue, though.

"I am. Two more weeks, then I'm done with them."

"I'll follow you home tonight . . . You know, just to make sure there aren't any problems," he said before punching in his code.

Just because he wanted to make sure she wasn't hassled didn't mean anything.

"Thank you. I appreciate it."

As he entered K2's inner sanctum, her words registered. She was leaving the Booby Palace? Good, then he could stop worrying about her.

He backed up a step. "You're welcome." Now that he stood behind the receptionist's counter, he could see she wore a black skirt that stopped several inches above her knees. His gaze followed her long, shapely legs down to the black do-me heels with little straps. Somehow, whatever she wore always seemed to be a mix of classy and sexy. Very sexy.

It had been years since he'd allowed himself to even think of having wild monkey sex, but lust slammed through him with the force of a torpedo hitting its target. England's eggs, he wanted her. Right there, right then. On top of the counter, on the floor, he didn't really care.

"Jamie?"

He jerked his eyes up and felt his face flush. Was he blushing? What was it about Sugar Darling that made him want to throw all his rules out the window? She stared back at him, and he about bit off his tongue to keep from asking her out to dinner.

"What?" It was like being back in high school, trying to act cool around a hot girl and failing miserably. It was both awkward and exciting, but in the intervening years, he'd apparently lost his smooth moves.

She lifted one lovely shoulder in a shrug, the gesture pulling her blouse apart enough for him to see the creamy valley of her breasts.

There were times in a battle when it was wise to retreat and regroup, and he decided it was one of those times. "Well, have a nice day." What a total dork he was, but her eyes softened, and she smiled that gorgeous smile of hers, and he found himself smiling back.

"You have a nice day, too."

For the first time ever, he had trouble concentrating on his job. All he could think about was Sugar Darling, imagining her naked except for her do-me heels. He pictured her under him, over him, in a bed, and against the wall. Wild monkey sex—he wanted it, and he wanted it with her. From the way she looked at him, she was definitely interested.

What was he going to do about it?

Since the accident, he'd not questioned his self-imposed rules. There were times he'd like a beer or glass of wine, but it was an easy enough rule to follow. He especially didn't miss the drugs. Did miss the cursing a bit though.

But the sex . . . He'd accustomed himself to reining in his needs and had believed he'd been successful. As he sucked on a lemon drop, he swiveled his chair and stared at the map on the wall, trying to concentrate on the red pushpins where K2 had active operations underway. Annoyed, he threw his pen on the desk. He'd wasted an entire morning thinking about Sugar.

Did he want her? Absolutely, unequivocally yes. More than he'd wanted another woman in years. He was hard just thinking about her, but she was a threat to the rules he'd put in place.

For months after the wreck, he'd been lost in a haze of drugs and booze in an attempt to dull the pain of what he'd done. Then the day came when he had to appear in court. Although he'd hit black ice, and that was determined as the cause of the accident along with his high rate of speed, he'd tested positive for marijuana and alcohol.

To his dying day, he would thank his lucky stars to have gotten the judge he had. His attorney had advised him to plead not guilty because Jamie didn't have any priors, and it could be argued he was speeding to the emergency room because his father was having a heart attack. The lawyer had thought it likely Jamie would only get his hands slapped.

Refusing to take the advice, he'd pled guilty, hoping the court would throw him in prison where he belonged. Instead, the wizened old judge had been sympathetic of Jamie's loss and *strongly* suggested he join the military.

"If you want to honor your father's and mother's lives," he'd said, "do something with yours that would have made them proud."

That night, he'd gone to the house that was no longer a home with parents who loved him even when he'd screwed up, and, in a rage that he hadn't been locked up and the key thrown away, he had gotten stoned dead drunk.

He'd blown everything. The college football scholarship he'd lost the summer after graduation when he'd hurt his shoulder playing a game of football with friends, all of them high. The homecoming queen—his girlfriend—had broken up with him when it turned out he wasn't going to be a college football star.

Then he had killed his parents, and every screwup that came before paled in comparison.

What kind of judge turned loose a man who ruined everything he touched? The next morning, he'd stood in front of a mirror, bleary-eyed and swaying, staring at himself as he contemplated his choices. Out of all the things said in the courtroom the day before, one thing kept hammering over and over in his mind. The judge was right: his parents wouldn't be very proud of the man looking back at him.

Jamie gave himself three days to sober up, then went to the closest recruiting office—which happened to be the navy—and enlisted. When the opportunity arose, he tried out for the SEALs and managed to get through the elimination process by the skin of his teeth. By that time, he'd already instituted the rules he would live by, and it was no surprise when his SEAL teammates nicknamed him Saint.

The last thing he wanted in his life was a woman who called to the man who was far from a saint. There'd been women who had tempted him to fall back into his old ways, but it had been a quickly passing urge, easy to resist.

Sugar threatened rule number three: no anything-goes sex. Because he knew down to his toes that's how it would be between them. If he gave in, which rule would fall next? He'd already cursed twice because of her, even if it was only in his mind. Next thing he knew, he'd slip and say one aloud. Doing drugs didn't worry him. He'd never touch the stuff again. But alcohol? Different story.

When would he decide there would be no harm in joining her in a glass of wine over dinner? No, he had no choice but to resist Sugar Darling. He lived his life to honor his parents, and nothing else mattered.

# CHAPTER SIX

G od, she was tired. Going from one job to the next was taking its toll. The numbers on the computer screen blurred, and Sugar pushed away from her desk. The music blaring from the strip club didn't help her pounding headache, and the three cups of coffee she'd downed to stay awake weren't doing it any good either.

One more week and she'd never have to come back to the club. Robert hadn't given up trying to talk her into staying, but she was so ready to be gone. The one plus—Kyle had avoided her like the plague. She'd been a little worried he would ignore Jamie's warning, but apparently Jamie's message had come through loud and clear.

She powered off the computer and tidied up her desk. A tropical storm had moved offshore and it was raining so hard she could hear it hitting the roof even over the music. After slipping on her raincoat, she grabbed her umbrella and purse. Wouldn't want to keep Jamie waiting.

True to his word, he'd been parked behind her car every night when she walked out the door. He didn't get out, didn't talk to her, just followed her home and waited until she was inside her condo before driving off into the night.

It was kind of weird, like having a phantom guardian angel. She'd tried to tell him the day before when she was at K2 that it wasn't necessary, that Kyle wasn't bothering her. He'd just grunted and walked off.

That was weird, too. After his one day of being nice to her, he was now ignoring her completely, to the point that she actually missed the grouchy Saint. Strangely, he intrigued her more each day. After what she'd learned about him on the Internet, she'd come to the conclusion there were depths to him he kept hidden.

It was as if there were two different Jamies: the one before the accident that had killed his parents and the one after. Unable to resist, she'd spent hours studying the pictures of him in high school, and in almost all of them, he was either laughing or had a big smile on his face. She could understand the grief and guilt he must have suffered, but it was as if he had banished forever the boy who had always been happy.

She thought back to the day she'd found Junior in the alley. Her cat had not been pleased when she'd trapped him and carried him home. He'd hissed and spit; he'd hidden for days under her bed. Since he couldn't talk, she could only try to imagine what he might have gone through trying to survive. Considering his bent tail and the missing part of an ear, at some point, he'd obviously either been in a fight or had been tortured.

With extreme patience and determination, she'd slowly won him over. When Jamie had given her a manly grunt the day before—after she'd told him he didn't need to worry about protecting her—a lightbulb had gone off. If he was worried about her, that must mean he cared, even if he couldn't admit it to himself. Could she win Jamie over as she had Junior with the same kind of patience and determination?

"Here, kitty, kitty," she murmured as she opened the door to step outside the Palace. With a new purpose in mind, she brought up her umbrella and the wind promptly tore it out of her hands.

"Get in the car!"

Sugar jerked her gaze from her departing umbrella to the car parked two feet in front of her. Jamie leaned over his console and pushed the passenger door open, and she scurried inside.

"Wow, did you see that?" Crap, in the few seconds it had taken to get in, she'd gotten soaked and was dripping water all over his leather seats. That should make him happy. When he grunted what she took to be a yes, she had to bite back a smile. Oh, yeah, kitty, kitty kitty was hissing.

"Where ya goin'? You just drove past my car." She twisted and stared at the receding car until it was lost in the rain.

"You can't drive worth a . . ."

"Shit?" she supplied at his pause.

"On a clear day under the noonday sun," he finished as if she hadn't spoken. "You'd be a menace to yourself and others on a night like this."

"But I need to get to work tomorrow."

A longer pause this time. "I'll pick you up in the morning and take you to get your clown car."

"I think my car just got insulted." She pretended to be offended by adding a huff and staring out the window. When she'd ignored her cat during the you-can-trust-me stage, he'd soldier-crawled to the edge of the bedframe where he could keep watch on her. Out of the corner of her eye, she waited to see if Jamie would look at her. He did. One point to her.

"Admit it, Sugar, that thing is an easy target for ridicule."

Convincing herself she'd heard a smile in his voice, she shifted toward him. "Torture me if ya want, but I'll admit no such thing." Well damn, his eyes heated and his nostrils flared. She was onto something it appeared. Just what, she wasn't quite sure yet, but she'd

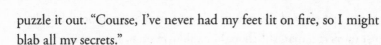 

puzzle it out. "Course, I've never had my feet lit on fire, so I might blab all my secrets."

"Had your feet held to the fire," he said, the slight crinkle of amusement at the corners of his eyes contradicting his scowl.

"That, too." The windshield wipers slashed back and forth on high speed, and the car's lights were overpowered by the heavy downpour. It was probably a good thing she wasn't driving in this mess.

Inside it was warm and cozy, and the man next to her smelled damn good, the spicy scent of his aftershave making her want to press her nose to his neck and breathe him in. He wore a button-down, white Oxford shirt with the sleeves rolled up to his elbows. She laced her fingers together to keep from trailing them over his arm to see if it was as muscle-hard as it looked.

A sign ripped from its moorings flew across the road in front of them. Sugar screamed and grabbed Jamie's thigh. He swerved to the left without changing speed, and continued down the road as if flying signs were an everyday occurrence.

"Wow, I'm impressed. I woulda crashed us into one of those parked cars."

"The reason I'm driving and you're not."

It wasn't until his leg twitched under her palm that she realized she still had her hand on him. She almost snatched it away, but that was what Hannah would have done, so she left her hand where it was. If he didn't want it there, he wouldn't hesitate to let her know.

It felt good to touch him, but she'd known it would. His heat seeped through her skin and up her arm, warming her. Probably, she shouldn't caress his leg the way she wanted. Hannah had been taught about sex by Rodney, and she'd hated having those cruel hands on her. Sugar wanted those memories replaced by good ones, but she'd yet to meet a man she thought could live up to her fantasies.

Until Jamie.

She'd rented endless romantic movies over the last two years, studying couples falling in love and how they treated each other. At first, the love scenes had made her physically ill, but as time went on and she continued to watch them, she'd started to understand Rodney was a sicko and how it had been with him wasn't the way it was supposed to be.

Jamie pulled up in front of her condo, leaving the car running. During the ride, he'd not spoken since he'd informed her why he was the one driving, nor had he pushed her hand off his leg. On an impulse, she leaned across the console and gave him a quick kiss on his cheek.

"Thanks for the ride." She grabbed her purse before turning to open the door.

"Sugar," he said, sounding like a pissed off, growling dog.

Pulling her back to him, he curled long fingers around the nape of her neck and covered her mouth with his. The revulsion she'd been afraid would rear its ugly head the first time a man's mouth touched hers was nonexistent.

*Oh, God.* So that was how it felt to be kissed by someone who she actually wanted to kiss her. It was wonderful, marvelous—spectacular even. He teased her lips with little nips, and then he slid his tongue inside her mouth.

Afraid he would stop if she responded the way she wanted, she tentatively touched her tongue to his. He tasted like tart lemons, and she gave a little sigh of pleasure. Remembering she'd wanted to touch his arm, she placed her hand on his forearm, feeling his muscles flex under her palm. She sensed he held back, but she didn't

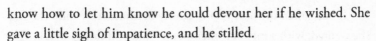 

know how to let him know he could devour her if he wished. She gave a little sigh of impatience, and he stilled.

Damn. Damn. Damn.

His hand slid away from her neck and he pulled away. It was too dark to see his eyes, to know if there was regret in them. "That was nice," she said, then cringed at how mundane that sounded considering her body was tingling all over.

"Pink pikes," he muttered.

Judging by his tone, he wasn't happy. "Word games again?"

"Go inside, Sugar." He stared straight ahead.

"Okay, but please don't be sorry you kissed me. I'm not."

He finally looked at her. "I'll pick you up at eight to take you to your car."

All righty then. He wanted to act as if it hadn't happened. "Thanks again." She opened the door and the wind slammed it closed. "Well, hell."

Needing to get away before she begged him to kiss her again, she pushed hard on the door and scrambled out of the car. Having lost her umbrella, she put her purse over her head and ran to her condo. Once inside, she peeked out the window just in time to see his taillights disappear into the downpour.

"Meep."

"Hey, Junior, my boy. Guess what?" She picked him up and carried him into the kitchen, setting him on the counter. "Since you're not going to hear a word I say until your belly's full, I'll wait to tell ya my news."

Opening a can of cat food, she spooned it into his bowl, then poured herself a glass of wine. In the living room, she turned on her stereo and curled up on her couch to wait for Junior. As she sipped her wine and listened to Adele, she studied the room.

It had taken the past year to slowly decorate the condo the way she wanted, with a mix of contemporary and odd things that caught her interest. She was renting it, but some day, she'd like to buy the place if she stayed in Pensacola. Of course, it depended on whether or not she continued to feel safe.

She glanced at the silver frame holding the picture of her make-believe parents. Pretending they were her mom and dad was kind of stupid if she thought about it too hard, but sometimes she would look at the couple holding the hands of the child between them as they walked along the beach and remember the good times, before her mother died and her father started drinking.

One day her mother had been fine and the next, she was gone, an aneurysm at the age of thirty-three. Ten-year-old Hannah had come home from school and found her mother sprawled on the kitchen floor, and life had never been the same after that.

She had not only lost her mother that day, but her father as well. In his own personal grief, he'd all but forgotten he had a daughter. One he'd used to lovingly call his sweet sugar. Two years later, the bank had foreclosed on their home, the only one Hannah had ever known, and her father moved them to public housing on the wrong side of Charleston's Calhoun Street.

Junior jumped gracefully onto the couch and began studiously washing his face. Glad to have her depressing thoughts interrupted, Sugar picked him up and sat him on her lap. "Forget about your bath, I have something important to tell ya. Are you listening?"

He blinked green eyes at her, and she took that as a yes. "Okay, so get ready 'cause the most amazing thing happened tonight. Jamie kissed me. Yeah, I know. Surprised the hell out of me, too. But, Junior, it was sooo incredible. I wasn't sure I'd like it . . . you know, because of Rodney."

Rodney's slobbery kisses had disgusted her to the point that she never thought she'd want to be kissed again. Then she'd met Jamie and started wondering if it would be different with him. She could now truthfully say: hell yeah.

"He didn't slobber all over me, and he tasted like lemon drops." She was going to buy a supply of the candy so that all she had to do to recall Jamie's kisses was pop one in her mouth. She'd probably end up spending a fortune on the things.

"Oh, and I think I've figured out his word game. He doesn't curse, but when he wants to, he says whatever comes to mind."

Junior apparently didn't care as he curled into a ball in her lap, tucked his nose under his tail, and went to sleep. "Okay, you're not impressed, but I sure as hell am. I just need to figure out how to get him to kiss me again."

Jamie pulled up in front of Sugar's condo a few minutes before eight the next morning and turned off his car. He moodily stared at her front door. Because of her, he'd not had a decent night's sleep. He still didn't know why he'd kissed her, and he wished he hadn't. What was it about kissing her that made him feel like he'd climbed Mt. Everest, exhilaration pouring through him as he stood on top of the world? He would like to believe it had been a onetime thing, but all he'd thought about was having his mouth on hers again.

At precisely eight, Sugar opened her door and sprinted down the sidewalk to his car. A point to her then for being on time. A light rain still fell, the remnants from last night's storm, and it struck him the women he normally dated would have an umbrella over their heads to protect their hair. Sugar acted like she didn't care. He kind of liked that.

"Hey, you," she said, water dripping from the tips of her eyelashes.

"Morning." He handed her a cup of coffee with extra cream and sugar. She wore a white silk blouse, and her eyes were blue. The white lace of her bra peeked from the edges of the shirt's vee. His doom sat next to him, a shy smile on her face as she accepted the cup.

"Thank you," she said with a breathiness that seemed to imply gifts were rare in her life.

It was just a cup of coffee, not a big deal in any way. She took a sip, closed her eyes and sighed, the sound very much like what she'd made the night before when he'd kissed her. Blue butter. Jamie threw the car in reverse and stopped himself just in time from peeling out of the complex. He needed to get her out of his car.

"It's perfect," she said, turning her thousand-watt smile on him. "Lucky guess?"

"No, I've seen you make it at work." Too much information. It sounded as if he paid attention to her. To keep from talking, he concentrated on driving. Unfortunately, he could smell her, and her scent made a man think of burying his face between the valley of her breasts and licking her.

To take his mind off her very fine breasts, he subtly studied her hair. Dampened from the rain, it was a darker shade, closer to the color of her eyelashes. He couldn't see any darker roots though. Maybe she didn't color her hair and it was just lighter than her lashes.

She craned her neck. "You just passed the turn to the Booby Palace."

As if he'd let her get behind the wheel of her car on wet roads. "I know."

"Okay, I guess I'll ask Maria to run me over at lunch."

"I'll take you to work tonight." Jamie was at a loss to explain the need to protect her.

"You're starting to make me feel bad, playing taxi driver for me and all. I know ya must have better things to do, and I really can take care of myself."

It was only the discipline he'd developed as a SEAL that kept him from snorting at the last part of her statement. Someone needed to keep an eye on her, and after the way things had ended with Jill, he actually didn't have anything better to do.

"Don't worry about it," he said as he pulled into the parking lot at K2. She gave him a look that said she couldn't figure him out, and he wished her luck with that. He'd not known what he was about since she'd picked him up at the airport.

"Trust me, I have bigger things to worry about than you. Thanks for the ride."

What did that mean? As he started to get out of the car, she suddenly disappeared from sight in front of his hood. He hurried to her and found her pushing herself up from the pavement.

"What happened?" he asked as he offered her his hand.

"I tripped."

A quick survey around her turned up nothing that would have put her facedown on the pavement. "On what?"

She grabbed hold of his hand and pulled herself up. "Hell if I know," she said, sounding so irritable he wanted to smile.

"You okay?"

"Everything's good but my pride."

"So we're just going to ignore your skinned knee?" When she tried to pull her hand away, he held tight.

"Right now, I'm wishing you'd ignore all of me."

"Not a chance, Sugar," he said, and found he meant it.

# CHAPTER SEVEN

Jamie spent the morning with Jake Buchanan planning an extraction of four kidnapped aid workers—one woman and three men—from Syria. Once they'd picked the team, they brought in Stewart, who would be the lead.

"Our intelligence reports that one of the men is sick and the other two aren't in much better shape," Buchanan said. "Ryan O'Connor comes on board tomorrow, and he'll be a part of your team, Elaine."

Jamie glanced at Stewart to see his reaction to having a team member he'd never met before.

Nicknamed Elaine because he was head over heels in love with Elaine on *Seinfeld*, Stewart shrugged. "I've heard good things about Doc. If we've got sick hostages, then I'm glad to have him. The woman's in good health?"

"As far as we know, she wasn't tortured like the men." Jake handed Stewart the dossiers on the aid workers.

As the two of them went over the files, Jamie turned his mind to Doc. He looked forward to seeing his friend again. It had been over a year since they'd last met and almost that long since O'Connor's wife had died. They'd talked on the phone a few times, but their conversations had been awkward. Once a happy man, deeply in love with Kathleen, he'd seemed to close up tighter than a clam after her death.

It would be good for Doc to be back with the team, and with him coming to work for Kincaid, only two of the original six of their SEAL team would be missing. Jamie was aware the boss had also offered Cody Roberts a job. If Dog accepted, they'd all be together again except for Evan Prescott, who'd been killed on their last mission in Afghanistan.

"Let's take a lunch break," Jake said, bringing Jamie's attention back to the present.

"Sure." At the mention of food, he realized he was hungry.

Stewart stood and stretched. "I'm gonna pass. I need to run by the bank and sign the papers on my car loan."

Jake snorted. "Bet you had to promise your firstborn, too."

"Your firstborn for a Corvette sounds fair to me," Jamie said.

"Nah, just my paycheck for the next twenty years." Stewart stopped at the door. "I've dreamed about owning a candy-apple red Vette since my older sister dated a guy who had one. Only reason she went out with him. Car's a babe magnet."

"How old are you again? Seventeen?" Jake asked with a roll of his eyes.

Stewart flipped them a finger as he left.

"I want to check and see if Maria's free to go to lunch with us," Jake said. "Meet you out front."

Jamie made a pit stop and then headed for the lobby. He'd expected Jake and Maria to be waiting for him. Sugar, not. She glanced over and smiled, and his step faltered as a funny flutter tickled his chest at seeing her. What was wrong with him? It wasn't like he hadn't seen her only a few hours ago.

"Where to?" he asked, stopping next to her.

"Maria wants to go to Captain Jack's. That good for the two of you?" Jake asked.

"Works for me." As Sugar passed, he caught her scent. Pink pansies, she smelled good.

"I've never been there, but I love seafood," Sugar said.

Jake unlocked his new Jeep Sahara, and Jamie opened the back door for Sugar, then walked around to the other side.

"Nice ride," he said, eyeing the black, soft-top Jeep's interior. "Like it better than your Challenger?"

Jake met his gaze in the rearview mirror. "Mostly. Maria does, for sure." He waggled his brows. "Says there's a lot more room in the backseat."

"Jake!" Maria punched him.

Everyone laughed, and it struck Jamie that since the death of his parents, he'd built a wall, shutting out anyone who tempted him to have fun. Even with the team, he held back, not letting any of them get too close. What had he been afraid of? That if he had fun, he'd slip back into his old ways?

In the beginning, it would have been a strong possibility, so the rules he'd put in place had kept him on track. Yet, as the years passed and he'd matured, he could have eased up a little. Until one bad driver with violet-blue eyes, he hadn't been tempted.

She scared him. She excited him. Did he dare give into temptation, take a time-out from his wife search and just have a bit of fun for a change? He glanced at Sugar, and when he caught her looking at him, she gave him a smile that almost seemed shy. His heart did a funny little thump.

Once seated in the restaurant and after their orders were placed, he sat back and listened to the other three discuss a movie they wanted to see. His mind was still a jumble of conflicting thoughts: the angel on one shoulder counseling Saint to ignore his base needs, the little devil on the other tempting him with promises of pleasures long denied.

"Well, hell."

Conversation at the table came to an abrupt halt and three pairs of eyes fell on him.

"What?" Why were they staring at him all wide-eyed?

Maria grinned. "Saint just said *hell*."

He'd cursed and even spoken the word aloud? His gaze slid to Sugar, who stared back at him in false innocence. There was nothing innocent about her; she was a sin he wanted to indulge in. She would be his downfall, but suddenly, he didn't care.

"Interesting," Jake murmured.

Jamie pretended not to notice the way Jake's all-too-seeing eyes darted back and forth between him and Sugar. Heat crept into his cheeks, and if he was blushing, he'd never forgive her. Before he could think of something to say to get their attention away from him, the waitress appeared with their food.

The conversation turned back to the movie and before Jamie realized what was happening, he'd agreed to make it a foursome to Saturday night's showing.

"Why don't we meet at our house for dinner, then we'll catch the one starting at nine," Maria said.

"What time should I be there?" Sugar asked.

No way was Jamie letting her drive around late at night. "I'll pick you up."

She studied him a moment, then shrugged. "Okay."

At some point since meeting her, his mouth had apparently disconnected from his brain.

Saturday morning, Sugar emptied her meager closet in an attempt to find something to wear. It wasn't like Jamie had actually asked her out on a date, so it really shouldn't matter what she wore, should it? She considered calling Maria to ask what she was wearing, but that seemed so high schoolish.

Although when she did shop, she tried to buy nice things that would last, she didn't spend a lot of money on clothes. After paying the rent, buying groceries, and covering small, miscellaneous expenses, the rest went into one of her money market accounts. If the day came when she had to run, she had determined early on that she would have access to money.

When she'd left Rodney's house, she had three hundred dollars to her name. It would have been easy to steal more than she needed from bad cop and bad cop, but then she would have been no better than them.

On the floor in her closet was a packed duffel bag with clothes, toiletries, and five thousand in cash. Also in the bag was a new identity under the name of Nikki Swanson. But she'd grown to like Sugar Darling and didn't want to have to become someone new.

Shaking off the unwanted thoughts, she decided to splurge on a new outfit for the evening to come. Leaving Junior asleep on top of a pile of clothes on her bed, she grabbed her purse and keys, and slipped on her sunglasses. As she walked down the sidewalk, she noticed a man knocking on the door of the condo Jake used to own. He turned to look at her, his gaze following her as she walked to her car. Dressed in a suit and holding a briefcase, she pegged him as a salesman, probably peddling insurance, or magazines. Glad she'd be gone when he made it to her door, she headed for the mall.

Three stores later, she was on her way out with her purchases when she spied Victoria's Secret. Not that she expected anything to happen between her and Jamie, but she decided on the spot that it was time to buy some sexy Sugar things.

When her doorbell rang, Sugar took one last glance in the mirror. "Whatcha think, Junior?"

"Mowwl." He yawned.

"That good, mmh?" She brushed her hands over the gauzy, colorful skirt, loving the soft feel of the material. The rose-colored camisole felt silky and sensual against her skin, and the strappy sandals were a perfect match to the camisole. Upon spying them in the shoe department, she'd let out a little squeal of delight.

Although she'd reminded herself a thousand times it wasn't a date, her heart picked up speed with each step she took toward the door. Even though no one but her would see them, the silk bikini underwear and lacy bra she wore made her feel sexy. She'd only intended to buy one of each, but the colors were all so pretty, and when she couldn't choose, she'd splurged, buying seven matching panties and bras, one set for each day of the week.

"Hi," she said after opening the door. "Come in, I'll just be a minute." Her mouth had gone dry at the sight of Jamie standing in her doorway, drop-dead gorgeous in a blue button-down shirt with the sleeves rolled up, and black pants. She rushed into the bathroom and lapped water from the faucet.

All the guys at work, including Jamie, wore T-shirts, cargo pants, and boots most days. He looked hot in what she thought of as the K2 uniform, but the man standing at her door could have walked off the cover of a magazine.

Glad she hadn't settled on a pair of jeans and a T-shirt, she grabbed her purse and after touching up her lipstick, she took a deep breath and returned to the living room.

"Junior, no!" Her cat was doing his figure-eight thing around Jamie's legs.

"Meep."

"You already ate, silly boy." She grabbed him, horrified by all the cat hair on the bottom of Jamie's pants. "He thinks you don't know he's had his dinner and hopes you'll feed him again."

Jamie glanced around. "Junior? Is there a senior I should beware of?"

She walked down the hall and tossed her cat into the bedroom, closing the door. Junior immediately made his displeasure known. Over his howls, she dropped her purse on the end table and snatched up the lint brush.

"Nope, no senior to be found. He's Dale Junior, you know, after the race car driver." Dropping to her knees, she busied herself with removing the hair from his pants. Without thinking, she curled her hand around the back of his leg as she brushed. A muscle flexed under her palm, sending little shivers up her arm. Oh God, she was touching him kind of intimately. She lifted her eyes, but only made it as far as his crotch. The material of his trousers twitched, and she watched in fascination as the area at the level of her mouth tented.

*Holy Toledo.* He was getting hard because of her? Something made her heart beat faster, and she wasn't sure if it was fear or excitement. She lifted her gaze to his face. He stared down at her—his eyes a darker blue than usual—with an unreadable expression.

"Sugar?"

"Mmm?"

"If you don't get off your knees right now, you might be surprised at the consequences."

"Okay." His voice had changed, turning low and raspy. A throbbing started down deep, something she'd never felt before. For the first time in her life, she understood what it meant when someone said they were turned on. She knew how it looked when a man was hard, had been forced not only to touch Rodney, but to put him in her mouth. Never had she thought to want to do it again with any man, but suddenly she wanted to know if it would be different with Jamie.

Although, as Sugar, she'd practiced flirting with a few guys, she'd never encouraged them to ask her out. If a man seemed too interested, she'd bolt like a scared rabbit racing for the safety of his hidey-hole. From the day she'd met Jamie, though, she had been attracted to him. That in itself amazed her, and her interest in him had grown each time she'd been around him. Unable to resist, she moved her hand and covered his erection. It jerked against her palm.

"Sugar," he growled, and pulled her up. "You're playing with fire, girl."

His mouth came down on hers, and she dropped the lint brush to the floor. Like before, he tasted of lemon drops. Although she'd bought several bags of the hard candy after he'd kissed her the first time, she discovered they weren't as good as tasting them on him. He angled his head and slid his tongue past her lips. She grabbed his waist when her knees threatened to buckle under her. In response, he wrapped his arms around her back and pulled her hard against him.

His erection pressed low on her stomach, and when he ground himself over her, she couldn't stop her moan. Heated blood rushed through her when he slid his hands down her back to her bottom, cupping her cheeks. Their tongues dueled for supremacy, but sensing he would be relentless in conquering her, she surrendered.

Melting against him, a sigh shuddered through her. Rodney's goal had always been to control her through fear and intimidation. With Jamie, she somehow knew if she said stop, he would.

He broke the kiss and leaned away, peering down at her. "Where'd you go just now?"

Oh, God. He was too perceptive by half. Now she was being stupid. There was no way he could know what she was thinking.

"I don't know what ya mean."

"You're staring at the buttons on my shirt. Look at me, Sugar."

She did. Was that concern she saw in his eyes? No question, she was out of her depth. What would he say if she told him he was only the second man she'd ever kissed, and the first one she actually wanted to? Considering where she worked and how she sometimes acted around him, he probably thought she'd kissed lots of guys.

He moved his hands back up to her waist and stepped back. "We need to go." When he dropped his arms to his sides, her skin still tingled where he'd touched her.

"Okay." Although sorry she'd somehow ruined the moment, she was glad he hadn't pursued his question. She didn't want to lie to him, but she could never tell him about Rodney.

"Maybe you should let your cat out. He's doesn't sound at all happy."

"That's because he hates closed doors."

He glanced down the hallway. "No kidding."

She picked up the lint brush and dropped it on the table before letting Junior out. To keep him from heading straight for Jamie, she took him into the kitchen and gave him a few treats. What did a girl say to a man who'd just kissed her like there was no tomorrow? *Thanks, when can we do it again?*

Standing in the middle of her living room, his hands in his pockets, and his face unreadable, his gaze followed her as she hurried and grabbed her purse. At the door, she turned to see he'd not moved an inch.

"You coming?"

He muttered something under his breath she didn't quite catch before following her out. Her new neighbor stood in the small front yard of her condo as her little Yorkie sniffed the grass.

"Hi, Mrs. Sims. How's Cricket doing?" The older woman babied the animal something terrible, and she'd been worried the dog was coming down with a cold.

"Much better, my dear. She only sneezed once today."

"Good, I'm glad to hear it." Sugar started to walk on.

"Did the nice man talk to you yesterday?"

A chill slithered down her spine, and she turned back. "What man was that?"

"He was all dressed up in a suit and tie. Not like the kids today in their baggy pants and big shirts. Such a handsome gentleman he was, and so polite." Mrs. Sims eyed Jamie. "Not as handsome as you though."

Jamie's eyes twinkled as he gave the woman a big smile. "Thank you, ma'am."

Any other time, Sugar would have rolled her eyes, but at the moment, she felt as if the world had stopped turning. "Was he selling something?" It had to be the man she'd seen the day before.

"No, he was from the condo management company. Said he was just checking in with everyone, making sure we all were happy. Asked since I was new here if I'd met any of my neighbors yet. I told him about you and what a nice young lady you are."

The condo's management had never sent anyone around to check on them before. Her stomach gave a sickening roll at the thought of strangers asking questions. What if Rodney had sent someone?

# CHAPTER EIGHT

Sugar swayed, and her cheeks lost their color. Afraid she was about to faint, Jamie slipped an arm around her back. She leaned into him as if she knew he could keep her safe from whatever frightened her. The feeling of protectiveness shouldn't have taken him by surprise. He'd felt it before, more than once where Sugar was concerned.

What had her turning as pale as a ghost, and what had put fear in her eyes? Was someone looking for her? A boyfriend or worse, a husband? He discounted a husband. It had been obvious when he'd kissed her that she wasn't very experienced. That shouldn't have pleased him, yet it had.

Color returned to her face, and she pushed away. After saying her good-byes to her neighbor, she turned and walked toward Jamie's car. As he followed, he couldn't help admiring her long, shapely legs and the way her hips curved out from a trim waist.

The outfit she wore was a man magnet, and he felt the pull as if he were made of metal. When he opened the car door for her, his fingers itched to trail a path up her bare arms to her shoulders where he might or might not stop.

"What was all that about?" he asked once they were on the road.

"I have no idea."

He didn't believe her. She kept her face turned toward the window, and sensing he'd get nothing more from her, he let it drop. For the time being. They rode in silence for a few minutes, and when she made no effort to converse, he searched for a safe subject.

"So you named your cat after a race car driver?"

"Yeah. I'm a big Earnhardt fan."

Something they had in common. "Danica Patrick for me," he said because he knew he'd get a reaction.

She finally turned to him. "Because she looks good in a bikini?"

Ah, there it was, that spark he'd wanted to see. "There is that, but she's actually a good driver. It surprises me you're a NASCAR fan."

"Why? Because I'm female? I have a thing for numbers, and there's numbers aplenty in NASCAR. Think about it. There are so many things to figure out during a race."

As she listed all the ways numbers needed to be crunched, he found himself revising his opinion of her. His first impression had been that she was flighty and not particularly bright. Cheerful and chatty, yes. But a woman who could tell every pit chief on the track when his driver needed to come in for gas? He'd not come close to cataloging the real Sugar Darling.

A lesson learned. Sometimes he could be wrong. He'd apparently hit on the right subject, and as he listened to the excitement in her voice when she talked about something she loved, he wondered what it would be like if she were ever that enthused about him.

Even though he'd managed to get her to talk, she wasn't her usual chirpy self. Somehow he needed to get her to trust him enough to tell him if she were in trouble. If he could help her . . . but did he really want to get that involved with her? Just because he'd accepted he couldn't resist her and wanted her in his bed didn't mean he was ready to take on her problems.

"Have you ever been to a race?"

"Talladega two years ago with Buchanan and Stewart. It was

pretty awesome." He pulled into the Buchanans' driveway and turned off the ignition.

"Oh, I'd love to go someday," she said, bouncing a little.

Jamie smiled. Any minute, she was going to start clapping. Her excitement reminded him of a kid at Christmas, and he found himself thinking he'd like to be the one to take her to a race. She'd probably want to visit all the pit crews to wrangle their strategy, then would tell them where they erred in their calculations. It would be fun to stand behind her and watch her dazzle them as she spouted mileage, and speed, and whatever else it took for a car to end up in the winner's circle.

Then her eyes dulled, and she sighed. "A pipe dream, considering."

Considering what? Something or someone had her running scared, and he wanted to beat the crap out of whoever stole the sparkle from her eyes. Maybe it was time to run a background check on her, see what skeletons were in her closet. He'd have to think about it first, decide if he had the right to invade her privacy.

At her door, he offered his hand—liking that she'd waited for him to help her out of the car. Placing his palm on her lower back, he walked beside her. Tension radiated from her, and he about bit off his tongue to keep from interrogating her.

After ringing the doorbell, he impulsively gave her a quick kiss. Violet-blue eyes blinked up at him in surprise. "If you ever need to talk, I'm a good listener," he said just as the door opened.

"Hey." Maria said. "Jake's on the back patio." She gestured toward the French doors. "You know the way, Jamie. I'll join you in a sec."

Jamie took Sugar's hand and led her to the backyard. Jake stood over a grill emitting massive amounts of smoke. "Whatcha burning, Tiger?"

Jake glanced up. "Hope you like your burgers blackened."

Sugar reached for the grill fork. "You two go do whatever it is men do when their women are busy in the kitchen."

*His woman?* Jamie didn't know whether to kiss her senseless or dig a foxhole and hide from the barrage of feelings raining down on him. He settled on something in-between. Pushing the fork away from doing serious damage, he slipped his fingers behind her neck and pressed his lips to her forehead.

"Don't burn my dinner." He turned away before she could respond, but he could feel the glare she trained on his back. It was likely he was in serious trouble. So why was he grinning?

Jake handed him a root beer, opening a bottle of Dos Equis for himself. "What's Sugar drink?"

Jamie glanced at the bar. Someday, he'd like to have a home like the Buchanans'. A crystal-clear, emerald-green pool shimmered under the setting sun, and the patio/bar area was pretty awesome.

"Red wine." How did he know that? Had he seen her drink wine before? A memory from three or four months ago returned. A group from K2 had been at Jake and Maria's house, along with Sugar. She'd sat on the edge of the pool with her feet dangling in the water, a glass of dark red wine in her hand. Angry he hadn't been able to keep his eyes off her long legs and pink painted toes, he'd left early. Even back then, he'd been paying attention to her; he just hadn't wanted to admit it.

He took the glass from Jake and carried it to Sugar. She expertly flipped the burgers, then closed the grill lid. Their fingers brushed when he handed her the wine, sending a powerful current up his arm.

"Thanks." She lifted the glass to her lips, peering at him over the rim.

Once, as a young boy, he'd fallen headfirst into a neighbor's pool. He'd been told to stay away—that the pool was dangerous—but hadn't been able to resist the allure of the sparkly water. Sugar Darling was as dangerous and irresistible to him as that pool had been. Swallowing hard, he skimmed his thumb over the top of her lip.

"You had a drop of wine there." When he brought his finger to his mouth to lick it off, she caught his hand.

"You don't drink." She leaned forward and sucked the wine from his thumb.

Dancing bananas, he was definitely in trouble.

"Sorry, I was on the phone with Angie. She's coming for a visit next month."

He and Sugar jumped apart and turned to Maria. Jake sat on a chaise, staring at him with a smirk on his face. How had he forgotten Buchanan was there? Jamie scowled at him out of principle.

"Who's Angie?" Sugar asked.

"A high school girl I met last year in Tallahassee."

"When she was kidnapped," Jake added, his mouth turning down in a scowl.

Sugar turned wide eyes on Maria. "Who was kidnapped? You or Angie?"

"My wife," Jake growled.

As Maria related the story, Jamie took over keeping an eye on the burgers. It still bothered him that the man Maria had thought at the time might be her father had gotten his hands on her during his watch. He had no desire to hear it rehashed.

"About time you got interested in someone with a pulse," Jake said, coming to stand next to Jamie.

"Who says I'm interested?" Was that how the team viewed the women he went out with? What business was it to anyone else who he dated?

Jake snorted. "You can't take your eyes off her."

Refusing to take the bait, he glanced at Sugar to see she and Maria had moved to chairs on the other side of the pool and were in quiet conversation. Was she confiding in Maria, telling her friend why she was upset? Ignoring the streak of hurt that she hadn't trusted him enough to tell him why she was afraid, he turned his back and loaded the burgers on a platter.

"Dinner's up," Jake called.

The October evening was still warm, and Maria had set the patio table. Still irritated, Jamie pulled out a chair for Sugar, taking the seat next to her. As everyone reached for the mustard, mayo, and ketchup, Jamie stole a glance at her. The sparkle he'd grown used to seeing in her eyes was still missing—the one that said life was fun and she didn't want to miss a minute of it. If someone was messing with her, one way or another, he'd find out.

The first game of the World Series had been played the night before, and talk turned to the fierce pitching battle that had taken place between the two teams. When Sugar spouted averages—RBIs, ERAs, WHIPs—Jake sat back and blinked at her in surprise.

"Numbers," Jamie said. "She likes them."

She smiled at him, he smiled at her, and the world came to an abrupt halt. Her lips—full, lush, kissable lips—were stained red from the wine. He'd start with her mouth, then work his way down her throat to her breasts. From there, he'd slowly lick his way to his goal, to the place he wanted to taste the most. Red-hot fire sizzled through his blood. He already knew how delicious she tasted . . . how would it feel to be buried to his balls inside her?

A little shudder passed through her, her eyes turned from violet to a dark blue, and her lips parted. God above, he ached for her, wanted her. It was the clearing of a throat that made him realize he'd leaned toward her, fully intending to kiss her into oblivion.

Apparently, she'd also forgotten they had an audience because she jerked back in her seat, her cheeks turning bright pink. If the heat creeping up his neck was any indication, so were his. How did she do that to him? How did she make him forget his surroundings? Even in his wild days, women had never had that kind of effect on him.

He should put a stop to it before he sacrificed everything he'd worked toward for the last ten years, but he'd passed the point of no return, and Sugar Darling was lined up in his sights.

Jamie glanced up to see Jake and Maria staring at them, Jake again smirking, and amusement glittering in Maria's eyes. Maybe he'd start a fight just so he could wipe that smug expression off Buchanan's face.

"You got a problem, Tiger Toes?" Maria's pet name for her husband was supposed to be a secret, but there were no secrets among the team.

Jake burst into laughter. "Nope." He slipped his hand into Maria's and brought it to his mouth, kissing her fingers. "No problem at all."

The two of them exchanged a look so full of love that Jamie felt gut-punched. A longing for what his friends had seared through him, so strongly it hurt. The years he'd spent looking for it, for what they had, what his parents had, suddenly seemed wasted. Had he been searching for the wrong woman all this time? He glanced at Sugar to see her staring at Jake and Maria in fascination.

Was there yearning in her eyes, too? Had she grown up with parents who adored her, or had she had a lousy childhood? Was she wanting something she knew and understood, or something she'd never had? Was she only looking for a good time, or did she want something more?

It occurred to him that where she was concerned, he only had questions. He knew nothing about her except she had eyes he could drown in and a mouth he could kiss for a month without coming up for air. She never talked about her past or even if she had family. It was time to find out just who Sugar Darling was.

"When's your last day?" Maria asked.

Her last day? Was she quitting her job at the Booby Palace? She'd said something about that several mornings ago, but he had been distracted by a blouse that had slid open and the do-me heels she wore. He waited for her answer, hoping that was what Maria meant.

Holy Batman, Robin. Jamie had almost kissed her in front of his friends, and Sugar would've let him. The man could make her forget her own name, all of them.

She blinked, focusing on Maria. "Next Friday."

Sitting close to him, she could feel his heat, could smell him. Sandalwood, maybe? Whatever it was, it made her think of leather and woods and sex. Not the kind of sex she'd known with Rodney, but the kind that could be good. Really, really good. More than anything, she wanted to press her nose against his skin and inhale him deep into her lungs. If anyone could replace memories of the smell of Old Spice and sweat, sloppy, wet kisses and pain, it was Jamie.

That was all she wanted from him. Bad memories replaced by good ones. Anything more, like a future and love, wasn't in the cards for her. At some point, she would pack up and run. As it appeared someone might be on her trail, it would likely be soon.

"You're quitting your job?"

She lifted her gaze to Jamie. "Yes, Maria offered me a position at K2, and I accepted."

"Good."

Did his slight hesitation in answering mean anything? Maybe he wouldn't like her working where he did. Too bad. She'd trade Junior for a chance to get away from the Booby Palace. Okay, not Junior, but almost anything else.

When she'd earlier told Maria about the man knocking on doors at her condo, she'd fully expected to have the offer withdrawn. Not only had that not happened, but her friend wanted her to stay at her house for a few days, just to be safe. Not used to anyone caring about her well-being, it'd been all she could do not to cry.

Although appealing, she'd declined. Not that Jake couldn't hold his own in a fair fight, but Rodney was a devious snake. If he found out she was under their protection, he'd go after the one he considered the weakest: Maria. No, she was grateful to have friends in her life, but she would not put them in danger.

"We need to leave soon if we're gonna make the movie," Jake said.

Sugar stood and picked up her plate.

"You two sit." Maria took her plate away. "Jake and I'll get this, you finish your wine."

When she started to protest, Jamie slipped his fingers into the waist of her skirt and tugged her down. "You heard the lady."

When they were alone, she tried to think of something to say, but the feel of his hand pressed between her waistband and her skin scrambled her brains. She couldn't figure him out. Only a week ago, she would've sworn he couldn't stand her. Yet, he'd shown up at the Booby Palace and saved her from Kyle's advances. He'd appeared every night thereafter and followed her home, making sure she arrived safely.

He'd kissed her. More than once, and all she could think . . . when would he do it again? She grabbed her wineglass and lifted it to her lips, gulping down the little bit left.

"Sugar."

The low rumble of her name sent heat pooling between her thighs and she squeezed them together. "Mmm?"

"I want to kiss you."

Her eyes snapped up to his. "You do?"

"Yes." His gaze settled on something behind her. "But not now. Time to go."

Seriously? He could practically melt her bones with the heat in his eyes, announce he wanted to kiss her, and then expect her to stand on legs she was sure no longer worked?

Seriously?

# CHAPTER NINE

When Jamie pulled up in front of her condo, Sugar debated inviting him inside. Was he expecting her to, or would he think her too forward? If he asked her how she'd liked the movie, she wouldn't know what to say. She hadn't paid attention to one minute of it. How could she, with scrambled eggs for brains?

Sitting next to him in the dark theater, all she'd been able to do was inhale the spicy man-scent of him, feel the hairs on his forearm brush against her skin, and think about kissing him some more. When he turned off the engine and shifted to face her, every nerve ending in her body crackled with anticipation. Hannah—the shy, scaredy-cat girl—would've jumped out of the car and run inside.

So, Sugar did the opposite. She unbuckled her seat belt, leaned over the console, and touched her lips to Jamie's. He grunted and wrapped his arms around her back, crushing her against him, his tongue invading her mouth. His hand fisted in her hair, holding her in place. The console hurt her ribs, and she tried to shift away from it.

He broke the kiss and gave a breathless chuckle. "The last time I made out in a car, I was in high school. I'm hurting you."

Although she wanted to deny it so he'd keep kissing her, it had hurt. "Would you like to come in?" Damn, her voice sounded like she'd run a marathon. She sat back in her seat and inhaled air in an attempt to calm her racing heart. "If you don't want—"

"I want."

*Thank you, God.* As they approached her condo, doubts set in. Were they going to have sex? Did she want to? What if she disappointed him? Her only knowledge of what happened between a man and a woman was with Rodney, and that hadn't been close to normal.

At her door, he took her key and unlocked it. Junior pounced as soon as it opened, almost tripping her. "Silly boy." She picked him up and kissed his nose. "At least let us get inside before you attack."

"Meep."

"Little liar. I fed you before I left." She glanced at Jamie to see him watching her, a rare smile on his face. "*Meep* is his word for *feed me.* I'll indulge him this time, or he'll never leave us alone."

"You speak cat? I'm impressed."

She laughed. "It's not a difficult language to grasp. *Meep* is *feed me* and *mowwl* is everything else, from *pet me* to *leave me the hell alone.* You want a root beer or some coffee?"

"No thanks." He followed her into the kitchen and made himself at home at her little pub table. She tried to ignore the way his eyes tracked her every move.

As soon as he heard the can opener, Junior ran his figure eights around her legs. Her nerves hummed a loud tune through her body, which she attributed to having Jamie's attention so focused on her. The way his gaze skimmed over her from head to toes sent her heart into a jittery dance. God, she'd have a meltdown if he didn't stop staring at her like that, as if he wanted to gobble her up.

*Men are all alike. He's probably no different than Rodney.* "Shut up, Hannah," she murmured.

"Did you say something?"

"No." Sugar put the dish on the floor for Junior, angling away from Jamie to hide her face and the doubt she wasn't sure she could conceal. She suddenly felt confused as to who she was. Hannah wanted to crawl under the covers and hide from the raw I-want-you look in his eyes. Sugar wanted to know if Rodney had it all wrong.

"Come here, Sugar."

At the low, rumbling sound of his voice, she turned to see Jamie spread his legs, inviting her to walk between them. Jesus God help her, she went to him. He put his hands on her hips and pulled her against him, his erection pressing just below her stomach. She'd made him grow hard? She, Hannah? How many times had Rodney drilled into her head she wasn't the kind of woman a man wanted, that he was only doing her father a favor?

Too many to count. By all that was holy, she hoped he'd been lying. *Stop thinking about Rodney, Sugar. Just stop.*

Jamie slid his hands down, cupping the mounds of her ass, and she forgot the bad memories. Her legs threatened to give out, but he kept her upright, the muscles in his arms flexing. She lifted her gaze to his eyes. The heat in them could start a bonfire.

"I don't know what to do," she whispered, immediately regretting she'd admitted that much.

Confusion clouded his eyes. "Please tell me you're not a virgin."

Now there was a loaded question. Technically, the answer was no with extenuating circumstances, but never in a million years could she tell him Hannah wasn't a virgin but Sugar was. Nor could she ever tell him the hell Hannah had lived through before escaping.

"Of course not." By the relief in his eyes, she knew he would have pushed her away and walked out the door if she'd said yes. Silly, honorable man.

"Thank God." His mouth covered hers, his tongue scraping over hers, the fingers of one of his hands spreading over her bottom, the other slipping under her blouse. Heat from his palm warmed her back as he traced the curve of her spine, sending shivers spiraling

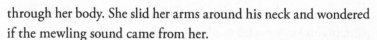 

through her body. She slid her arms around his neck and wondered if the mewling sound came from her.

"Bedroom," he growled and scooped her up as if she weighed no more than her cat.

Was she really going to go through with it? If she stopped, however, she didn't think she'd ever find the courage to try again. She would never know if being with a man was something she could enjoy.

If anyone could prove to her sex was all it was cracked up to be, it was the man who'd just kicked the door shut in Junior's face. Ignoring the cat's howling protest, Jamie came to a stop at the edge of her bed, and still holding her, lowered his face, his mouth covering hers.

Holy bejesus, the man could kiss.

He let go of her legs and she slid down his body. It was like sliding down a wall of rock-hard muscles. To keep from ending up in a boneless pile at his feet, she grabbed his waist and plastered herself against his chest. Totally by accident, her ear ended up pressed over his heart, and she heard it pounding like a jackhammer on turbo speed. It boosted her confidence to know she could do that to him.

Jamie's eyes grew wide as he surveyed her bedroom. "Wow."

She followed his gaze as he took in a room rivaling that of any brothel's. Although the rest of her condo was tastefully decorated, she'd gone a little crazy with this room in a weird attempt to conquer her fears of what went on behind closed doors. What she'd ended up with, she still didn't understand, but she liked it because Hannah would hate it with a passion.

A sinfully thick, white throw rug covered the oak floor next to a bed blanketed by a deep-burgundy comforter, and matching velvet drapes covered the windows. She'd splurged on expensive cream-colored silk sheets, and they were heavenly to sleep on. Old-fashioned lamps with crystal beads dangling from the bottoms of the rose-colored shades graced each night table. A ceiling fan that appeared to be dried palm fronds lazily circled overhead, creating a soft breeze.

The highlight of the room though—and what Jamie intently stared at—was a four-foot-square painting of a nude man and woman entwined in each other's arms.

"Sometimes I lie here at night and wish a man would look at me the way he's looking at her," she said, then squeezed her eyes shut. What was wrong with her? Well, that's what happened when she stopped thinking—things popped out of her mouth she'd never want to admit to anyone, especially him.

She felt his body shift toward her, felt his thumb trace the outline of her lips. The sleeve of his shirt brushed her arm, prickling her hairs. Her senses heightened, she inhaled his scent and her mouth watered. When she started to open her eyes, he lightly pressed his fingers over her eyelids.

"No. Keep them closed."

Her heart stumbled at the huskiness in his voice, and she willingly obeyed. It was easier to accept his touch with her eyes closed, when she didn't have to look into his and wonder if he only thought of her as a convenient screw. No, that wasn't Jamie, not the man she'd come to know the past few weeks.

*Oh, God, let him be a kind lover. Please let me enjoy what is about to happen.*

"And stop thinking," he growled next to her ear, startling her.

She thought he might be asking the impossible, but he didn't know Hannah was also screaming in her ear to run. *Please go away, Hannah. Please don't ruin this for me.*

"Sugar?"

Her eyes popped open. "What?"

"Close your eyes and stop thinking."

FALLING FOR HER

There was desire in his eyes for her, yes, there was. She was sure of it. A little piece of her fell in love with him then, but that was all she could spare him. It was enough though for her to once again obey him. She closed her eyes and stopped thinking.

His thumb returned to her mouth, pushing its way inside. She tasted the saltiness of his skin and licked her way from one end of it to the other before starting over. Next thing she knew, she was naked. He'd stripped her with the experience of a man long used to undressing women. She refused to think about that.

"Now you," she said urgently, opening her eyes, wanting to see his beautiful body. She wasn't disappointed. By the time he'd shed the last of his clothes, she was close to drooling.

A broad chest tapered to abs so hard she was sure she could bounce a ball off them. Narrow hips came next, then . . . then his erection. She tried to be all cosmopolitan about seeing him . . . seeing *that*. She really did. She failed. It pointed at her as if it were an arrow aiming straight at her and, oh God, it was huge. It would never fit inside her.

Hannah surfaced, screaming that he was going to hurt her.

Sugar's stomach rebelled.

Jamie froze at the panic in Sugar's eyes. She'd seen a man aroused before, she'd said so. She wasn't a virgin so why did she look as if she were about to lose her dinner?

"What the hell?" The only answer was Junior, yowling to get in.

Her color turned pea green, and she ran into the bathroom, slamming the door behind her. More confused than he'd ever been in his life, he stood, naked, in the middle of a bedroom a whore would die for and tried to make sense of the inexplicable. She wasn't a virgin. She had silk sheets and a nude picture on the wall, so why had she taken one look at his erection and turned green?

83

And what was with all the night-lights? Every outlet had one plugged into it, and that was just weird.

Retching sounds came from behind the door. His erection shrank at the thought of her being sick. Ignoring his briefs, he grabbed his pants and slipped them on. The door was unlocked, so he went in to find her with her head hanging over the porcelain rim of the toilet.

He positioned himself behind her and gathered up her hair. She tensed at his touch, and he murmured soft words to her. Damn, he hated seeing her like this.

Jamie refused to consider that he had been cursing left and right since he'd walked in her front door. What did confuse him, though, was how she'd gone from all soft and dreamy when he'd touched her, to hugging the john. Something was going on inside her head and he'd sure as hell like to know what.

She grabbed a wad of toilet tissue and swiped it across her mouth as if she was angry at the world. There was only one thing he could think of that would cause her to shy away from being touched. Someone had hurt her. He wanted a name, someone he could pay a visit and show the man—because it had to be a man, didn't it?—how it felt to be on the receiving end.

Did he really want to play hero to a woman he'd never consider as a mother to his children? She was too flighty, too . . . too Sugar for the role. The time with her was only supposed to be for fun, something he'd denied himself for years. Had he mistakenly convinced himself she was looking for the same thing?

Although he eyed the door with longing, he couldn't bring himself to leave her. "Hey, you okay?" he asked when she leaned back against him, refusing to acknowledge how right it felt for her to curl her body into his.

"I'm fine. Really. Something I ate, probably."

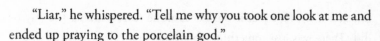 

"Liar," he whispered. "Tell me why you took one look at me and ended up praying to the porcelain god."

She shook her head and tried to crawl away, reaching for a towel.

"Stubborn girl." He grabbed it and wrapped it around her, picked her up and set her on the counter. The way she hung her head, listless and defeated, tore at something inside him. The last thing he wanted was to feel tender toward her. He wet a washcloth in warm water and gently wiped her face.

Violet-blue eyes peered up at him, and he wanted to beat the daylights out of whoever had put the hurt in them. "Talk to me, Sugar."

"Mouthwash," she murmured.

Not what he'd wanted to hear, but he opened her cabinet and found a bottle of mouthwash, handing it to her. After she'd rinsed her mouth, he picked her up, carried her to the bed, and leaned back against the pillows, settling her in front of him.

She brought up her legs, wrapped her arms around them, and buried her face against her knees. "I'm sorry."

The words were whispered, making him want to comfort her, but until he knew what caused her distress, he wasn't sure what to say. "Do you want to talk about it?"

The back of her head shook vigorously. "You should probably go."

He probably should, but much to his surprise, he didn't want to. Her shoulder-length hair fell forward, exposing a soft expanse of neck. As he stared at the spot he'd like to press his mouth over, he tried to recall exactly when she'd flipped out on him. When he'd undressed, she'd eyed him like he was a piece of candy, her gaze roaming over him. Her eyes had widened when she'd lowered them to his erection. That was the moment she'd turned green, and why was that?

She claimed she wasn't a virgin, but she sure as hell acted like one. And when he got home, he was going to have to wash his mouth out with soap. The woman was annihilating his self-imposed rules, one at a time. Not that it was her fault he reacted to her the way he did. There was just something about her that called to him . . . to a time when he'd been on top of the world.

It was something he needed to think about, but later. What he really wanted was the reason she'd gotten sick at the sight of him. He almost snorted. Not the reaction he was used to, even from the women Jake referred to as "Saint's nuns." It wasn't until Sugar, though, that he realized just how colorless they were.

Here goes nothing, he thought as he considered his first question. "You have been with a man before, right?"

She nodded.

It appeared he was doomed to have a conversation with the back of her head. "So you've seen a man's penis?"

She held up one finger.

One man? The part of him that was pleased with her answer worried him, something else he'd think about later.

"If you've seen a man aroused, then why did looking at me upset you?" She muttered something he didn't understand, and he leaned forward. "I'm sorry. I couldn't hear you."

"You're so big."

His ego certainly liked her opinion of him, and although he was an inch or two over standard issue, most women were happy about that. "I'm pretty much the same as most men."

A vigorous shake of her head accompanied her hand rising above her shoulders, her thumb and index finger spread apart.

"Four inches? You thought a man aroused was only four inches?" Her towel slipped down her back, and as he waited for her answer, he narrowed his eyes at a faded scar that looked suspiciously like a whiplash.

What in God's name had been done to her?

# CHAPTER TEN

Sugar was mortified. By the shock in his voice, it appeared she was clueless about a man's appendage. If true, then Rodney was defective. The thought sent a surge of satisfaction through her. Was that the reason he'd used the big vibrators—and other things she tried to forget about—on her with a roughness she knew was meant to hurt, and in places she could never speak of?

When she'd spied the size of Jamie, memories of her time at Rodney's hands had slammed into her, making her ill. Stupidly, it now seemed, she'd thought all men were small there and that a kind lover wouldn't hurt her. But if men were normally that big, then she wanted no part—especially *that* part—of them, even one belonging to Jamie.

Surely he'd realize there was nothing for him here and leave.

"Answer me, Sugar. Have you been living in a cave . . . never watched a dirty movie, read a sexy book?"

His finger traced the scar, and she willed herself not to shudder. If he asked about it, she had a story ready. The tone of his voice commanded her to answer, yet there was an underlying gentleness in his words and in his touch. She didn't want to talk about Rodney with him, not really. It would be like opening the door and inviting evil into the room. Yet, she sensed some small part of Jamie cared, and the temptation to share something of her life—a very edited version—with him was irresistible.

He pulled her back against his chest and combed his fingers through her hair. Her eyes closed in the sheer pleasure of a man touching her with kindness.

"Talk to me."

"You're a stubborn man, Jamie Turner." The expelled breath from his chuckle blew warm on her neck, and she sighed.

"So I've been told."

He went silent after that, and she had the feeling he'd sit there all night if that's what it took. She reached for a pillow, brought it to her chest, and hugged it—body armor of a sort. As she considered what to tell him, he continued to massage her scalp and she came close to purring. His touch calmed her, and she realized she needed to guard her heart because he could steal it if she wasn't careful.

"I-I was in a . . . relationship for a few years. He's the only man I've ever been with or seen naked. No, I've never watched a dirty movie, and yes, I've read sexy romance stories. I always thought . . . I just thought they exaggerated the size of a man's erection. You know, for the story."

God, she sounded like a country bumpkin. Never mind Rodney had told her women practically drooled when they saw his junk. By the number of times he'd boasted about his prowess in the bedroom, she should have suspected he was lying his damn face off.

Jamie's hands moved down to her shoulders, kneading the tense muscles, and she leaned forward on a moan, giving him better access. As she hugged the pillow, luxuriating in the massage, she couldn't help but wonder why he hadn't left. Why wasn't he bored silly? There must be women in his life who could show him a better time than what he was getting from her. Although, after meeting his girlfriend, maybe not.

Which begged the question. "Why aren't you with your girlfriend, instead of here playing masseur?"

His hands stilled. "She's not my girlfriend."

The relief at hearing that made her smile into the pillow. Not that there was a chance of her ever being his girlfriend. Not only would he not want someone like her with all her hang-ups, but with her new knowledge of men's anatomy, she wanted nothing to do with them.

"Let me see if I have this straight," he said, his hands gliding down her arms, then back up, causing her skin to break out in goose bumps. "Because I'm bigger than what you've ever experienced, you think I'll hurt you? So much so that it made you lose your dinner?"

In a nutshell, but it was the things Rodney had done to Hannah that had her on her knees, hanging her head in the toilet. She nodded.

He pulled her against him, palmed her cheek, and turned her face up to his. "I promise you on the SEAL oath . . . which I'd uphold with my life, that I'll never hurt you. Will you let me prove to you that sex can be a wondrous thing?"

She didn't believe him. "I don't—"

"With just my hands for now. If you don't like something, or if you think I'm about to hurt you, all you have to do is say stop."

Hannah wanted him to go far, far away, which gave Sugar the motivation to agree. If she didn't do this with him, she would forever be the cowering, frightened girl she'd tried to banish. She glanced over her shoulder and nodded. He must have seen the surrender in her eyes because he smiled, and it was the sweetest, kindest one a man had ever given her.

"Remember, all you have to do is say stop."

"Okay." That alone was more than Rodney had ever given her, and she made a little more room in a corner of her heart that would always belong to Jamie.

"Lean your head back on my chest. If you can, close your eyes and just feel."

He let go of her face, and she settled against him, trying to ignore the panic building in her stomach. He wouldn't hurt her, would even stop if she asked. He'd promised.

"I'm going to take the pillow away, but you can keep the towel on."

He pried her fingers loose, then the pillow disappeared. Not sure what to do with her hands, she folded them over her stomach, then moved them higher, then to her sides.

"Put them here."

Taking a peek, she saw he'd put them on his legs, just above his knees. "I'm ready," she said, striving for braveness.

He chuckled. "No, you're not. You're shaking like a leaf, but that's okay. If I'm as good at this as I pride myself on, you'll soon be shaking for a good reason."

Sugar doubted it, but if true, it would be a welcomed miracle. "What do you want me to do?"

"Other than hush and close your eyes, nothing. Just feel, Sugar. That's all I want you to do."

Her grip tightened on his legs as she waited for him to invade her vagina. Wasn't that the goal of every man? Surprising her, he brushed the tips of his fingers across her forehead, then trailed them down her cheeks before his thumb traced the outline of her mouth the way he'd done earlier.

As he continued his gentle exploration of her face, her tension slowly seeped away. What he was doing was nice. Her head swayed in a soothing rhythm with each inhale of air he took into his chest. If he would just do that all night, she might be able to sleep without the nightmares.

Sooner than she was ready, his hands lowered down her neck to the swell of her breasts. When she tensed again, he shushed her. She bit down on her bottom lip to keep from telling him to stop.

Twisting her nipples until she was sure they would fall off had been one of Rodney's favorite punishment games. One of many.

"You have beautiful breasts, Sugar. I'm just going to loosen the towel and slip my hand inside. You'll like it, I promise."

As he continued to talk, telling her what he was doing or about to do, she began to relax again. How he knew it helped to hear him explain, she didn't know, but he was right. She did like what he was doing.

"Feel how your nipple is peaking when I touch it?" He flicked a fingernail across the tip. "Now I'm going to pinch it a little."

"No! Don't." Her nipples had experienced more than their fair share of abuse and she didn't think they could handle anymore.

His hand stilled. "My intention is not to hurt you, sweetheart," he murmured, his mouth close to her ear. "It's a kind of pleasure most women enjoy, but I promised I wouldn't do anything you didn't want me to." He returned to caressing her breasts.

*Stop being a coward, Sugar.* It was a night to conquer her fears, and he was a man who could help her do it. He'd sworn on the SEAL oath no less that he wouldn't hurt her. Even if he hadn't, she still trusted him, knowing he wasn't like Rodney.

"Okay, you can pinch me, but just one time." There was no way she was going to like it.

"You sure?"

Not really. She fisted the material of his pants. "Yes."

Okay, so she was wrong. The pinch had been a kind of strange pleasure pain. Not the kind of hurt Rodney had inflicted on her. *No more thinking about Rodney, damn it. Stop comparing everything Jamie does to that bastard.*

"Do it again," she surprised herself by saying.

His mouth was now pressed to the side of her face, and she felt his lips curve in a smile—likely a pleased-with-himself one. Well, he should be. He'd taken her further than she'd expected, and he wasn't done yet. For the first time since he'd begun, excitement tickled her stomach.

"Have you ever played with yourself, Sugar?"

"No." Why bother? She was dead in all the places that gave a woman pleasure.

He took her right hand and brought it under the towel, pressing her fingers to her right breast. "You play with that one, and I'll concentrate on this one. Let's see which one of us your girls like the best."

Even though embarrassed heat traveled up her neck to her cheeks, she didn't snatch her hand away. He'd made it a game of competition, something fun. She mirrored his actions, and damn, it did feel good.

"I'm going to spread the towel apart so you can watch our hands. Okay?"

When she nodded, he kissed the top of her head, as if pleased with her.

"Open your eyes, sweetheart," he breathed into her ear. "This is too beautiful to miss."

She obeyed and saw his large hand, with its elegantly long fingers, strumming over her nipple as if he were playing a musical instrument. Compared to his, her hand looked small and hesitant.

"Put your palm underneath and test its weight. Like this." He demonstrated. "How does that feel?" he asked when she held her breast.

"Good. Soft."

"Oh, yeah. Soft," he agreed.

It did feel good when she did it, but nothing like the way her left breast felt in his hand. As he molded the shape to fit his palm, he flicked his thumb over her nipple. She shivered, and hot liquid pooled deep in her belly.

Amazing! She was actually getting wet. She'd read about that happening to women in every love scene of every book she'd devoured. Never had she expected it to happen to her; she had pretty much thought it was pure fiction.

"You like what I'm doing. Don't deny it." He followed the declaration by swirling his tongue in the whorl of her ear.

Dear God. She wanted to tell him she hated it, but it would be a lie. Her nipples pebbled, her clit throbbed, and her mind went blank.

"I think you want me to touch you here," he said as he danced his fingers over the skin of her stomach to the edge of her pubic hair. "Right here, in fact." He pressed the tip of his index finger to her clit and stilled.

She wanted to yell at him to stop, that she couldn't do any more. But he'd made her want something she didn't quite understand, and her hips rose to meet his touch.

"Oh, yeah," he murmured. "Thank you."

He was thanking her? Shouldn't it be the other way around? If he knew what the night meant to her, he would probably take a hike faster than a jackrabbit could flee from a circling hawk.

"Come for me, Sugar." The finger playing with her clit slipped inside her, his thumb replacing it.

He'd made a sneak attack—had been telling her everything he was going to do until then. If she'd known he was about to touch her there, she would have told him to stop. But any words of protest died in her throat.

As he explored her and his thumb continued its relentless assault, a primal moan crawled its way up her chest, past her throat, and out her mouth before she could stop it. A raw, low humming sound from Jamie answered her.

Every nerve ending in her body felt electrified, and she wasn't sure what to do with herself. A part of her tried to fight against the sense that she was going to irreparably shatter into so many pieces that she'd never be the same again. But she couldn't fight the intense pleasure building deep inside. As it spread its way through her, she pressed back against Jamie, needing him to hold her.

"I'm here," he said, as if he understood.

That was all it took, and a feeling such as she'd never known crashed through her like a tidal wave, and the force of it consumed her. She said words, but they sounded like gibberish to her ears.

As she floated back to earth, marveling that she'd finally had her first orgasm, Jamie held her tight against him. Although what had just happened had been all for her, his chest heaved as he drew air into his lungs. That he was turned on simply by pleasuring her sent her heart into a tumble.

"Wow," she said once she could breathe again.

"Yeah, wow." He pulled her hair away from her face and kissed the corner of her eye. "I wish you could see how beautiful you are when you come, sweetheart. There's so much passion inside you, and I could spend all night proving it to you."

She felt something poking her in her back and reached behind her, her hand freezing when she realized it was him. His erection jerked against her fingers, and she snatched her hand away. Oh, God, she wasn't ready for *that*. But it would be selfish to refuse him after the intense pleasure he'd given her.

Gathering her courage, she twisted to face him, resting on her knees. Tentatively, she put her hand on him, and he grew even larger under her touch. Suddenly, she was glad he still had his pants on so she couldn't see him. Her stomach made a sickening churn. His gaze bored into hers as if he saw deep into her mind and understood her distress.

"Come here."

Next thing she knew, he'd arranged them so he was behind her, spooning her. As she lay in front of him with his arm resting on her hip and his fingers spread over her stomach, she realized the last time she'd felt this protected was when her mother was still alive—when she'd had the love of both her parents.

"I'm sorry," she whispered.

He nestled tighter against her. "Hush. You have nothing to be sorry for."

Oh, but she did. "Thank you for tonight, Jamie. I never knew. I want . . . I want to do the same for you." If she said it enough, maybe she'd start to believe it.

His chuckle tickled her neck. "And I want you to, believe me." Pushing up on his elbow, he peered down at her. "I'll never lie to you, Sugar. Right now, I'm as hard as an ironing board and suffering a severe case of blue balls. The thing is, I've got a problem with putting my most private part inside a woman who turns green at the sight of me. But now, you've become a challenge."

With that announcement, he lowered himself down. What was she to make of that?

"I'm going to teach you to want me, and I'm going to love every minute of it. Consider yourself warned, sweetheart."

"I'm afraid you're going to be disappointed." *Afraid* wasn't even the right word. *Petrified*, more like. Why did a man like him even want to waste his time on her?

"I don't think so." He brushed her hair back and then kissed her eyes closed. "Go to sleep, baby, and I'll watch over you for a little while."

If he knew she'd just fallen in love with him, he'd run straight through the bedroom door, leaving an outline of his fleeing body. It didn't matter though, she thought as she slipped into sleep to the feel of his hand caressing her. She was going to be selfish and cherish her time with him for however long it lasted.

# CHAPTER ELEVEN

Jamie listened to Sugar's even breathing and considered what he was doing. Didn't have a clue, truth be told. What had possessed him to issue a challenge? He slid his hand up to the underside of her breast, warm and soft. She was like a wounded bird, hurt and wary.

Whoever the man she'd been with; he'd done a number on her. Jamie would like to have a few minutes alone with him, see how he liked being hurt. What made a man want to abuse a woman, a person without the physical strength to fight back?

Did he even want to know the details? She'd fooled them all though, with her happy-go-lucky disguise. His initial impression of her couldn't have been more wrong, and it shamed him.

And then he'd gone and given Miss Sugar Darling her first orgasm ever, promising to teach her to want him. Either he was about to embark on a fascinating journey, or he was the biggest fool in the world.

Slipping out of the bed, he pulled the covers over her. She sighed and rolled onto her stomach, and he was caught for a moment by the way her lips parted on another soft sigh. He'd tasted that mouth and found it to be as sweet as her name.

He collected his clothes, turned out the lamp, and opened the bedroom door. Her cat shot up from where he'd curled himself on the other side and took a flying leap onto the bed. Junior plastered himself on her back and because of the light provided by all the night-lights, Jamie could see the creature glaring at him.

"I don't like you either," he murmured, then left.

Once he'd made sure all her windows and doors were locked, he tossed his shirt, briefs, and shoes onto the passenger seat of his car. Driving home, he analyzed the events of the night.

The one thing he kept coming back to was the way she'd turned green at the sight of him. What kind of cruelty did it take to cause such a reaction? What kind of hurting had she been put through that she could only sleep if every outlet in her room had a night-light plugged into it?

Even so, she'd been responsive to him, more receptive than any woman he'd been with since the accident. Although he would be wise to end whatever it was growing between them, he knew he wouldn't. If nothing else, maybe for the time they were together, he could help her put her fears to rest.

Once home, he tossed his keys into the bowl on his kitchen counter and headed straight for the shower. As hot water pulsated over his head, all he could think about was the expression of wonder on her face when she'd climaxed. And all he wanted was to see that again.

He was royally screwed.

The next morning, Jamie rummaged through his kitchen cabinets, finally locating an empty jar, and stuffed seven one-dollar bills into it. One for each curse word he could remember thinking or saying. At the end of his time with Sugar, he would take the jar crammed with money—he didn't doubt it would be—to the Humane Society and insist it be put toward the adoption of a cat.

That he'd even conceived of such a plan was proof his cock had taken control of his brain. Heaving a big sigh, he dug another dollar out of his wallet and added it to the others. It would probably be a good idea to stock up on singles.

After slipping a chain holding his house key around his neck, he locked his door and doubled his normal five-mile run. Even though he'd taken the edge off in the shower a few hours ago, he was still hot and bothered. The erotic dreams he'd had of a certain violet-eyed woman hadn't helped.

By the time he returned home, the late-October day had warmed up enough that he was drenched in sweat. A quick shower cooled him down, and he followed it with a breakfast of scrambled eggs and toast, two cups of coffee, and a banana. Another hour was taken up with some housekeeping while he half paid attention to CBS's *Sunday Morning* show.

One of the segments featured a bestselling erotic romance author and he paused to listen, amazed at the number of books she sold. When the interviewer read aloud a heavily bleeped passage, Jamie realized he'd been right there in that scene, back in the days before he was Saint—before the Great Jamie Makeover. Many times.

As he remade the bed with clean sheets, he contemplated the necessity of maintaining the stringent rules he'd put in place. They had been necessary at the time, the things he needed to do to change the destructive direction in which he was headed. His motivation to be a man his parents would have been proud of had kept him from slipping at a time when he was metaphorically walking on ice. Those days were long past, and maybe it was time to ease up.

He stuffed the pillows into their cases, then sat on the bed. "You're messing with my head, Sugar," he muttered. Thinking back on it, he considered it amazing no woman had crossed his path in the last ten years who called to the man he'd once been in the way Sugar did.

And when it did happen, what did he get? A wounded bird who turned green at the sight of his erection. Chuckling, he shook his head. Life was full of surprises, and whether this one was a good one or not remained to be seen.

A promise had been made though. Before he was done with her, she would want him. And he always kept his promises. He glanced at the clock to see it was eleven. She should be up. He pulled a lemon drop from his cargo shorts pocket, unwrapped it, and popped it into his mouth. Grabbing his cell out of the charger, he clicked off the TV and dialed Sugar's number. That he'd got it from Maria and programmed it into his phone a week ago should have been a warning.

Sugar squinted at the alarm clock, blinked, and looked again. She never slept until eleven. Junior had awakened her at seven and she'd fed him, then crawled back into bed, intending to grab another hour of sleep. But it had been the most restful night she'd had in years. No nightmares, no tossing and turning, no staring at the ceiling fan circling above her while listening for noises that didn't belong.

"Thank you, Jamie," she whispered, wishing he hadn't left. When she'd come back to bed after feeding Junior, she'd pulled the pillow that still held his scent to her face and fallen back to sleep inhaling his smell.

Her phone buzzed, no identity on the caller. She almost answered, but remembered the stranger asking questions and let it go to voicemail. When the beep sounded, signaling a message, she listened, her heart taking a happy bounce when she heard Jamie's voice.

"It's Sugar," she said as he answered her return call.

"You up?"

"Yes," she lied.

"You have plans for today?"

"No." She never had plans other than to go to work, come home, feed Junior, surf the Internet for the latest news on bad cop and bad cop, sleep, then go to work again. Saturdays and Sundays were spent doing . . . absolutely nothing. What was there to do when she didn't have friends, much less a boyfriend?

"Good. I'll pick you up at two. Wear a bathing suit. A bikini would please me," he said, using that sexy voice of his.

"Okay." Holy moly wow! He was actually asking her out. The line went dead. She threw off the covers and shot out of bed. There was just enough time to go to the mall and buy a bikini.

As she returned home with her tiny bathing suit, a gauzy, white cover-up with a giant parrot hand-painted on the back, and a new pair of glittery beach flip-flops, she wondered if she'd gone a little overboard. She glanced at the passenger seat. Oh, and a yellow straw hat with a red ribbon that trailed off the back. Yeah, she'd gone overboard, but what the heck. It wasn't every day a hot guy called, invited her to the beach, and in a husky voice said a bikini would please him.

When she'd taken on the persona of Sugar, she'd cut and dyed her hair, lost twenty pounds, and adopted a personality completely opposite from Hannah. If she was going to hide from two very bad cops, she had to be someone they'd never think to look for.

It hadn't helped the night before, though. At the sight of Jamie in all his glory, Hannah had popped out and freaked, big time. Sugar didn't want to be that girl, the one who didn't know how to enjoy life . . . or a man.

Sugar wanted to want Jamie, and after the orgasm he'd given her with just his fingers, she held out hope he would prove up to the challenge he'd issued. If tiny bikinis and sparkly sandals excited him, then it was money well spent. If it made her a little sad that whatever happened between them was a temporary thing and he'd never know the real her, she would just have to deal with it.

*I'll never lie to you.* His words echoed in her mind as she painted her toenails cherry red. She pushed Junior away from her wet toes and flopped back on the bed, covering her face with her hands.

"I have no choice but to lie to him, Junior, but if he ever finds out, he'll hate me for it. I don't want him to hate me, but I really, really do want him to make good on his promise."

"Mowwl."

"That's easy for you to say; you're neutered." His face pressed against her hands and she moved them so he could smash his nose on hers. After giving her a sandpapery lick, he curled into a ball on her pillow and went to sleep.

"Big help you are," she said. Jamie would knock on her door in thirty minutes, and to calm her nerves, she made a cup of chamomile tea and carried it into the bathroom where she'd left the bathing suit. She jumped into the shower and shaved her legs, under her arms, and for the first time in her life, gave herself a bikini trim.

"You're just having yourself all kinds of adventures today, Sugar." After putting on the bathing suit, she held a mirror between her legs to make sure she'd done adequately on her shave job. No hairs peeked out of the crotch, so she was good to go.

Lord, the thing was small, she thought as she turned in a circle in front of the mirror. The bathing suit hadn't looked this tiny at the store. No way could she go out in public wearing only two strips of material. Somewhere, she had a one-piece. The doorbell rang just as she yanked open the drawer she thought the suit was in. Crap!

Okay, so she would just put the parrot cover-up on and not take it off. Not even for Jamie. Probably. She snagged the straw hat and the tote she'd filled with some bottled waters, the two new beach towels—men didn't own beach towels, did they?—she'd also bought, then jogged to the front door, practically out of breath by the time she opened it. What was left of the air in her lungs expelled at the sight of Jamie standing there, wearing a blue T-shirt that matched his eyes and a pair of boardshorts that stopped a few inches above his knees. Good God, look at those legs.

"Hey, you," she said, managing not to drool.

"Hey you back."

The way his gaze roamed over her, slowly perusing the line of her body all the way down to her toes, his eyes promising more of the kind of pleasure he'd already shown her, short-circuited her brain. She gave into the urge to squeeze her thighs together. A knowing smile crossed his face as he leaned toward her. Thinking he was going to kiss her, she closed her eyes. He chuckled and she felt his breath at the side of her neck. What was he doing?

"You smell nice," he said, then took her hand.

As she walked beside him to the car—Jamie's large hand curled around hers—it struck her how intimate the act was. She'd been too closely watched as a teen to even consider having a boyfriend, had never held hands with a man before. Whenever she'd walked beside Rodney, his hand was always at her neck, his fingers digging into her skin, a constant reminder that she belonged to him.

When they reached the car, Jamie backed her up against the passenger door, braced his arms on either side of her head, and lowered his mouth to hers. All morning she'd found herself touching her lips and wondering if she'd only imagined how great he kissed. She hadn't.

"Mmm. Nice," he murmured, then stepped back. "I've been wanting to do that since I tiptoed out of your bedroom last night."

"Really?" God, she sounded so juvenile. Why couldn't she think of something sophisticated to say?

"Yes, Sugar, really. If you'll move that beautiful ass of yours, I'll open the door."

"You just said *ass*," she blurted. *Stop talking, Sugar, until you have something intelligent to say.*

"Your fault, sweetheart. Entirely your fault."

From his grin, she knew he was teasing her, and that in itself was a novelty. She liked it, but he was still a mystery to her, this man his friends called Saint. Like the hard rock music blaring out of the radio. She would've guessed he'd go for oldies, maybe country.

She did want him to kiss her and hold her hand again, and . . . and do that magical thing he'd done with his fingers the night before. It still astounded her she'd had her first orgasm, something she'd accepted would never happen for her.

"A penny," he said and turned down the radio.

Caught at her thoughts, fire lit her cheeks, and she knew they'd turned bright red. "Ahem, I wasn't really thinking anything, just listening to the music."

"Little liar." He took her hand and put it on his thigh. "You were thinking about last night. At least, I hope you were."

"Some. A little. Maybe." His leg muscle flexed under her palm, as if he were pleased with her answer. Unable to help herself, she circled her fingers over the material of his shorts, wishing she had the nerve to move her hand to his bare skin.

After crossing the bridge to Gulf Breeze, he turned onto a narrow lane leading to a marina on the bayside of the island. "I thought we were going to the beach." She'd never been on a boat in her life, and wasn't sure she wanted to be on one with him. If she got sick, she'd die of embarrassment, especially after barfing her guts out in front of him the night before.

He pulled into a space in front of the marina office and shifted in his seat to face her. "I have something much better in mind than sitting on the sand, surrounded by hot, sweaty, screaming kids. For what I have planned for us, we need privacy."

The last was said in such an intimate, compelling voice that she could only nod her assent. Did more privacy mean he would do those things to her again?

"I'm on board." She helplessly snorted. *Really, Sugar. On board?* Already, she was boat-talking. His lips curved into an amused smile, as if he knew her every thought. God forbid.

"Just remember, on a boat, the captain's the boss. Whatever he says goes." He got out of the car and came to her side, opened the door and leaned in. "The first mate's job description is to obey the captain, no questions or arguments. Got that?"

Sugar barely refrained from saluting. "Aye, aye, captain."

"That's my girl," he said with a pleased, downright sexy grin.

That's *my* girl. She was in deep shit, falling for a man who would never love her back. But what the hell! As long as he wanted her, she was his. She ignored how pathetic that sounded.

Well, she would be his for as long as he wanted her unless she had to run.

# CHAPTER TWELVE

Jamie backed the twenty-three-foot Sea Ray away from the dock. Sugar sat on the padded seat next to him, her arms wrapped tightly around her own waist. He loved his boat and wanted her to love it, too. Why that mattered, he chose not to think about.

By the color of her face, however, he thought she was only minutes from hanging her head over the side. It hadn't occurred to him to ask if she was prone to seasickness, but they were only a few yards from the marina, the water as smooth as glass.

To divert her attention, he slipped his arm around her and pulled her onto his lap. "You steer."

"Shit, no."

She tried to scramble away, but he held on to her. "Easy, sweetheart. Just put your hands here." He brought up her unwilling hands and wrapped her fingers around the wheel. Her knuckles turned white. "I won't let you run into anything."

An annoyed breath huffed from her. "Shows what you know. If there's anything within a hundred miles I shouldn't run into, you probably won't be able to stop me. Have you already forgotten the beer truck near miss?"

"I remember. Gave me nightmares." Jamie pressed his mouth to the side of her neck and grinned, although the reminder should probably have had him quaking in his flip-flops and in fear for the life of his boat. Whether she wanted to admit it or not, she liked having control. Already, her fingers were turning back to a healthy pink, and the green was fading from her cheeks.

As she darted alert glances left and right, he eased up the throttle, giving her a little more speed. Minutes later, she gave a delighted laugh as they bounced over the small waves coming in from the inlet.

"Where am I supposed to be going?" she called over the roar of the motors.

"Straight ahead." He wrapped his arms around her waist, liking the feel of her against his body.

She peered back at him, her eyes as wide as saucers. "In the ocean?"

"You a scaredy cat?" Unless he missed his guess, the woman wouldn't refuse a dare.

Her lips thinned into a determined line. "Hell, no."

It took every bit of his control not to laugh when she tossed her straw hat aside, stood, and practically pressed her nose to the windshield. Any desire to laugh died at the sight of her eye-level bikini-clad bottom clearly visible through the gauzy cover-up. Unfortunately, the parrot painted on the back blocked out the enticing parts of her. Figuring more speed would keep her focused on her driving, he moved the throttle forward some more.

"Just keep going in the direction you are. You want to keep inside the red and green buoys." He'd checked the weather before inviting her, and knew there'd only be slight swells on the gulf.

"Piece of cake," she said, and he heard the excitement in her voice. "I can do this. I can do this. I can do this."

Her steady stream of self-encouragement brought a grin to his face. "What are you, the little choo-choo that can?"

Laughter flowed from her. "Yep, that's me."

Giving in to the need to touch her, he placed his hands at her knees, then trailed his fingers up her legs, his thumbs stroking the soft flesh of the inside of her thighs. He slipped under the cover-up, and when he reached that lovely ass in front of his face, her rounded cheeks rippled as the pads of his fingers danced over her skin. So, she liked that.

And he liked the little yellow bikini. Very much. All he had to do to get it off was pull the bows dangling down the sides of her hips. To test her reaction, he gave one a light tug and got swatted.

"Stop it." She brushed his hand away. "I can't concentrate when you do that."

He'd get her out of it before the afternoon was over. He hoped. For now, she was coming up on the inlet, and she didn't have the experience to get them through the pass. Standing, he pressed against her and eased back on the throttle. With his hands on her shoulders, he talked her past the shoals and incoming waves.

"I did it!" she cried when the last of the rock wall was behind them.

"You certainly did." The excitement dancing in her eyes when she looked back at him reminded him of a child on Christmas morning. Once into the Gulf of Mexico, the boat rode the gentle swells as easily as a bobbing cork. He reached his arms forward and put his hands over hers, turning the wheel to the left.

She laughed, then pushed his hands away. "This is so great. I've never been on a boat before, and I love it."

Jamie sat back down, letting her have the wheel. His Sea Ray was his one true love, and his heart gave a little flip at her words. The October day was perfect, warm enough not to be chilled by the wind, but not so hot they were sweltering. A line of pelicans flew overhead, their fat bodies and long beaks outlined by the stark blue sky.

When they took the lead, Sugar bounced on her feet. "Can we go faster? Please. Oh, pretty please."

"The throttle's there at your right hand. Just remember, we're not on a NASCAR racetrack and you're not Earnhardt."

She let out a shriek and pushed the throttle forward, catching up with the pelicans. "Y'all have nothing on me, ya beady-eyed bastards," she yelled heavenward, shaking a fist at them.

Her enthusiasm was contagious, and laughter spilled out of him, coming from places he thought he'd closed and locked the doors to forever. He tried to imagine Jill—or any of the other women he'd dated the past ten years—racing a flock of birds and . . . giving them the finger?

"Sore losers," she muttered.

Jamie glanced behind him to see the pelicans veer off toward shore. "Appears they are. Is this where I'm supposed to soak you with champagne?"

"A simple, 'you're awesome, Sugar,' will suffice." She glanced back and shot him a grin.

The woman *was* pure awesome, a fact he couldn't deny. A funny thing happened then. As clear as day, he saw a fork in the road. One kept him going in the direction a scared, young man once decided was his destiny, a way to honor the parents he'd killed. The other might lead him to hell or heaven. There was no way to know which, only that a beautiful, vibrant woman with the unlikely name of Sugar Darling dared him to follow.

She'd put her hair up in a ponytail before they'd left the dock, and he tugged on it, pulling her down onto his lap. "You are awesome." He put his hand under her chin, turned her face to the side and kissed her. "I surrender," he whispered against her lips, knowing she couldn't possibly understand.

The boat swerved crazily to the left when she wrapped her arms around his neck, and he grabbed the wheel. "Time for me to take over."

"Ooops," she said, then giggled. "You made me forget I was driving, so it's your fault."

"A good sea captain never forgets he's at the wheel, no matter the circumstances," he said, just to rile her.

Surprising him, she turned so her body faced his, her legs straddling him, and her eyes glittered with mischief. "Is that so? Makes me wonder. What if I did this?" After making a quick scan of her surroundings, she put her hands on the hem of her cover-up, lifted it over her head, and tossed it to the seat. Then she reached behind her and pulled the ties to her top, baring her breasts on a level with his mouth.

The boat swerved crazily to the right.

"Jumping junipers, Sugar." He righted the Sea Ray. "I could've killed us." Although he couldn't argue it would be a good way to go out.

"A good sea captain never forgets he's at the wheel, no matter the circumstances," she mocked, her lips forming a smirk.

"Little witch." He pulled the throttle back and cut the engine before covering her breasts with his hands. "Fair warning, I have plans for these." When he flicked his thumbs over her nipples, they puckered. In anticipation, he hoped.

Something that looked a little like fear flickered in her eyes, and she buried her face against his neck, hiding before he could be certain. To say he was confused was an understatement. He caressed her back, rubbing his hand over skin that felt as soft as a baby's.

"I'm not sure how to go on with you, Sugar. One minute, you yank off your top, displaying your girls in all their glory." He kissed the side of her cheek. "And believe me, they are glorious. Then I think I see fear in your eyes. Talk to me. Tell me what you want."

A shudder passed through her body, then she let out a long sigh. "I'm trying to be brave, okay? I want to be normal."

"What makes you think you aren't?" Was he about to find out what had happened to her?

"I don't want to talk about it," she said, her lips still pressed against his neck. "Was it wrong to take off my top? I should know these things, shouldn't I?"

The woman was worming her way into his heart without even trying. Her vulnerability called to his need as a man to protect her, something he'd not planned for. He wasn't sure how to deal with it, but for her he had to try.

"This is important, so listen to me, sweetheart." He leaned away, forcing her to look at him. "If it feels right to you to take your top off, then it's right. Here's what you have to remember. I'll never hurt you, okay? If I ever do something that makes you uncomfortable or scares you, all you have to do is say stop. Simple as that." A strand of hair had come loose from her ponytail, and he curled it around his fingers. "You trust me?"

Her eyes shifted to the horizon a moment before returning to him. "I want to."

Not the answer he wanted, but it would have to do for the time being.

As if suddenly remembering she was bare from the waist up, she crossed an arm over her breasts. "All I have to do is say stop?"

He nodded.

"Then I'll trust you until you give me a reason not to."

Humbled by her faith in him, he cradled her face with his hands. "Thank you." He brushed his lips over hers, holding back from kissing her the way he wanted. Although he knew she liked his kisses—thank God for that much, anyway—he sensed it was not the time to thrust his tongue into her mouth and devour her the way he wanted.

He handed her the bikini top. "I need to anchor us before we end up in the Keys." When she started to put it back on, he grabbed it. "Oh, no you don't. No hiding that killer body from me."

Going to the bow, he dropped the anchor, noting he could still easily see bottom. Could he convince her to do a little skinny-dipping? If he could, he'd consider the day a success. If what frightened her the most was the sight of a man's penis, then if they were naked while in the water, maybe it would be easier for her to get used to him. He just wished he knew the reason for her fear. It would give him some idea on how to go forward.

He turned to make his way back to Sugar and stilled. She'd put her straw hat back on and a pair of sunglasses, but that was all. Sitting on the rear bench, her long legs stretched out in front of her and her face tilted up to the sun, was a goddess come to earth. Although she still wore her bikini bottom, her magnificent breasts were in full view. More aroused than he'd been in too many years, he headed for her.

Sugar forced her hands to stay at her sides and not cross them over her chest. What had possessed her to bare herself to him? The exhilaration of racing his boat, the wind on her face, and just being near him had stolen her sense of self-preservation. How could she want something and not want it at the same time?

The only reason she wasn't swimming for shore was because he'd said she only had to say stop if he did something she didn't want. Well that, and she couldn't swim.

The marvel of it was: she believed him. The last time she'd trusted a man was her daddy before her mama had died. If Jamie knew how momentous her being able to trust him was, he'd probably freak. He'd see it as some kind of hero worship, and he wouldn't want that from her.

If she did think of him as a hero, then that was something she'd just keep to herself. The boat rocked as he made his way back to her, nimbly traversing the narrow ledge just inside the railing. After he jumped to the deck, he whipped off his T-shirt, then came to stand over her.

He slipped his sunglasses down his nose and peered over the rims. "I might have said this before, but it bears repeating. Beautiful."

It took effort, but she managed not to squirm under his leisurely perusal of her body. As determined as Rodney had been to have her, he'd never looked at her the way Jamie was doing, as if she really were beautiful. And desirable.

It had never occurred to her to wonder before now, but if she hadn't been either beautiful or desirable—or both—to Rodney, why had he been so doggedly resolute to own her? Not wanting to ruin this afternoon with Jamie, she shelved the question for later consideration.

Deciding it was only fair to return the favor, she let her eyes roam over his body, starting with the broad shoulders toned to perfection by all the training exercises the guys practiced. A dusting of golden hair crossed the top of his chest, and a darker blond arrow of hair on his stomach pointed to parts below. A trim waist, narrow hips, and long, muscular legs combined with the rest of him made for a pretty spectacular package.

As her gaze traveled back up, she noticed the front of his board-shorts was tented, and as her eyes paused there, the material moved. He was hard and aroused. She jerked her gaze away. How had she missed that on her inspection down his body? Swallowing hard, she forced herself to look at his face. The puzzled but intense expression she saw there said he was trying to figure her out. Not gonna happen, she thought.

"Let's go swimming."

Terror with sharp talons grabbed her heart. Not in a million years. "N-No, thanks." Damn, even she heard the fear in her voice.

Jamie picked up her legs, slid under them, and sat. "You've had a bad experience with water?"

She nodded.

"Want to tell me about it?"

No, no, and no. The man was entirely too perceptive. How could he know she'd almost drowned just by the shakiness in her voice? She pulled her legs from Jamie's lap and tucked them under her.

"Sugar, the blood's drained from your face." He pulled off her sunglass. "And your eyes have gone wild. Talk to me."

She shook her head. Suddenly remembering she was naked from the waist up, she grabbed her cover-up from the back of the bench and clutched it over her chest.

He scooted closer and tucked her under his arm. "The only way to conquer a fear is to confront it. Did you almost drown when you were a child?"

Why couldn't he leave it alone? She had no desire to confront that particular demon.

"Did you?"

"No." She eyed the shoreline, wishing she had the ability to walk on water.

"All grown-up then. So you'd never learned to swim?"

If she didn't answer, maybe he'd give up.

"I'll take your lack of response as a no. Were you alone?"

The full force of her terror that day as she sank to the bottom of the pool—swallowing water all the way down and knowing those few precious seconds were her last on earth—slammed through her.

"No, I wasn't alone!" she screamed, losing all hope of containing the storm roiling inside her. "I wasn't alone," she said, softly. Tears streamed down, hot on her cheeks. "The man I told you about, the only one I've been with, he-he threw me in the end of a pool to teach me a lesson."

"And what lesson would that be?"

Even through her tears, she could see the rage welling in Jamie's eyes, could hear the anger in his voice. For her? She brought the edge of her cover-up to her face and wiped her cheeks.

"That he held my life in his hands." When Rodney had pulled her out and made her throw up the water she'd swallowed, he'd said exactly that.

She could still hear his voice, close to her ear as he'd tugged her head up, his hand fisted in her waist-length hair. "I own you, Hannah. I decide whether you live or die. If you displease me again, I may not pull you out the next time. You know I can make your body disappear so no one will ever find it." It was the calm, cold way he'd said it that made her believe him.

"Did I hear you correctly? A man who supposedly cared for you tried to drown you to teach you a lesson?"

Oh, God, why had she admitted that? "I'm here, aren't I? Obviously, he didn't drown me. He pulled me out of the pool in time." Embarrassed she'd told him even that much, she wrapped her arms around her knees in an attempt to fold into herself. "No more. I think you should take me home."

He spread his arms across the back of the bench seat like a man who had all the time in the world and was going nowhere. "No."

No? Furious, she dropped the cover-up and came at him the way a riled, spitting cat would. So livid she couldn't see straight, she beat on his chest. And he let her.

Finally, his arms came around her. "I'm not him, Sugar, but if it helps to pretend I am, then have at me."

Who was this man that he'd offer to be a punching bag for all her pent-up rage? Feeling like liquefied butter, she melted into him. "I'm sorry. I don't know what just happened. I'm sorry."

"Shhh, sweetheart." He caressed her bare back. "There's nothing to apologize for."

For a few more minutes, she let him hold her and pet her. At some point, she was going to have to lift her face from where it was buried against his neck and look him in the eyes. That she was embarrassed was an understatement. For the life of her, she couldn't comprehend how she'd so outrageously lost control.

"You said you wanted to trust me, and I want that from you. You trust that I'd never do anything to hurt you, right?"

Warily, she leaned back and searched his eyes, wondering what the catch was if she said yes. She saw no trickery in his steady gaze, just the clear, honest stare of a man who'd so far never lied to her.

"Y-Yes."

He chuckled. "That was a half-hearted yes. Say it so I know you mean it."

"Yes," she said with conviction. "I know you will never hurt me."

"Good girl." He took her hands in his and brought one to his mouth and kissed her fingers. "I want you to come into the water with me."

Her heart took a dive to her toes. "No, absolutely not."

"Listen. I'll be right with you, and I promise I'll keep you safe. When I was a SEAL, water was our second home. I'm not asking this to scare you, but to help you face your fear so you can spit in the face of that asshole who lost the right to call himself a man."

*No, please don't do it,* Hannah screamed in her head. Hearing that frightened voice, she made her decision. She was Sugar, and

Sugar could do anything she set her mind to. It had been her mantra from the day she'd escaped her husband.

She should tell Jamie she was married, but she couldn't bring herself to say the words. He would hate her for lying. Not that she'd lied, because he hadn't asked, but a lie of omission was still a lie. She justified keeping her secret because her time with Jamie wouldn't last, so it didn't really matter, did it? Willing to do anything that would enable her to spit in her husband's face—even if metaphorically—she nodded her assent. She would jump into the damn water. It would be another victory over bad cop, and although it would mostly be for Sugar, it would be a little bit for Hannah, too.

A grin spread across his face, so big that Sugar couldn't help grinning back. It didn't mean she wasn't shaking like a leaf in a windstorm.

"That's my girl."

*His girl.* She loved when he said that, and how she wished it was true. He was a man who when he loved, he loved with all that he was. Or so she believed. Maybe not, but she liked thinking it was true. And she wanted to please him, to make him proud of her. So she would get in the water and pray she didn't panic and drown.

As if reading her thoughts, he said, "I'll keep you safe, I promise." His gaze lingered on her bare breast for a moment before he leaned forward and gave her a soft kiss on her mouth, and it was so sweet that she just wanted to crawl into him and live there.

He dropped his hands and stood. "I'm going in first so I'll be there for you."

The panic returned. "I can't jump in, I just can't."

"You don't have to. I'm going to hook a ladder on the stern, and you'll come down it."

Oh, God, what had she been thinking to agree to this? She watched with misgiving as he opened a bin and pulled out a ladder and life vest, the sight of which eased her anxiety a little. But only a little.

"Do I get to wear that?"

"You get to hold on to it." He gave her a wicked grin. "But I'd rather you hold on to me."

She'd rather hold on to him *and* the vest. After hooking the ladder on the back of the boat, he set the vest near it, then dived into the water. Startled, she jumped up and peered over the side where he'd disappeared. The gulf was emerald green and crystal clear, and she watched as he swam to the bottom as if he'd been born a fish. He grabbed something, then shot to the top like a torpedo. His body popped halfway out of the water before sinking back down to his neck.

Wow. Maybe he really was part fish. He swam to the side of the boat and held up his hand, showing her a bright orange starfish.

"Oh, that's so cool." She touched it with a finger and when it moved, she snatched her hand away. "It's really bumpy. You're going to let it go, right?"

"Hold out your hand."

When she did, he put it in her palm.

"Just stay like that and it'll crawl off and back into the water."

It tickled when it moved, and sure enough, it fell off and plopped back into the gulf, and she watched it return to the bottom. She glanced at Jamie to see him looking at her, a smile on his face. Her heart did a funny dance, and she knew she was in trouble. The day he tired of her, or if the day came she had to run, it was going to hurt worse than anything Rodney had ever done to her.

# CHAPTER THIRTEEN

"Time for you to join me." Jamie moved to the back of the boat and grabbed hold of the ladder. "Come, Sugar."

She stared down at him and then eyed the water surrounding them before shaking her head. "I don't want to."

It was obvious she was scared, and she had every right to be considering what had been done to her. He'd wanted to demand the man's name because whoever he was, he deserved a beating.

"Come, sweetheart," he said, holding out his hand. If she panicked once he talked her into getting in the water, he'd get her back on the boat. If they were going to spend some time together, he wanted her to love boating and the water as much as he did.

He also believed she needed to confront her fear. What if she fell in a pool someday, or off his boat if he took her out again? She needed to know how to swim, at least enough to float on her back until she was rescued.

"You said you trusted me, right?"

She crossed her arms over her breasts, and her gaze darted from him to the water, then back to him. "I changed my mind."

"You changed your mind about trusting me or that you'll come in with me?" The bastard had done a real number on her. If he'd been willing to almost drown her to exert his control over her, what else had he done to her?

"Both," she said.

"Put your hand in mine, sweetheart," Jamie said, still holding up his arm.

Her feet slid forward a few inches, then stopped. "You promise you won't make me put my head under the water?"

"You have my word. You're safe with me, Sugar." A visible shudder traveled through her, and he almost gave in. Just as he opened his mouth to tell her she didn't have to, she reached out and placed her hand in his. Because she was doing this for him, a tenderness he'd never felt for any woman before slipped its way into his heart.

"Turn around and climb down backwards," he said when she eyed the ladder with misgivings. "I'll be right behind you." It took a few minutes as she descended at the pace of a sloth. Once in, with the water at shoulder level, she held on to the ladder with an iron grip and white knuckles. Her eyes had gone so wild, he didn't think she even saw him.

He grabbed the life vest and floated it in front of her. "Sugar, look at me." Whether it was the command in his voice or just plain desperation, her gaze locked on his, her eyes beseeching him to save her. "Easy, sweetheart. I'm right here."

Hoping to make her feel more secure, he grabbed the ladder, caging her next to his body and lifting his leg to her bottom to form a seat. He'd thought to have the vest for her to hang on to, but her fear was just too great.

"I'm going to put this on you," he said, "but you're going to have to let go so I can slip it up your arms." The leg he'd put under her seemed to help. She let go of the ladder and wrapped her arms around his neck in a death grip.

"I'm not usually such a coward."

No, she wasn't. She was a brave, brave girl who trusted him not to let her drown. "Actually, you're amazing." Although he had to peel her fingers out of the ends of his hair, he managed to get the vest on her. Once it was snapped up, he decided the next best thing to do would be to kiss her.

She responded immediately; whether from the pleasure of having his mouth on hers or because it took her mind away from fearing she was going to drown, he didn't know. Didn't care. All he knew was kissing her was even better than double-chocolate chip cookies, and those, he loved. As her back was now to the boat and she hopefully wouldn't notice, he floated them both away.

Her legs were wrapped around his waist so tightly he'd probably need a crowbar to pry her away, but he had no desire to. For a few minutes he allowed them to drift, letting her get used to being in the water. Too bad there was a life vest between his chest and her breasts. If he could get his mouth on them, they would taste seawater salty. Soon, he vowed.

When he felt some of the tension drain from her body, he dog-paddled back toward the boat, keeping one arm around her waist. Now to see if he could get the rest of her suit off.

"Hold on to the ladder for a minute."

She didn't let go of him. "Why?"

"I need to do something. I'm not going away," he added, before she could protest. As soon as he had his hands free, he slipped off his shorts and tossed them into the boat.

"What're you doing?"

"Just this." He quickly tugged on the ties of her bikini bottom and pitched it over the side.

"Jamie!"

"Mmm?" While her attention was on her newly nude state, he took her hands and pulled her with him, away from the boat. "Having fun yet?"

She snorted. "Seriously? I'm in the middle of the ocean, and the only thing I'm wearing is a life vest, and you want to know if I'm having fun?"

"Then my work here isn't done." Whether she realized it or not, she was more at ease and was even treading water. No longer plastered around him like she'd been glued to him, she only had the fingers of one hand curled around his wrist as he dog-paddled them in place.

"When can we get back in the boat?"

"Soon." He pulled her to him, sorry for the vest she wore. "But first this." Careful to keep his erection—the one he'd had from the moment he'd removed her bikini bottom—from touching her, he angled his head and covered her mouth with his. She put her hands on his shoulders and parted her lips. It was all the invitation he needed.

Water lapped gently around them as he explored her mouth, her taste one he could come to crave. He slid his hand over the back of the vest to her bottom and cupped a taut, rounded cheek in his palm. It was cool to the touch from the sea, and little goosebumps rose on her skin as he caressed her.

Unfortunately, in his lust-induced haze, he forgot his intention to keep the lower parts of their bodies separated and pulled her against him. She wrapped her legs around his waist, putting her right where he wanted her. The head of his erection nudged itself past her folds, seeking entrance.

Her body went instantly stiff, and she tried to push away. "Jamie!"

"Sorry." He put his hands on her waist and moved back. "That wasn't intentional, Sugar." Distrustful eyes stared back at him in accusation. Irritated she didn't believe him, he slipped his fingers through the vest's snaps and towed her back to the boat.

Was she worth the trouble?

Probably not, but he couldn't deny he wanted her. If he could figure out why that was, maybe he could find a cure. The girl had issues, that was certain. Yet, the way she responded when he kissed her and touched her told him there was a sensuous woman inside her screaming to get out of whatever prison she'd been locked into. The temptation was there to find the key that would unlock the cell door.

"Jamie, I'm sorry."

He slipped an arm around the ladder and turned. If he'd accomplished nothing else, at least he'd helped her face her fear of the water. She probably didn't even realize she'd let go of him and was using her hands to keep her in place. Or that the water was so clear he could see her pubic hair and long, sleek legs. The red polish on her toes flashed in and out of sight as her feet busily dog-paddled.

How long would it take him to get her to come in without the life vest or her bathing suit so those magnificent breasts of hers would float tantalizingly near the top of the water? That he was asking the question told him he'd answered another one. He would do his best to prove to her some unnamed bastard had it all wrong, would prove to her that sex with the right person was a thing of beauty.

She grabbed the opposite side of the ladder. "I'm sorry."

"For what?"

"I panicked," she answered, her gaze on the horizon as if she were too embarrassed to look at him.

Jamie put a finger under her chin and turned her face back to him. The tears filling her eyes tore at his heart. "There's no denying I want you. I want to slide inside you and lose myself in you. I want to make love to you so badly I'd give up my boat for it." He slid a glance at his beloved Sea Ray, wondering if he'd really just said that. "Okay, maybe not quite that bad, but close. So damn close, Sugar."

She gave him an adorable scowl. "Why are ya all of a sudden cursing? Not that I don't, but it's just weird when you do."

Good question. He put his hand on the boat and pushed away from her. To answer her question, he'd have to tell her why he'd hit the delete button on cussing in the first place, and why she had him saying words he hadn't said for ten years. To avoid going there, he decided to turn the tables on her.

He forced a chuckle. "I just told you how much I want you and your response is to ask why I'm cursing?"

Sugar didn't know what to say. When she'd first met him and started this game, she'd flirted with him the way she thought a woman who was attracted to him would. For a while, it had been a safe flirtation because he'd made it clear he didn't like her. Knowing he wouldn't put any moves on her, her behavior had grown more outrageous in her attempts to get a reaction out of him. It looked like she had.

She understood she was at a crossroads with Jamie. There was probably not another man on earth who would tolerate her fears the way he had and continued to do. But for how much longer? When she'd felt him poking her down there, she'd transported back to Rodney and the cruelty she'd suffered at his hands.

Logically, she knew she wasn't being fair to the man waiting for her response; she knew he wouldn't hurt her. Not like that, anyway. How could she explain the punishments she'd been subjected to so he'd understand, without spilling her pathetic story? She didn't want his pity, nor did she want him to feel like he needed to avenge her. Already, he'd asked several times for Rodney's name. Why? So he could track her husband down and teach him some kind of lesson?

Although she'd tried without success to put out of her mind the man knocking on the condos' doors and asking questions, the idea that Rodney had found her scared the bejesus out of her. No way did she want to involve Jamie in her problems. But if she had a week or two before she had to haul ass, maybe he could get her past turning into an icicle at the touch of a man.

And if her heart decided to stay behind with him . . . well, it was a risk worth taking. So what if she couldn't wear mascara for the next six months because she couldn't stop crying? All she had to do was gather up the courage Sugar pretended to have and . . . she swallowed hard. She could sleep with him without losing her lunch. She could!

First she had to climb the ladder, her rear end in all its naked glory available for his viewing pleasure. No way would she let him go first and stay in the water by herself. Although if he did go first, she'd be the one ogling him.

Tempting, but she wasn't ready to do a solo swim yet. Admittedly, as long as he was with her and she had the vest on, he'd helped her face her fear as he called it. When he'd kissed her, she'd even forgotten she was in the water. If she liked kissing him that much, would sleeping with him really be as bad as it had been with Rodney? There was only one way to know and that was to just do it, to face another fear. On the positive side, it wouldn't kill her like drowning in the ocean would.

"You could probably fill a book with all the thinking you've just done. I'd give anything to know what's going through your head."

She lifted her gaze to his. Blue eyes stared patiently back at her, and that was another thing she wasn't used to: a man's patience. "I was only thinking if I don't get out of this water, I'm going to look like a prune."

"Oh, there was more than that going on in your head, but after you," he said, sweeping an arm up.

"Close your eyes."

One side of his mouth curved up in a wickedly sexy grin. "So not happening, sweetheart."

"Pervert," she grumbled, reaching for the ladder.

A low chuckle rumbled out of him. "No, just a man who appreciates the sight of a beautiful woman and her sexy bottom."

If he wanted to put it that way, who was she to argue? When she lifted her ass out of the water, he growled and put a hand on her butt to help push her up. She had to admit it was a heady feeling to have a man like him make throaty sounds because he wanted her. At the moment, with him, she'd give anything if she were a normal, sex-is-a-good-and-wonderful-thing kind of woman.

*Hope you rot in hell someday, Rodney.*

She scurried over to the bench seat and sat, pressing her legs together and placing her hands over her lap. How had Jamie managed to talk her into the gulf, strip her of all but a life vest, and have her almost enjoy the experience before it was over?

A water god rose from the depths and stood over her, glistening seawater dripping down a body that took her breath away. Mamma mia, someone should coat his lovely self in plaster and stick him in an art gallery. Women the world over would beat down the doors to get a glimpse of such a magnificent specimen.

Her gaze slid to the one part of him she wasn't so keen on. It didn't look too threatening, shriveled up in a nest of golden curls. It must have realized she was eyeing it because it moved, grew a little. She wished it wouldn't do that.

"He's not going to hurt you, Sugar."

Were all her thoughts scrawled across her forehead for him to read? "I know," she whispered. But that was a lie. She summoned her courage and met his unwavering gaze. "Actually, I don't know it. I-I want it to be true. It's just . . . there are things . . ." No, she wouldn't go there.

"Touch me. See for yourself I'm harmless." An amused smile curved the corners of his mouth. "I can't believe I just said that."

It was the humor in his voice and the kindness in his eyes she couldn't resist. If she didn't do this now, she never would and it would be a regret she'd have to live with for the rest of her life. She forced her hand to lift and touched the tip of him with her index finger. It reached for her the way Junior did when he needed a pet.

A laugh escaped, surprising her. She trailed her finger down the side of him, amazed and pleased with herself that she was touching *that*. His skin there was hot and velvety. As she explored him, he grew and grew and grew. Her stomach gave a churning dip, then settled as if even it knew he was safe.

His pubic hair was still damp and springy to the touch. When she trailed her hand under him and held his balls in her palm, the muscles in his legs flexed. From above, she heard a growl and looked up to see his attention was focused on her hand and what she was doing to him. Then his lashes lifted, his gaze landing on her face. Heat shimmered in eyes gone as dark as the midnight blue of a sky.

"Sugar."

Her name was spoken in two drawn-out syllables, sounding almost as if he was in pain. Even as clueless as she was about these things, she understood he wanted her and he wanted her badly. For the first time in her life as a woman, she had a glimpse of the power that was hers to command if only she dared.

# CHAPTER FOURTEEN

Jamie gritted his teeth. It was obvious Sugar didn't know what she was doing, yet her fingers were like magic, leaving tingling sparks everywhere she touched him. The slow glide of her hand down his shaft to his balls, then back up again, then back down, almost did him in. Just as he started to drop to his knees and beg her to let him show her how good they could be together, he heard the sound of a boat motor.

A cigarette boat traveling at maximum speed seemed to be aiming straight for them. What the heck? He grabbed her cover-up and thrust it into her hands. "Get below," he ordered, reaching for his shorts.

She blinked back at him, confusion in her eyes. "Below?"

The speeding boat continued on its course, and he scooped her up. With three long strides, he arrived at the door to the cabin, opened it, and tossed her onto the bunk. "Don't come out until I tell you to."

"What's happening?"

"I don't know. There's another boat going way too fast, headed straight for us."

Faster than a crab caught on top of the sand after a wave, she scrambled for cover, pulling the bunk sheet over her. "Is it him?"

He'd been about to close the door when her words stopped him. "Is it who?"

"No one. I don't know what I'm saying. It's just that you're scaring me."

"Stay here," he said, pulling the door shut. If she entertained the chance that the mysterious *him* could be in the other boat, then he wouldn't discount the possibility.

After pulling on his boardshorts and T-shirt, he opened the compartment near the steering wheel and removed the loaded Glock 19, slipping it behind his back, into the waistband of his shorts. Deciding it best to be ready to flee, he started the engine and eased the throttle forward, turning the boat toward the open water. As sweet as the Sea Ray's engines were, he'd never be able to outrun the Marauder 50 if the occupant was up to no good.

The sleek, silver boat veered off at the last minute and circled them. Jamie recognized the driver, a loud-mouthed, pot-smoking man in his late twenties who didn't seem to work as he was always hanging around the dock. Because he hadn't trusted the dude, Jamie had previously done some checking up on Roger Blankenship, not surprised when he'd learned the man was a drug dealer. Just what was he up to?

There was only one question Jamie wanted an answer to, however. Who was the man in the passenger seat? The way the guy was looking over the Sea Ray, like he was searching for something, made Jamie uneasy. *More like he's looking for someone, Saint, and just who might that be?* Willing Sugar to stay out of sight, he slipped the gun from his back and held it down by his leg.

"Roger, can I help you with something?" he called.

The other man said something to Roger that Jamie couldn't hear over the noise of the engines. Growing more suspicious by the minute, Jamie slid his finger over the trigger.

"You out here alone?" Roger yelled.

Jamie glanced around his boat as if checking to see if anyone else was with him. "Appears so. What puzzles me though is why that's any of your business."

A seemingly tense conversation ensued between the two men, and Jamie took the opportunity to give the Sea Ray a little more power, putting more distance between him and the Marauder. He didn't want trouble, would avoid it if at all possible, but his gut said trouble was brewing.

So far, he hadn't seen any weapons in evidence, but he didn't doubt the men were armed. Considering Roger was a drug dealer, Jamie had to assume the man carried at all times, and considering the shaved head and all the tattoos visible on the other man—especially because of the inked teardrop just below his left eye—Jamie wouldn't be surprised if he was an ex-con. Was that the man who had hurt Sugar? If so, Jamie itched to put a bullet right between his eyes. Yet, he just couldn't picture her with the dude. If not him, then was he a hired gun? Someone sent to find her and bring her back to whomever she had escaped from? That was more likely, he decided.

"He wants the woman," Roger said.

Now there was a surprise. If he had the slightest chance of outrunning them, he would push the throttle to full power and take off that minute. But there was no way he could leave the high-powered cigarette boat behind. His best chance was to outsmart them, and if that didn't work, he'd have to shoot them. That would end up being a hot mess.

"I thought we just established I'm alone. Can't deny I wish I had a woman, but sorry, can't help you with something I don't have."

The second man stood and brought up a 9mm, aiming it Jamie. "I want the woman, asshole."

"Can't have her, *asshole*." As he spoke, knowing any words would have the effect of delaying the man's reaction as he listened, Jamie brought up his Glock, aimed, and fired. Being a crack shot, he hit his target, and the 9mm was jerked out of the man's hand and went flying into the water.

"Fuck," the dude cried out as he shook his hand.

Jamie didn't doubt that had hurt, but the man should consider it his lucky day he was still breathing. The mood Jamie was in at that point, he'd just as soon have followed through on his first thought and put the bullet between the man's eyes.

"Yeah, that hurt, didn't it? Next time, there won't be any pain because you won't be alive to feel it. Before you go back to whatever hole you crawled out of, I want you to tell the man you're working for that no one takes what's mine."

That probably hadn't been the smartest thing to say as it would be a challenge to Sugar's nameless man. His buttons had been pushed, though, and putting a claim on Sugar had popped out of his mouth before he'd thought better of it.

Pointing his weapon at Roger, Jamie said, "You have exactly three seconds to disappear." He didn't doubt Roger would take off, but what was to keep them from coming back? Then an idea occurred to him, and he lowered his weapon and fired three times, making a three-inch hole in the boat's hull just below the waterline.

"What the hell, man?" Roger screamed.

"I estimate you have just enough time to make it back to the dock before that pricey boat sinks. You should probably get going."

The inked man leveled a stare full of hatred at Jamie. "You haven't seen the last of me," he spat.

"Then you're a dead man," Jamie said just before Roger gave the cigarette boat full throttle, causing the Marauder to practically rocket out of the water with the grace of a soaring killer whale.

Until the boat disappeared around the cove, Jamie didn't move, nor did he put away his gun. What kind of trouble was Sugar in? He turned to the closed door of the Sea Ray's cabin. There hadn't been the slightest squeak from her since he'd tossed her onto the bunk. Time to get some answers.

He reached for the handle and opened the cabin door. "The man who almost drowned you, is he looking for you?" The anger raging inside him died at seeing her curled into a ball with the pillow pulled over her head. She gave no sign that she heard him. He sat on the edge of the bunk and leaned over her.

"Sugar?" Lifting the pillow, he peered down at her face. "Sweetheart, you're safe."

She blinked up at him, and he'd never seen such fear in anyone's eyes before. Jamie brushed her hair away from her face. "The man who hurt you, does he have tattoos?"

"What? No, I don't know anyone like that." Her gaze darted to the doorway. "Are they gone? I heard gunshots."

"Who would they be, Sugar? You need to tell me what's going on, or I can't help you." Her reaction to his question puzzled him. The eyes he thought beautiful blanked, and he got the feeling she had just shut down all her emotions. The second her gaze shifted away from him and she stared at the wall in front of her face, he knew she wasn't going to tell him.

So be it. She clearly didn't trust him enough to confide in him. He'd wanted to make a full day of her first time on his boat. In the small fridge was a platter filled with a variety of cheeses and fruit. Assorted crackers and chocolate chip cookies he'd made himself were tucked away in a cabinet along with a bottle of wine. All intended to be enjoyed while tied up at the dock at sunset.

Change of plans. She was in no condition for a romantic evening. Leaving her on the bunk, he went topside. He started the engines, pressed the throttle down, and headed back to the marina.

As the boat skimmed over the water, he thought about the woman below and all he knew about her.

From the first, he'd jumped to conclusions about Sugar Darling that he was learning were so off base that he'd not even been in the right ballpark when sizing her up. Her tough exterior hid a vulnerable and somewhat naïve woman, one who apparently needed a protector. He was the wrong man for the job. The people he loved ended up dead.

*Is that why you choose the women you do, Saint? Ones you'll never fall in love with even though you claim that's what you want?*

Did a part of him believe he'd find a way to kill the next person he loved? It was a disturbing insight—if that's what it was.

*What if Sugar was the one?* Even though she was a conundrum with her combination of soft and hard, courage and fearfulness, and innocence and brashness, he liked her. Who was he kidding? He'd passed *like* when he'd held her in his arms and given her the first orgasm of her life.

Still, she had baggage he didn't want to open, and he didn't have it in him to be what she needed. He'd been doing just fine in his search for a wife before Sugar had blown into his life like a whirling dust devil. Okay, not entirely true, but maybe he hadn't been putting enough effort into it, and that he could change.

Having a disruptive, mini tornado—with the potential to turn his life into chaos—for a wife didn't bear consideration. The woman he married would have a calm temperament like his mother, would bake double-chocolate chip cookies for him and their kids, and wouldn't call to his base emotions.

As he slowed in the no-wake zone, his tormentor poked her head out. "Do I need to do anything to help you land?"

"Dock. We don't land, we dock." She flinched at the harshness in his voice, and he sighed. Granted it was because of her his head was spinning like a kid's top, but that was no reason to snap at her.

"Okay, what should I do?"

She really did have beautiful eyes, and they were looking everywhere but at him. "I think you should stay out of sight until I get things put away and we can leave."

"I'm sorry," she said before disappearing back into the cabin.

So was he.

Normally, he washed down the Sea Ray after taking her out, but all that mattered now was getting Sugar home and hopefully finding the adage *out of sight, out of mind* to be true.

"That's a cool name for a boat," she said as he hurried her up the dock toward his car.

He followed her gaze to see a fifty-something-foot yacht named *Therapy*. "Uh-huh. Come on, let's go." So they were going to pretend their afternoon hadn't been interrupted by gunfire.

"Why doesn't your boat have a name?"

"Just never got around to it." That wasn't true, but he wasn't about to tell her he planned to name the Sea Ray after his wife, whoever she might be. It was bad luck to change the name of a boat, so he'd not picked a temporary one. He headed up the dock, keeping an eye out for Roger and his friend. The Marauder wasn't in sight, and Jamie hoped it was sitting on the bottom of the gulf. He slowed his strides when he realized Sugar was jogging to keep up with him.

"You should name it. Something cool, maybe *Saint's Pleasure*."

"It's a she, and no, I'll come up with a name for her when I'm ready." *Stop talking, Sugar, just stop.* He didn't want to listen to that musical southern voice of hers; he didn't want to feel her body heat as she walked next to him; and he didn't want the scent of her in his nose.

"Is that the bathroom?" she asked, pointing to a building off to the side.

"Yeah, you need to use it?"

She nodded and without waiting, veered off. He trailed after her, refusing to let her out of his sight. Just because he hadn't spied Roger and friend didn't mean they weren't around. As he waited outside the building, Roger came around the corner and when he saw Jamie, he froze. Then he gave a slight shake of his head before backing up.

Jamie had already palmed his weapon. "If you take another step, I will shoot you. Don't think I won't."

Roger stilled and put his hands up, palms facing out. "Look, man, I don't know what that was all about. The dude gave me a thousand bucks to follow you. It's gonna take every bit of that to fix my boat." He narrowed his eyes. "Hell, man. Since you put the hole in it, you should pay to fix it."

Jamie snorted. "Not happening. That's the kind of thing you should expect when you play with the bad guys. You saying you don't know his name or what he wanted?"

"No. You could say he ain't a sharing kind of man."

That was likely true. "I'm gonna give you some valuable advice, Roger. He comes around again, it would be in your interest to refuse any request he might make. Second, you get any thought in your head to come after me or the woman, you'll regret it. Trust me, I'm badder than I look."

The drug dealer nodded his head as if he were one of those bobbing-head dolls some people put in their cars. "Look, man, I don't want no trouble. I ain't never seen shooting like that. Not many coulda done that. I got things going on I don't wanna mess up, you get me?"

That the man's drug deals were his priority eased Jamie's mind about having to keep an eye out for Roger. "I get you, and I'll take you at your word unless you prove I shouldn't. We good?"

Roger began to nod again, then his gaze slid past Jamie's shoulder, and his eyes widened. Jamie knew before he turned what he'd see. "You give him one of your guns?"

"No, man," Roger said, vigorously shaking his head.

Jamie spun and took off after the man dragging Sugar toward the parking lot. He dismissed shooting at a moving target, afraid he'd hit her. Nor did he want anyone to call the cops. The man was his, and he wasn't in the mood to share.

Although she was gagged, Sugar screamed through the cloth while fighting like a furious tigress as she tried to kick the man in the groin with the heel of her foot.

*Good girl, sweetheart. Slow him down.* As Jamie closed the distance between them, he saw the moment she realized he was coming for her. The panic in her eyes slowly receded as she locked her gaze onto his. She knew he would save her. Even as he put on a burst of speed, his heart, his brain, his body surrendered to Sugar Darling. She was his, and any man who thought otherwise would live to regret it.

If the man had a second gun, he would have used it by then, so Jamie leapt through the air without fearing he would be shot. The front of his body hit her first, and he wrapped his arms around both her and the man, forcing them to land on top of the bastard who had dared to touch her.

Once they rolled to a stop with him straddling her, and her lying over the man's chest, Jamie pressed his hand hard over the man's face, pushing the back of his head into the pavement. Then he turned his focus onto Sugar and winked. It wasn't what he wanted to do. He wanted to kiss the fear right out of her eyes, but there was still a man needing a lesson before he could tell Sugar Darling—a woman he'd never thought to want in his life—that he had changed his mind. He removed the gag.

"I want to go home," she said, then turned her face away.

That was all she had to say after everything that had happened? "Fine." He pulled her up and handed her his car keys. "Here. Lock yourself in while I take care of some things."

With a foot pressed hard against the man's chest and his weapon aimed at his head, Jamie made a quick phone call to K2 and had a brief conversation with the boss. After hanging up, he jerked the man up, and at the point of the gun, prodded him to the back of his car, and then pushed him back against the trunk.

"You even sneeze, I'll pull the trigger," he said.

For the fifteen minutes it took Kincaid and Jake to arrive, Jamie kept his gun pointed at his prisoner. The questions he asked were met with stony silence. He knew how to get the man to talk, but Sugar was in the car, and she'd had enough trauma for one day. Kincaid and Jake arrived and hauled off the man.

Jamie slid into the driver's seat and started the car. "Tell me everything."

It was a command Sugar would not obey. Jamie could have been killed out there on the water because of her. That she could not live with. She would return to Rodney first.

"There's nothing to tell," she answered, keeping her gaze on the passing scenery. If she looked at him, she would see his disappointment in her. He wanted her to trust him, and she did. If she told him, though, he would go after her husband. She could live with knowing she was hurting Jamie by her silence if it meant keeping him alive.

A battle raged in Sugar's head between herself and Hannah. When the other boat had come at them, soon followed by gunshots, the chance that she would be taken back to Rodney had paralyzed her. In her despair, Hannah had taken over, curling herself into a ball with the pillow over her head. Helpless. So damn helpless.

Even now, Hannah begged . . . for what, Sugar no longer knew. But Sugar was supposed to be fearless, willing to fight for the new life she had created for herself. Run or stay and fight? Because there was no doubt Rodney had found her.

She glanced at the man driving the car. He'd been stonily quiet since she'd refused to answer his question. She had so many regrets where he was concerned.

They turned into her complex, and he pulled up next to her car. "Go inside and pack enough to get you through the next few days," he said as he stared straight ahead.

"I'm staying here." There was no way she was going home with him. If Rodney somehow found her with another man . . . she didn't even want to consider the consequences. What she wouldn't tell Jamie was that she had no intention of staying in her condo knowing Rodney was close. She would check into a motel while she decided what to do.

He looked at her then, his eyes hard and determined. "No. You're not. If I have to tie you up and take you where you'll be safe, I will. You're staying with Jake and Maria. It's already been taken care of, and Maria's expecting you."

Funny that she was hurt he didn't want her with him when that wasn't what she wanted either.

After dropping Sugar off at Maria's, Jamie headed straight for K2. He wanted in on the interrogation. He found Kincaid and Jake in the back warehouse area that they used to set up mock houses, or sometimes small villages, when they had an upcoming mission. Kincaid believed in being prepared in every way possible, and they would re-create the interior of a house or village if they could get that kind of information from an informant, then spend days practicing as if it were the real deal.

In the far back was an area that had two windowless cells for the rare occasion they needed to interrogate someone. Knowing that was where he would find them, he crossed the warehouse floor.

Jake met him outside the cell door. "Figured I'd see you here. You take Sugar to my house?"

"Yeah. Foolish woman wanted to stay at her place. Told her I'd tie her up if I had to." He glanced at the closed door. "Learn anything?"

"Name's Jax Harrison. Served time for armed robbery. Got out four months ago, and obviously didn't waste any time getting involved with the wrong crowd. He doesn't know anything. Says a dude approached him in a bar, offered him three thousand bucks to do a job."

"Not even a name?" Jamie wanted to get his hands on the man inside the cell, even knowing he'd get nothing more out of him after Kincaid had been at him.

"No, but here's the interesting thing. The man knew our guy. Knew his name and that he'd recently been released. Threatened to send him back behind bars. Said he had the power to do it."

"Does that sound like a cop to you?"

Jake nodded. "Unless he was bullshitting our guy."

They pretty much had nothing then. "How was he supposed to get back in touch once he had Sugar?"

"With a burner phone. Unfortunately, he claims to have lost it."

"That's bull. He tossed it somehow."

"That's what the boss is discussing with him as we speak," Jake said, his gaze on the cell door with a look that said he wished he was in the closed room.

Frustrated, Jamie swiped his hand through his hair. "What's Kincaid plan to do with him?"

Jake grinned, and it wasn't pretty. "He's to be our guest for a few days until he finds Jesus."

At least Sugar would be safe from Jax Harrison. But who would come after her next time? The man who wanted her back, or would he send someone else?

# CHAPTER FIFTEEN

The next morning, Jamie poked his head into Jake Buchanan's office, but Jake wasn't there. Sugar hadn't been at the reception-ist desk when he'd arrived, and he needed to make sure she was okay. Ryan O'Connor had arrived and was in the operations room with Stewart. Jake would want to sit in with them on the operation's final planning stages, but where the doggone was he? Probably with Maria.

Turning on his heels, Jamie strode across the open area between offices. Maria's door was slightly ajar, and he raised his hand to knock.

"Normally, we fingerprint all our employees, but I'm going to have a momentary lapse and forget to do yours."

Who was Maria talking to?

"I don't want ya to get in trouble. Thing is, I think it's time for me to move on."

No mistaking that southern accent. At the sound of Sugar's voice, Jamie lowered his hand. She would just up and leave without a word to him? If nothing else, that told him that he didn't mean anything to her. He wasn't prepared for the hurt that hit him square in the gut. Damn her, he thought, and made a mental note to put a dollar in the swear jar when he arrived home. Kincaid headed his way, and Jamie reluctantly moved away from the door.

He followed the boss into the war room and spent the next hour planning the extraction of the aid workers out of Syria. It was great to have Doc back on the team, and Jamie was glad to see him hit it off with Stewart. A part of him regretted he wouldn't be going on the operation, but since he'd just returned from Somalia he wasn't up on the rotation. The way he was feeling, he wouldn't mind an ocean between him and Sugar.

As soon as they wrapped things up, Jamie headed to his office and spent the next ten minutes staring at his computer. Who was Sugar Darling? He typed her name and held his finger over the Enter key. Did he want to know? She obviously didn't want him to know her secrets, and he didn't understand why. Didn't she realize he—all of K2, in fact—could help her?

"You daydreaming on the job?" Ryan O'Connor asked.

Jamie pressed the Delete key and leaned back in his chair. "Yeah, and she's every man's dream woman." The comeback was safe because his teammates knew Saint never mixed business and pleasure. Doc snorted, giving Jamie the reaction he'd wanted.

"Didn't get a chance to talk to you before the meeting. It's good to see you, Saint," he said, taking a seat.

"Back at you. So, whatcha think?"

"It's great to be back with the team. Can't believe Romeo's married. That was a shocker when I heard, but now that I've met Maria . . ." He waggled his brows.

"Don't let her hear you call him Romeo. He's Tiger these days."

Doc had married his childhood sweetheart, and had never caroused with the guys. When she'd been murdered a year ago, he had opted out of the navy and literally disappeared. Jamie could relate to losing a loved one.

"I wanted to come to the funeral, but I was in Afghanistan. You doing okay?" Jamie asked when the conversation lagged.

Pain flashed in Doc's eyes, and he glanced away. "Yeah, I'm fine."

Subject closed. But his friend wasn't fine, and Jamie wished he had something better to say about the loss of a wife other than "you doing okay." If Sugar and Maria were having this conversation, they'd probably share all their feelings and hold each other while they cried. Obviously, Sugar had felt more comfortable confiding her troubles to Maria than to him. He hated that it bugged him.

"The receptionist's the hottest thing I've seen in a long time. She single? Didn't see a wedding ring, but these days, that doesn't always tell the story."

Jamie blinked, then mentally berated himself for showing too much. He blanked his face, hoping it wasn't too late. "Haven't a clue." Not a lie since there was someone looking for her. If it was a boyfriend or husband, how was he supposed to know? He forced himself to remain still under Doc's scrutiny.

His friend leaned his head back, stared up at the ceiling, and laughed. "Well hell, Saint's got a thing for a hot chick. About time."

Someone else had recently said "about time." Jake, maybe. What was it with his teammate's opinions of the women he dated? Before Sugar, that was, and she was an anomaly.

"So it's hands off?"

Jamie opened his mouth to say he didn't care if Doc hit on her. "Fucking A."

Doc laughed so hard, he lost his breath, bringing on a coughing spell. "Saint." Cough. "Said." Cough. "Fuck." He walked out, still laughing while muttering about needing water.

Jamie opened his wallet to see if he needed to run by the bank and get more ones on his way home. The swear jar was filling up fast.

"Hey, beautiful. I'm Ryan O'Conner."

Sugar knew who he was, but if anyone was beautiful, it was the man draped carelessly over the counter. Ryan O'Connor, or Doc as the guys referred to him, had the most unusual eyes she'd ever seen and she could probably stare into them for . . . well, like forever. Green was their primary color, but there were streaks of orange in the irises, and she'd never seen any like them.

A knowing grin crossed his face and she reared back, embarrassed to be caught staring. Other than his eyes, he did nothing for her even as drop-dead gorgeous as he was. He wasn't Jamie.

"I'm Sugar Darling," she said, then clamped her mouth shut to keep from apologizing for her delay in responding. Damn, those eyes made it hard to think.

"I know, and sadly, you're off-limits." He winked, then disappeared back into the inner sanctum.

Bewildered, she eyed the door as it closed behind him. What was that all about? Who said she was off-limits? The phone rang, and after giving a confused shake of her head, she answered, forgetting about the strange conversation.

After putting the call through to the boss, she eyed the clock. Although there was an hour left to the workday, she didn't intend to stay. First thing that morning, after tossing and turning all night, she'd made the decision to leave. Living with Jake and Maria for the rest of her life was out, so where did that leave her? Cowering in her condo waiting for Rodney to appear? No, it was time to introduce Nikki Swanson to the world, and for it to work, she would have to leave.

As for what it would do to her to never see Jamie again, she couldn't even think about that.

Maria and Jake were on their way to New Orleans for a few days to celebrate their anniversary. She was supposed to stay at their house while they were gone, and they had assured her no one could get past their alarm system. Also, they'd arranged to have one of the K2 guys keep an eye on the house. But she wouldn't be there.

Hannah had almost taken over in the cabin of Jamie's boat, her fear so paralyzing that Sugar wasn't sure she could recover. It hadn't been easy to soothe the scared girl inside her, but she had and had taken control again. It had showed her, though, that she wasn't strong enough yet to go up against Rodney. She had finally accepted that she would have to confront him one day if she ever wanted to be free, but she needed time to plan and prepare.

It didn't sit well to deceive her new friends, but she didn't dare tell them her intention to run. They would find a way to stop her, but she'd got it into her mind that the only way to keep everyone safe, especially Jamie, was to disappear. As for Jamie, he'd ignored her all day, and she hoped that he'd decided he'd had enough of her. The last thing she wanted to believe was that she'd hurt him in any way. Since he'd made it clear she wasn't what he was looking for, it was easy to convince herself that he would be happy to be rid of her.

When the clock reached four, she slipped out the front door and got in her car. Her cell phone rang as she pulled into her parking spot, and when she answered, no one responded. Was that the sound of breathing on the other end? "Pervert," she muttered and clicked off as another thought occurred to her. What if it was Rodney? That'd be just the kind of thing he'd do, call her and try to scare her. She dropped the phone back into her purse and hurried inside, locking the door behind her.

"Meep."

"Hey, baby." She picked up Junior and kissed his nose. "We're leaving on an adventure. What do you say to that?"

"Meep."

"Yeah, yeah. All ya care about is getting fed. Come on then." She carried him into the kitchen and filled his bowl with food. She planned to leave sometime after midnight, but before that, she needed to clean out her refrigerator. Stuck on a back shelf was a tin of caviar she'd bought on a whim the day after Jamie had given her the first orgasm ever. She'd bought it, along with a bottle of champagne, as a kind of celebration. Since it was a few hours before she would be driving, she opened the champagne and poured a glass, then took the caviar to the table.

"Okay, Junior, my boy, let's see what we think of this." As soon as the wrapping was off the caviar, Junior's nose twitched, and he jumped onto the kitchen table, his mouth jabbering like a cat on speed.

"You know you're not supposed to be up here." But she didn't have it in her to care. "How do you eat this stuff, anyway?"

"Meep."

"Hold your horses, kitty." Not sure what else to do, she scooped her index finger into the little red eggs and brought them to her nose. "Ewww."

Junior dug his claws into her arm and tried to pull the stinky stuff to him. "Meep. Meep."

"Ouch. Wait your turn." With the tip of her tongue, she tasted the caviar. "All righty then, not for me," she said, and set the small container in front of her cat. Sitting back and sipping her champagne, she watched him scarf up the roe.

"Don't expect that every day, kiddo. We're about to go on the run, and I don't think caviar's in our budget." She left him to his washing up and wandered into the living room, stopping in front of the pretend picture of her parents. "To the good old days," she said, raising her champagne glass to them.

The only thing she'd taken when she'd run was her mother's photo album. Some nights when she felt particularly lonely, she'd get it out and pore through the pictures, remembering a time when everything was perfect. If she looked at those old photos now, the ones of her mom and dad smiling at each other, or the ones with their arms around her, she'd probably start bawling and never stop.

How had she come to this? Oh, right. She'd made it possible for Rodney to commit a murder. Just how guilty was she in the eyes of the law? Hannah had suspected he planned to steal Mrs. Lederman's money but had been too afraid to tell anyone. Besides, who would she have told? Her cop father? He was so deep in Rodney's pocket that he was just as guilty as Rodney. Someone else in the town? Yeah, sure. They would have either gone straight to Rodney and ratted on her or would have been as scared as she about doing anything to stop him.

Mrs. Lederman had been such a sweet old woman, Hannah's only friend. Sugar liked to think that Hannah would have found a way to stop Rodney if she'd only known just how far he would go to put someone else's money in his pocket.

Maria was a lawyer; maybe she should ask her. But then she'd have to confess to her part in the sordid affair. As it stood now, Maria only believed Sugar was hiding from an abusive boyfriend.

And there was another lie of omission. A harsh laugh escaped, and she downed the remainder of her champagne. Although she'd love to pour another glass, she'd be driving her car in a few hours. Not only that, but one never knew when bad cop might come a calling, and she'd need a clear head.

If Rodney ever caught up with her, it would be bad. Very bad. Unfortunately, she knew him well, and even after two years, he'd still be royally pissed she'd found out his bank password and had transferred seven hundred thousand dollars out of it.

Oh, yeah, she'd pay dearly for that if he ever found her. Definitely time to run.

# CHAPTER SIXTEEN

Although Sugar's blinds were closed, Jamie could see the outline of lights at their edges. He'd been sitting in his car outside her condo since dark, a silent sentry, guarding her. Was she getting ready to run? It still burned, overhearing her tell Maria it was time to move on. Did she just plan to take off without a word to him?

She had disappeared before their workday ended, and no one knew where she'd gone. When he hadn't found her at the Buchanans' house, he'd just known she'd gone home, even though it was the most dangerous place she could be.

"Damnit, Sugar, what the hell are you thinking?" He automatically pulled two dollars out of his pocket, putting them in his cup holder. His damn cuss jar was filling up fast. He pulled another dollar out, adding it to the first two.

It appeared that it was a good thing he'd remembered how Jake had put a tracking device in Maria's purse before she had been kidnapped. If he hadn't thought to do that . . . well, none of them wanted to consider the consequences. Before he left K2, Jamie grabbed a device as he thought it a good bet his lady might need tracking, too.

Another thing he'd done before leaving work: he had finally relented and Googled her name. Only two things had come up on a Sugar Darling living in Pensacola. One was an accident report when she'd backed into another car in the grocery store parking lot.

Imagine that. The biggie though was the legal name change a little over two years ago from Sarah Dempsey to Sugar Darling. Funny that, as Sarah Dempsey had died forty years ago.

That had led him to research how to get a fake Social Security number, and he'd been surprised at how easy it was. So, she'd gotten a dead woman's identity and then changed her identity, which told him she didn't want a trail of her real name.

"Who are you, Sugar Darling?"

There was no record of her working at the Booby Palace, but that wasn't surprising. The owner probably paid half his staff under the table. There was no record of her working anywhere actually. Her driver's license was only a few months old, and for all intents, Sugar Darling was only two years old. If nothing else, the woman was smart. It also meant she'd lied to him when she said Sugar Darling was the name on her birth certificate. He should have taken her up on seeing it when she'd offered—although she probably had a fake one of those, too.

A car turned into the complex and he slid down in his seat. Anyone noticing him sitting in the dark, staring at the door of someone's condo, would think he was up to no good and would likely call the cops.

The dark-colored sedan's lights flicked off, and the vehicle slowed as it passed in front of Sugar's condo. What he wouldn't give for a pair of night-vision goggles. Why hadn't he thought to grab a pair of those, too, before leaving for the day? All he could tell was that a man sat behind the wheel. The car pulled into a space two doors down, and Jamie waited for the occupant to get out. Instead, the man slinked down until his head was barely visible over the back of the headrest.

After a few minutes' consideration, Jamie exited his car and slipped up behind the sedan, memorized the license number, then approached the driver's window. The idiot was so busy watching Sugar's door, he didn't even notice Jamie when he pointed his finger and whispered, "Bang, you're dead."

Jamie tapped on the window and the man startled, accidently blowing the horn. With a roll of his eyes, Jamie motioned for the incompetent idiot to roll down his window. "Help you with anything?"

The man pushed himself up and glared. "Who the hell are you?"

"Neighborhood watch." If the jerk hoped to intimidate him, he'd soon learn he was messing with the wrong person.

"I'm waiting on someone, so you can be on your way."

When the window started to roll up, Jamie reached in and bent the guy's index finger back. What was it with Sugar and these men he needed to protect her from?

"What the hell's wrong with you, man? I told you I'm waiting for someone."

The guy tried to pull his hand away but Jamie tightened his hold. "And I'm telling you I don't believe you. If you don't leave now, I'm calling the police. If you really are waiting for someone, the cops will get it sorted out." With his free hand, he removed his cell from his pocket and held his thumb over the nine.

"Asshole," the man growled, and then started his car.

Instinctively, Jamie knew the man was a private eye, working for whoever wanted Sugar. He let go of the finger and stood back, watching until the sedan disappeared down the road. *You get what you pay for, whoever you are, and obviously, you didn't pay much.* There wasn't a member on his team, including him, who would've gotten caught spying on anyone.

He shook his head in disgust, then eyed Sugar's door. "We're about to get some answers, sweetheart." His knock wasn't answered, so he knocked again, harder. "I know you're in there, Sugar. Open up."

The door opened the two inches the safety chain allowed, and she peeked out, only one eye showing around the edge. "Jamie?"

"In the flesh. We need to talk."

"Give me a minute to dress."

"Are you naked?" Parts of him hoped for a yes, but his saner self knew it'd be best if she wore a burqa, covering her from head to toe. Even then, she'd probably manage to look sexy in the thing.

"No, but—"

"It's important. Let me in." Preferably, before her watcher took it in his head to return and caught him talking to her. The door closed, the chain rattling against the wood. When it swung open again, whatever he'd been about to say vanished.

An almost-sheer white cotton top with thin straps did little to hide her perfect breasts. The hem of her shirt stopped about two inches above her only other article of clothing—purple boxers barely covering the cheeks of her bottom.

God help him if he started drooling like a slobbering hound on the scent. Unable to control his eyes, his gaze roamed over her, down to her bare feet and blue painted toenails. She hiked one foot up, curling it behind her knee.

"What do you want from me, Jamie?"

He jerked his gaze up to hers. *Everything.* He pushed past her and closed the door behind him. To get his mind settled and off her bare legs and the rest of her, he roamed her living room. Stopping in front of a picture of a couple walking on the beach, a child of around three or four between them, he picked it up.

"This you and your parents?"

"Yeah," she said, but her concentration was on the line her toes were making in the carpet.

The woman was lying through her teeth. Why would she claim as hers a photo of some miscellaneous pretend family? Unless he missed his guess, the picture had come with the frame. Setting the silver frame back in its place, he continued his inspection of her things with her following close behind. He was unnerving her, as was his intention. Nervous people tended to let things slip. Being close enough to feel her heat and smell her coconutty scent was setting him on edge—a thing he kept hidden. Barely.

"Stop touching my things, and tell me why you're here." She grabbed the porcelain cat from his hand and set it back on the shelf with a bang.

"Speaking of felines, where's yours?" Thinking he'd gotten his lust under control, he turned to face her. Wrong. As long as she stood before him in that skimpy outfit, he was going to have trouble focusing.

"Sleeping over there on the counter," she said, waving a hand toward the kitchen.

"What?"

She tilted her head, her brows furrowing. "Junior. You asked where he was."

"Right." The cat. *Pay attention eyes. Stay above neck level.* Because his disobedient orbs refused to listen and remained on her breasts, he turned away and strode to the dang cat. He was there for a reason, and it was not to see how fast he could get her undressed.

Jamie idly scratched Junior's chin as his attention turned to the laptop standing open next to the cat. On the screen, a headline from a newspaper article caught his eye, and he quickly scanned it. Unsurprisingly, Sugar slammed the lid closed when she realized he was reading it, but he'd seen enough to get a name and more.

"Who's Rodney Vanders?" Besides the chief of police of Vanders, South Carolina, who was currently on vacation in an undisclosed beach location.

"No one."

Right. Nobodies—one likely from several generations of nobodies—got towns named after them every day. How was he supposed to help her if she refused to trust him? Maybe he should walk away, putting Sugar Darling out of his life. He eyed the door. If he was smart, he'd do exactly that.

A breath of air huffed out of her. "You said you needed to talk to me. About what?"

She looked so vulnerable standing there in her bare feet, her eyes wary . . . or was that fear in them? "You're in troub—"

Her phone rang, scaring both her and the cat. Junior leapt off the counter and disappeared down the hall. Sugar held her hand over her heart and stared at the cell phone on the counter as if it might bite her if she touched it.

"Aren't you going to answer it?"

Wide eyes lifted to his, and she shook her head.

Jamie picked it up. Caller blocked. Interesting. He punched Talk and brought the cell to his ear, but didn't speak. At first, there was silence, then the sound of soft breathing.

Sugar tried to grab the phone from him, but he slipped his hand around her wrist and held on to her. He'd bet his next paycheck the breather was the chief of police of Vanders, South Carolina, and the bastard who had once tried to drown her to teach her a lesson. The man who'd put a scar on her shoulder with a belt or whip. The same one who had sent an ex-con to retrieve her.

After a brief internal debate, Jamie decided not to invite the man over for a little talk. Better to learn his enemy—rather, Sugar's enemy—first. Once he knew what he . . . she was up against, he'd arrange a discussion with Mr. Vanders and invite him to leave Sugar alone or else. Not that he expected the man to give up that easily, but it'd only be fair to give him a chance to live another day.

Sugar tried to pull her arm away from Jamie's hold on her. She desperately wanted to push him out the door, but his grip was unrelenting. Although she'd almost convinced herself earlier it hadn't been Rodney calling and breathing into her ear, this second time pretty much snatched the hope out from under her feet.

For sure, it was time to pack up and leave, but the blue-eyed warrior taking up too much space in her kitchen seemed to think he had the right to nose into her business. She could almost see him brandishing a sword while daring the villain to take him on, and she didn't know whether to laugh or cry.

But nothing about her life was funny, and that was the sad truth. Jamie wanted answers she couldn't and wouldn't give him. Rodney was not his problem. Not that she didn't think Jamie could hold his own against the biggest bully to walk the face of the earth, but why should he? He owed her nothing.

Lusted after her, sure. She could see the heat in his eyes when he looked at her. But that didn't give him the right to know the intimate details of her past. She'd be mortified should it come to that. Jamie was honorable, a man who'd gone to war to protect his country, a man who held himself to the highest standards while she was—as far as the law was concerned—a thief and an accessory to a murder.

No way could he ever love her.

"Let me go," she said when he set the phone back on the counter. He dropped his hold on her so fast she stumbled backwards before catching her footing. With as much dignity as she could manage, she lifted her chin and put her hands on her hips. "Go home, Jamie. I don't want you here." That just might have been the biggest lie of her life.

His lips thinned in obvious displeasure. "So you're okay with me leaving you alone even though there's a man watching your condo? If I had to guess, I'd say a private eye hired by someone to keep an eye on you." He glanced at the closed computer, then scowled. "Rodney Vanders, maybe? And what about the man we're holding at K2? You forget about him, Sugar?"

Oh, God. Her knees gave out, and she sank to the floor. It was just all too much.

Jamie squatted in front of her and put his finger under her chin, lifting her face. "Sugar, what's going on? You know I can help you. Why won't you tell me?"

No, she couldn't tell him. If she did and he decided to go after Rodney and got hurt, she'd never forgive herself. She had to leave as soon as she could get him out of her house. But first, there was one thing she wanted from him, to know how making love to a man was really supposed to be.

It would mean letting him put his penis in her, but he wasn't Rodney and wouldn't hurt her. That she knew to the bottom of her heart. Taking his hand, she stood, pulling him up with her, and turned toward the bedroom.

"Sugar?"

When he pulled her to a stop, she put a finger over his lips. "Don't talk. Don't ask questions. Don't do anything but follow me." No was in his eyes; she could see it clear as day. "Please, Jamie. I've never asked you for anything, but I'm asking for this. I need you to hold me, to make love to me. I need it like I've never needed anything in my life."

Lifting onto her toes, she put her hands on his waist and pressed her lips to his. Hands at his sides, he stood as still as a statue and almost as rigid as an unyielding slab of granite.

"Please," she whispered against his lips, wishing for the first time in her life she knew how to seduce a man. Instinctively, she licked her tongue across the seam of his mouth. Other than a slight flexing of his muscles under her palms, he gave no reaction. Defeated, heartbroken, she lowered her heels back to the floor and prepared to send him on his way.

"Damn you, Sugar."

Faster than she could blink, she was swept off her feet and carried to her bed, where she was unceremoniously dropped onto the mattress. Afraid she might say the wrong thing, she stayed silent as he stared down at her. His eyes had gone a turbulent blue and she couldn't tell if they reflected anger or desire. Maybe a little of both. Anger for sure if he was back to cursing, and the desire could just be wishful thinking.

He reached into his back pocket and removed his wallet, opened it and pulled out a condom. Sugar fisted her hands as anticipation warred with fear of what was going to happen. Setting the foil package on the nightstand, he tugged his T-shirt over his head and dropped it on the floor. She'd thought he would undress her first, but no. His jeans soon joined his shirt and he stood before her clad only in a pair of dark blue briefs.

God above, he was magnificent, and it was a sight she'd carry with her forever.

The thin arrow of golden hair running down the middle of his stomach caught her attention. Her gaze fell to the huge bulge in his underwear, and she swallowed hard. She wasn't Hannah, she was Sugar, a woman with no reason to be afraid of joining with a man. When he pushed the briefs down his hips and stepped out of them, she kept her gaze to his face.

"If you can't look at me without the panic I see on your face, I won't do this. Tell me you want me, Sugar."

The barest hint of warmth had entered his eyes, and she took courage in understanding he was giving her the choice of what happened next. That he'd purposely undressed first told her he remembered their last night together, and if she wanted him in her bed, she'd have to show him that seeing him aroused didn't make her feel sick.

For a moment, it did. But she swallowed the bile rising in her throat and gave herself a stern lecture that he wasn't Rodney, and she was being stupid. Jamie was what she wanted, and as the thought settled in, her stomach calmed and she lowered her gaze to his erection.

Oh, yes, she wanted him. "I do. I do want you, Jamie."

With a new resolve and heat traveling through her veins, she lifted her hand and circled her fingers around his cock . . . wasn't that what men liked to call it? Before Jamie, she'd thought of it as *that thing* she didn't want anywhere near her. Now, she had a whole new appreciation for the appendage, and wasn't that a wonderful thing?

"I wouldn't want to be a man if I had to walk around all day with that between my legs, but it's strangely fascinating." She sat up and traced the shape of it, then lifted it and peered underneath.

"What are you doing, woman?"

"Studying it," she answered, pleased to hear the amusement in his voice. "To address your concern, it's not at all as scary as I'd expected, and there'll be no repeat of my embarrassing behavior like last time."

"That's a relief." He took her hand away and sat next to her. "Are you sure about this? I won't deny the minute I first saw you, I wanted you. As much as I tried not to, I couldn't stop thinking about you." When she didn't reply, his eyelids lowered, and he shifted his face away from her. "Maybe I should leave."

"No." She placed her hand on his leg to stop him from standing. "I need you to understand I'm not looking for anything permanent. I just want . . ." How much to tell him? Enough so he'd understand that what would happen next meant something to her, but not so much to scare him away. "I was chosen by Rodney . . . I don't remember, did I ever tell you that was his name?" When he didn't respond, she said, "Anyway, when I was fifteen, and from then on, I was never allowed friends or outside interests. I don't think of him by anything but *bad cop*."

"He took you at fifteen? Where the hell were your parents?"

Never had she heard such anger in a voice, not even from Rodney at his worst. Although he didn't know it, his rage was on behalf of Hannah, a girl no one had cared enough about to protect, and Sugar willed herself not to cry.

"No, he *chose* me, but he waited to take me until after I'd finished high school. As for my parents, my mom died when I was ten, and my father changed after that, started drinking and not spending much time at home. Then he met Rodney. I-I don't want to share all the sordid details of my life after that. All I want is this one night with you, to know how it feels to have a man make love to me. I don't consider the things Rodney did making love."

"I'd like to have a word with your father. How could he—"

"Shhh. No more questions. Will you give me this one night? Please, Jamie." His thigh muscle tensed under her hand and she waited, half expecting him to get up and walk out.

# CHAPTER SEVENTEEN

How do I say no to that?" He should. The woman looking at him with uncertainty in her eyes had ghosts plaguing her, and Jamie had enough of his own ghosts to contend with. Hearing her speak of the man who'd chosen a fifteen-year-old girl—then had mistreated her so badly—made him want to break something, preferably one Rodney Vanders.

The last thing he wanted was a relationship with a beautiful, hurting woman needing the soft touch of a man. Even though she'd said just one night, he wasn't sure he'd be able to walk away if he laid her down on her bed and shared such an intimate act as joining their bodies.

Just lust, he thought, lying to himself. He'd lusted plenty up to the day he'd killed his parents and never had it felt like this. Still, as much as he should, he couldn't deny her. If all she wanted was one night, so be it.

"Thank you for not saying no," she said, her whispered words calling to something so deep inside him he couldn't begin to answer her.

Instead, he gently pushed her down onto the bed. Knowing that she'd been mistreated, maybe even brutalized, he was determined to touch her so softly she would think she'd made love to a gossamer angel.

Stretching out beside her, he lowered his hand over her stomach so that his palm covered her belly button, his fingers spread over her soft, silky skin. "You're dangerous, Sugar Darling."

"That's silly. I'm not even close to dangerous."

"To me you are," he said, lowering his mouth to hers. Slipping his hand under the little T-shirt as he kissed her, he brushed his fingertips over a breast. So soft. So warm. He flicked her nipple with his thumb, causing her to sigh into his mouth.

What kind of fool did it take to not see how innately sensual she was, instead, mistreating her so badly she'd gotten sick at the thought of making love to a man? If he could give her nothing else, he'd show her how it was supposed to be between a man and a woman, how good it could be. Deep in his bones, he knew she planned to leave. If nothing else, he would be doing her a favor, and the next time she met someone she liked, she'd know sex didn't have to hurt.

If it bothered him to think of her with another man, he'd get over it.

As he gently caressed her other breast, he understood this woman needed tender, kind hands on her. The last time they'd been in bed together, it had seemed to help when he'd talked to her, telling her what he was going to do.

"I'm going to take off your shirt, sweetheart, so I can see these beautiful breasts I'm touching. Okay?"

Her lips curved up as she grinned. "I was beginning to think we were going to do this with you naked and me clothed."

Knowing some of her past, the trust in her eyes—darkened to a deep violet now—would have brought him to his knees if he'd been standing. "You're definitely going to end up naked, baby. Shirt off." He helped her pull it over her head and sucked in a breath at seeing the pale pink nipples peaked from desire. There should have been warnings tattooed on her body that read, "Jamie, no return past this point."

"You ready for your shorts to come off? And you should know I might die if you say no." Her laugh rolled though him like some kind of healing balm injected straight into his veins, and he found himself laughing with her, although he couldn't explain what was so funny as they dissolved into gasping giggles.

Saint didn't laugh, something the guys had tried but failed to make happen for years with their stupid jokes and silly faces. There was a standing bet among them that the first one to set him off would collect five hundred bucks from the others. What would they think if they knew a beautiful but damaged woman had him giggling like an eight-year-old girl high on sugar at a slumber party?

"Tell me why we're laughing, Sugar," he said when he'd caught his breath and could speak. That set her off once more, and taking him by surprise, she twisted up and straddled him, dangling those beautiful breasts in front of his face.

"Because at this particular moment we're so happy we can't help it?"

"Could be." It was as good a reason as any. She rocked against him, settling herself so that the outer lips of her folds hugged his erection. Even with the barrier of her little boxers, her heat seared him, and he gritted his teeth against his raging desire.

"Can I take my shorts off now, Jamie?"

Never had he been asked a stupider question. "God, yes."

She lifted, standing on the mattress, and wiggled out of her last piece of clothing. His gaze traveled from her knees up to all the other parts of her. He noted in passing that her pubic hair was a different color than the hair on her head, more of a reddish tint to it than the honey blonde. At the moment, he didn't care if her curls were neon green.

"Sugar," he rasped, and slid his hands up her calves to the back of her knees. "Come down here and lay your body over mine."

Sugar gazed down at Jamie as she stood over him, wondering where the courage to be some kind of sex kitten came from. But she did know. It was him. His kind touch, the softness in his eyes when he looked at her, his laughter joining hers over their silliness. She stole her courage from him, from the beautiful soul that resided inside him.

As she lowered herself over his legs, she stared into his eyes, memorizing the way they turned to a blue so velvety dark she was reminded of midnight. In the nights to come when she was in some other city, in some other state, she'd walk outside at the stroke of twelve, gaze up at the velvet night sky, and think of him.

Always him.

Time was running out, though. "Are you ready for me?"

"In a sec." He grabbed the condom from the nightstand, and she watched as he rolled it on. For some reason, seeing him do that was just damn sexy.

"Now?" she asked when he finished and looked up at her with those angel eyes of his. At his nod, she slid up the length of him and waited for him to take over because she didn't know what to do next. Although she'd carefully kept her gaze off the part of him he would soon put in her, it was there in her peripheral vision, and it hadn't gotten any smaller since the last time she'd seen it. Her stomach lurched. What was wrong with her? Hadn't she just been studying it not five minutes ago, claiming it wasn't scary after all?

*Stop being a baby, Sugar. Hannah did this before, not you. Just remember that.*

To prove—if only to herself—she was no longer Hannah, Sugar gathered her courage and looked down, right at his erection, and her only reaction was fascination with the way it seemed to point at her.

Pleased with herself, Sugar smiled and lifted up. "What now? I just impale myself on you?"

"Tell you what," Jamie said. "I'm just going to lie here and see what you decide to do next. Just know this, Sugar. Whatever you decide, I won't hurt you. If it helps in your decision to know I might die if you end up hanging your head in the toilet again because of me . . ." His smile melted her heart like chocolate left in the hot sun. ". . . I'll leave. Even though it will kill me. My favorite flowers are . . ." he slid a hand up, from her knee to her hip, ". . . wildflowers. Send a batch of those to my funeral."

"You'd best not leave or die. Shut up, Jamie." If she hadn't loved him before, she would've tumbled head over heels that very second. He really would leave if she asked him to, and he'd do it without laying a hand on her in anger. The nerves she'd been battling since he'd removed his clothes disappeared, and she wrapped her hand around him, and lowered herself down.

"Just know this, Jamie Turner. You're not going anywhere. At least, not tonight." He filled her, and it didn't hurt! There were miracles still to be had in this world after all.

"Why the tears?" he asked as he reached up with both hands and brushed his thumbs over her cheeks.

So gentle his touch was. "Jamie," she whispered, and bent over him until their mouths were locked together.

His hands settled on her waist, and his fingers pressed into her skin, supporting her weight as he helped her lift up, then easing as she came back down. Up and down she went on him, finding a rhythm that seemed to excite him if his low growl was any indication.

By all that was holy, she'd never felt anything so good as having Jamie filling her, never dreamed a man could pleasure her into incoherency. Had never felt so complete. The tears continued to fall, and she couldn't stop them.

"Why, Sugar?" he asked, returning his fingers to her face, catching the watery drops.

"Happiness, that's all." *And knowing I'll never see you again after tonight.* The crisp hairs on his thighs rubbed against her sensitive skin as she moved steadily over him, and it was like she was a harp, and her strings were being plucked to create a masterpiece, one that would never be heard outside her bedroom. She'd never in her life been so sad and so happy at the same time.

Suddenly, he flipped her and loomed over her. "Can I take it from here?"

"Yes, please." The blue of his eyes turned three shades darker, and just seeing how his desire for her changed their color did funny things to her heart.

"Thank you." He rocked against her, burying himself deeper. "Sugar," he whispered, then wrapped his lips around the nipple of her breast and sucked.

Red-hot fire spiraled through her, sending what felt like molten lava to the very core of her. If she burned to a crisp, she would welcome it. She raised her legs, bracing her feet on the mattress. His hands found their way under her, cupping her bottom, and he moved his mouth to the opposite nipple.

"Ahhh." Long past forming coherent words, Sugar gave herself over to the rush of pleasure streaming though her and met him thrust for thrust. Pressure built inside her starting at where they were joined, then raced through her, increasing to an unbearable level. The blood flowing through her veins hummed, her skin prickled, and her ears rang so loudly that she wondered if there was a church in the distance where someone was pulling on the bell ropes.

He'd pleasured her once before, bringing her to an amazing orgasm, but that one paled to this. Fearing she would shatter into irreparable pieces, she tried to hold back the oncoming tide of feelings threatening to consume her.

"No. Don't go away. Stay with me."

At the command in his voice, she opened her eyes. She caught his gaze and held it as stars, bright and shimmering, danced in her vision. A wave with the force of a tsunami crashed over her, through her, and deep inside her. It consumed her, then burned her, then healed her.

"Jamie!" *Oh, God, Jamie.*

"I know, sweetheart. I know."

Something flickered in his eyes, something soft and meant just for her. Something she'd treasure forever. She wrapped her arms around his neck and felt the shudders traveling through him as he climaxed inside her body. *I love you. I love you, Jamie Turner.* The words could never be said aloud, but they were there in her head, always would be.

The room settled into silence as their breathing calmed, and she greedily savored the last few minutes she'd have with him before finding the words to make him leave. His back was slick with the sweat of their lovemaking, and she glided her hands over his warm skin, wishing she could climb behind him and lick him dry.

*I love you,* she silently told him one last time. His body still covered hers, so strong and alluring. As much as she needed him gone . . . God, she didn't want him to leave. If she could just curl up in his arms and pretend she didn't know a man by the name of Rodney Vanders, she'd feel safe for the first time in years. Could she tell him just enough so he'd help her get away without being followed?

"Talk to me, sweetheart. I didn't hurt you, did I?"

The endearment about did her in, and she blinked against the tears burning her eyes. Once she got away, she'd never see him again, and that alone tempted her to confront Rodney just to put an end to everything. If she didn't live through it—a strong possibility—then so be it.

Junior jumped onto the bed and bumped her shoulder with his head, wanting to be petted. If Rodney knew how much she loved the stray she'd taken in and given a home, he'd kill the poor thing and make her watch him doing it. It would be the last straw, the one to finally send her over the edge. No, she had to run. There was no other way.

Before the last minutes, she'd never have dreamed of asking Jamie for anything, but there had been tenderness in his eyes for her, maybe even a little bit of caring. Enough to aid her without the explanations she couldn't bring herself to give him? Only one way to find out.

"I have to disappear. Will you help me?"

# CHAPTER EIGHTEEN

Jamie lifted onto his elbows and stared down at the woman who'd just given him the equivalent of an out-of-body experience. "That wasn't at all what I expected you to say."

The desperation in those beautiful eyes as Sugar asked for his help was next to impossible to resist, but she wasn't going anywhere until he got answers. He slid his legs over the side of the bed and grabbed his jeans, pulling them on. Obviously clued in by his abrupt movements, she pulled the sheet up to her neck, warily watching him as if he might turn on her at any minute.

Did she really think he was no different from her lowlife Rodney Vanders? Did she believe he was the kind of man who would strike a woman? That hurt him as much as it angered him. Especially after the way he'd felt being with her. Never had he known anything like being with her, making love to her. He couldn't compare it to any other woman. It had been like coming home.

The last time he'd felt like he was home had been ten years ago when he'd walked into the kitchen after spending the afternoon with his friends to find his mom taking double-chocolate chip cookies out of the oven. It had been the day before he'd gone and killed everyone he loved. He'd been stoned and suffering from a bad case of the munchies. Not waiting for them to cool, he'd grabbed a handful, and without even thanking her, had shut himself up in his room. Even all these years later, he could still see the worry in his mother's eyes as he'd stumbled out of the room.

Shaking off the unwanted memory, he tugged his shirt over his head and moved to the chair. Her painting of the nude couple caught his attention, and he suddenly understood Sugar's longing to know the kind of love shining from their eyes as they gazed at each other. For a brief moment there, he'd thought maybe he'd found it, and with a woman not at all like his mother, no less.

Fortunately, before he'd said something stupid he couldn't take back, she'd reminded him that someone was after her, had apparently found her, and she could be in danger. But she couldn't trust him with the truth. How would he even know if whatever story she told him was true?

"Who's after you and why?" he asked, settling a cold gaze on her, when what he really wanted to do was return to the bed, wrap her in his arms, and promise he'd keep her safe. "What's your real name, Sugar?"

Her gaze jerked to his at his last question, and as the light faded from her eyes, she pushed the cat aside and stood, dragging the sheet behind her as she disappeared down the hallway. With a disgruntled expression on his furry face at losing the warm lap, Junior blinked green eyes at him.

"Don't look at me. I'm as clueless as you about what's going on."

"Mowwl," Junior said, before leaping off the bed and scampering down the hall.

Jamie drummed his fingers on the arm of the chair for a moment, then rose and followed the witch and her familiar. If she couldn't be honest with him, he couldn't help her. In the living room, she stood, draped in the bedsheet, at her open front door.

He stopped in front of her, hissing out a frustrated breath. "Please, let me help you."

Not only did she not respond, but she refused to look at him. Fine. He could take a hint. She wanted him gone and he was happy to oblige.

"Damnit," he muttered when he hesitated with one foot out the door and one still in her condo. *Don't be stupid, Saint. Walk out and don't look back.* She obviously didn't want his help, and he forced his feet to move forward.

He didn't look back.

Sugar closed the door, sagging against it, and then followed it down when her legs decided they'd no longer keep her upright. Seated on the floor, she pressed her face between her knees when her lungs threatened to hyperventilate. He'd really left.

It shouldn't surprise her. When he had asked her real name, she'd realized she would have to tell him everything or nothing. If she told him all, he would hate her and would leave anyway.

Nor was she willing to put the man she loved in the sights of Rodney, a venomous snake if there ever was one. Yet . . . and yet, as she listened to the sound of Jamie's car fade away, she knew she'd made a mistake. She should have confessed all the shameful details, but she'd waited too long.

Finally getting air back into her lungs, she swiped at the tears and pushed herself up. It was done, and crying would solve nothing. She turned the deadlock, slipping on the chain. As always, she was alone. No problem. Hadn't it been that way since she'd come home from school to find her mother sprawled out on the kitchen floor?

"Mawww."

"You learn a new word, Junior?" She eyed him, sitting a few feet away, his tail twitching in agitation. Of course, he sensed her fear and needed reassurance all was well. Nothing was right, but she picked him up and stroked his chin.

"It's all right, baby. How would ya feel about us taking a vacation? Maybe Arizona or New Mexico? I hear there's lots of lizards in either state, so you'd like that, right?"

His purr sent calming vibrations through her, and she returned to the bedroom, with the only creature in the world who loved her, to pack what she would need to take. She'd get everything ready to go, and sometime after midnight, she'd load up her car and leave, hoping anyone supposedly watching her would be home in their bed, expecting her to be fast asleep in her own.

Before she left, she sent Maria an e-mail apologizing for accepting a job she couldn't keep. Although her friend knew enough to understand, she didn't know all. No one but Sugar and bad cop and bad cop did, and Sugar planned to keep it that way. It was the only way to protect her friends.

Everything she could take with her was piled by the door and one last time she roamed her apartment, saying good-bye to the things she'd have to leave behind. She considered taking the picture of her fake parents, but on reflection, decided she didn't love them anymore. She'd find new parents for Nikki Swanson.

"Nikki Swanson." She tested the name, listening to the sound of it on her tongue, getting used to hearing it. It was an okay name, but strangely, she'd miss Sugar Darling more than she'd ever missed Hannah Conley. Neither Nikki nor Hannah knew or would ever know a man called Saint.

With tears streaming down her cheeks, she loaded into her car the cat carrier with Junior in it, her laptop case, one suitcase for her, and a small tote with the things Junior would need. The oversized purse containing, among other things, her new identity and the cash she'd stashed for just such an emergency—along with an illegal gun—she tucked next to her.

Fortunately, Junior was an easy traveler, curling up and going to sleep as soon as she started the ignition. She circled the block a few times to make sure no one followed her. Although it hadn't been her intention, she found herself turning down the road to Jamie's house. She'd looked up his address on the K2 computer after their day on his boat.

Twice since then, she'd driven by when she knew he wasn't home, and stared at the house that seemed like one straight out of the pages of a romance novel. White with royal-blue shutters and a porch that ran across the front, the damn thing even had a white picket fence with an arbor entrance covered by climbing pink roses. What man owned a house like that? Maybe one who needed to reconstruct a past life when he'd been happy?

After seeing it the first time, she'd fantasized about living there with Jamie, a stupid dream if ever there was one. She slowed for one last look at the home of the man she loved, her heart splintering like shattered glass at knowing she'd never see him again. The garage door was closed, and his car would be safely tucked inside, no evil lurking at his door.

For a split second, she considered parking, walking up the steps, and throwing herself on his mercy, but she pushed her foot down on the pedal and sped past. He was too good a man to have her nasty troubles dumped on him.

"Good-bye, Jamie," she said as the house disappeared from view.

At that time in the morning, I-10 West was as empty as her heart, not a soul to be seen ahead or behind her. As she traveled through Alabama, she kept an eye on her rearview mirror, but if anyone was following her, they were too clever for her to see them.

Leaving Alabama behind, she drove through Mississippi, then into Louisiana. When her tires ran over the rumble strip, she jerked her eyes open and gave a violent shake of her head. Time to find a motel and get some sleep before she ended up in the swamp lining the road. The upcoming exit only had a Burger King sign, so she drove past.

The next one had several fast-food restaurants and two motels. Exiting the interstate, she saw the McDonald's sign was lit, and she turned into the drive-thru and ordered a large cup of coffee and one plain hamburger. Knowing the coffee would help to revitalize her, and that she was on the road that would take her into New Orleans, she decided to drive a little longer. When she reached the city limits, she picked the cheapest-looking motel with a name she'd never heard of. Once in the room, she tore the plain burger into pieces and set them on the dresser for Junior. Out of his cage, he jumped up and devoured them, then meeped for more.

"Sorry, kiddo, that's all there is." She removed a baking pan from the tote and poured a thin layer of litter into it, then stood back to see if Junior would use it. As his cat box was too big to fit into the bag, she'd thought herself rather ingenious to think of the pan. He circled it, sniffing the edges before sticking a paw in and digging at the litter. Seemingly satisfied with the make-do potty, he hopped in and squatted.

It would be a few hours before the bank opened and she could visit one of her three safety-deposit boxes spread out between Pensacola and San Antonio, five thousand dollars stashed in each one. It would have been nice if she could have gotten her money out of the Pensacola bank, but someday she would sneak back and get the cash she'd stashed there.

With the five thousand in her bag, the five she'd get when the bank opened, and the last five she'd pick up when she passed through San Antonio, she'd be in better shape than when she'd gone on the run the first time. Not wanting to repeat the desperation she'd felt back then, she'd come up with the idea of hiding money along the escape route she'd planned if the time ever came to leave. Whenever she'd managed to accumulate five thousand dollars over the past two years, she'd taken a little trip, the first one to San Antonio.

"I'm one smart cookie," she told Junior, feeling rather proud of herself for her foresight. Smart, alone, and lonely, that was her. No, she wouldn't go there. She'd made her choice, and she was Sugar, and Sugar looked on the bright side of everything.

Except she wasn't Sugar any longer; she was Nikki Swanson, or would be as soon as she walked out of the bank in New Orleans. The box in Texas was in Nikki Swanson's name. That would give her between now and her arrival in San Antonio to create a new persona.

So, who was Nikki Swanson?

# CHAPTER NINETEEN

Jamie had circled the complex after leaving Sugar, unable to get out of his mind the way she'd looked as he walked out the door. Not seeing any suspicious cars, he found a place to park a few spaces down from her front door. Then he snuck over to her little car and put the magnetic tracking device in her wheel well.

Two hours later, realizing he was nodding off, and since all was quiet and her lights were out, he decided it was safe to slip down to the convenience store a few blocks from her house. Inside, after a quick pit stop, he grabbed the largest cup and filled it with coffee. He was back in place in less than ten minutes.

Her ugly orange car was gone. Of course it was. Jamie slammed his hand down on the steering wheel. "Damnit, Sugar, you couldn't wait ten minutes?" What if she hadn't left willingly, but had been taken? He doubted they—whoever they were—would use the little car as the getaway vehicle, but he broke into her condo anyway. There was no sign of a struggle, which was a relief. The refrigerator was empty, but he had no idea if she cooked when home. Most telling, her cat was gone. If someone had come for her, they wouldn't have taken Junior.

After checking all the rooms, he left the way he came in, through the back door. A large garbage bag was set off to the side on the grass. He opened it to find cartons and containers of food, still cold to the touch.

She had run. No surprise there. He'd been expecting it, just hadn't planned for her to do it in the less than ten minutes he was gone. "What am I going to do with you, Sugar?" he asked as he returned to his car. It was a question to which he didn't have an answer.

At K2, Jamie determined her whereabouts, then picked up the phone. "Sugar ran and appears to be heading for New Orleans," he said into the phone.

"Kismet," Jake said, not at all sounding like he'd been awakened from sleep.

"What does that mean?"

"It means we're in New Orleans, and how ironic is that? Hi, Jamie."

The change from a male voice to a feminine one was a bit disconcerting. "Hey, Maria. I hate to bother the two of you, but I've got a bad feeling, and I need to find her. Are we on speaker?"

"We are," Jake answered, and Jamie heard the rustle of bedsheets.

"I'm headed that way now." He bit down on his anxiety, feeling guilty that he was interrupting their time away.

"Why don't you let us handle this end, and you keep tabs on her whereabouts."

Not gonna happen. "No. Don't approach her. She's running scared, and I don't want to spook her. I called Doc, and he's on the way in. He'll track her for us. Just keep an eye on her until I get there."

"I just checked my e-mail, and there's one from Sugar. She apologized for taking a job she couldn't accept and said she knew I'd understand," Maria said.

"I wish I understood." Ryan O'Connor poked his head in, and Jamie motioned him to take a seat.

"It'll take me a few hours to get there," he said. "Is there anything you can tell me, Maria, that will help?"

"Her real name's Hannah Conley. The rest you can get from her."

"Thanks." Hanging up, he brought Doc up to speed. "Sorry about dragging you out of bed, especially when I know you're supposed to be off tomorrow."

O'Connor's gaze shifted to the satellite map on the wall. "Not like I had anything better to do."

In the few days he'd been onboard, it was obvious that even after a year, his friend still had some deep hurt over the loss of his wife. Jamie could appreciate that. Almost eleven years had passed and his heart still mourned the loss of his parents. When things settled back down, he would make a point to get Doc out, introduce him around.

"Keep me updated," he said on the way out the door. Making a detour to the kitchen, he tossed some ice into a cooler, and then added four bottles of root beer. From the pantry, he grabbed a handful of energy bars. After a quick stop in the bathroom, he left K2 to hunt down his prey.

Once on the interstate heading west, Jamie flipped on his radar detector, bringing the car to fifteen miles over the speed limit. Nothing but questions tumbled through his mind. Was her final destination New Orleans? Did she know someone there? Was Hannah Conley her real name or just another alias?

Impossible to think of her as a Hannah. The name didn't fit the woman he knew. His violet-eyed, messed-up girl—one minute funny and confident, the next vulnerable and hurting—was a Sugar through and through.

When he caught up with her, he'd force her to tell him the story of her life, starting from the day she took her first breath. After he kissed her senseless for scaring a month off his life. As he drove, he listened to O'Connor give Jake updates on Sugar's movements, appreciating that Doc had thought to put them on a three-way call. By the time he reached the outskirts of New Orleans, he was confident he had a good plan. Get answers. Help her as much as he could. Then figure out what she meant to him.

Following the directions from Jake, Jamie pulled up next to the Buchanans' Jeep, where they'd parked across the street from a run-down motel just inside the New Orleans city line. He spied Sugar's orange car sitting in the motel lot. His dumb heart did flips at the speed of an exuberant gymnast. Clamping down on the excitement he didn't want to feel, he slid into the backseat of the Jeep.

"Sorry I screwed up your trip. Bring me up to speed, then you can leave."

Maria twisted in her seat and glared at him. "You think we don't care about her? I'm just glad we're here so we can help. I think you two should stay in the car, and let me go talk to her. She did confide in me after all."

That burned. "No, this is my operation from here on. I'd prefer it if you left."

"But—"

"No, Chiquita, let's leave Saint and his woman alone." Jake gave his wife a wicked grin. "'Sides, I've got plans for you. If the idiot sitting in our backseat had taken care of business and not let his woman get this far, I'd be feeding you hot *Beignets* and *café au lait* right now. In bed."

"But—"

"No buts, wife. Get out of my car, Saint. If you need us again, you got our number."

Jamie wanted to protest that Sugar wasn't his woman—at least not yet—but he wanted them gone even more. After they drove away, he eyed Sugar's car. What should he do next? Find out what room she was in, then knock on the door? What would he say? "Hi, I'm in the neighborhood and decided to stop by"? Would she welcome him in, or would she slam the door in his face?

"I was doing just fine before you wormed your way into my life, sweetheart." So he was talking to himself? Great. Nor did he appreciate how indecisive she'd made him. He was trained to make decisions on the spot, life-and-death ones, and it was time to confront the woman who'd run from him.

As he headed for the office, figuring he'd have to wake someone up, an older model Hyundai with a magnetic sign on its door turned into the motel parking lot. The driver's head angled to look at door numbers as he slowly drove by the rooms, then pulled up behind Sugar's car.

How had she found a pizza delivery at nine in the morning? He chuckled. "Oh, right, we're in New Orleans, and this is Sugar you're talking about." But the timing was perfect, and he grabbed two unopened root beers from the cooler on the passenger seat. Jogging across the lot, he came up beside the pizza delivery kid.

"Just popped over to the convenience store to get some sodas." He dangled the bottles in front of the boy's face. "Thought I'd beat you back. How much I owe you?" he asked, reaching for his wallet.

The teen's brows furrowed as he frowned at Jamie. "You don't look like a Janie Turner to me, dude."

The little witch had more or less stolen his name, but in doing so, she'd certainly made it easy for him. He flipped his wallet open and held it up so the kid could read the name on his driver's license. "Jamie and Janie Turner. Cute, huh? Well, my wife thinks so anyway. How much?"

"Eight bucks."

He handed the kid a twenty. "Don't have anything smaller, but if you disappear like right now, it's all yours."

The boy flicked a nervous glance at her motel room before shrugging and then returning to his car. Jamie waited until the taillights disappeared, then approached Sugar's—aka Hannah's, aka

Janie's—door. Giving it three knocks, he cleared his throat and changed his voice. "Pizza delivery."

At the sound of the lock turning, he stepped against the outer wall, keeping the pizza box where it could be seen if she kept the chain on and peeked out. If she swung the door wide open without checking first, he was going to dump the contents over her head for being stupid.

She saved herself from having pizza dripping down her face by keeping on the chain. At the sight of the box, she closed the door, slid off the chain, and when she opened it again, he stepped in front of her.

"Your pizza, ma'am." It was probably wrong to take such satisfaction in the wide eyes and open mouth. Then her expression turned guarded. She should be wary, considering he wasn't happy with her right now.

"Jamie? What're you doing here?"

"Beats me." He pushed past her before she could slam the door in his face. Moving to the middle of the room, he lifted the lid of the box and peered in. "What'd you order us, Sugar?" When he was sure he had her attention, he arched a brow. "Or is it Hannah today . . . oh, wait, it's Janie Turner according to the delivery man."

Her face paled, and he crushed the longing to scoop her up and hold her tight, safe in his arms. "I had to go to a lot of trouble to convince him to turn over the pizza, so I hope I can look forward to the benefits that come with having a wife." He'd never acted cruel toward a woman before, but this one pushed buttons he didn't know existed. It was either everything or nothing at all where she was concerned, and she'd sent her message by running. She wanted nothing from him.

She slid down, planting her butt on the floor. "I can explain."

"I certainly hope so." Making himself at home, he set the root beers on the bedside table, then settled on the bed and leaned back against the pillows. "Want a piece?" He held out the box.

"Not really hungry right now."

"What? Lost your appetite?" Her hair was wet, telling him she'd recently showered, and she wore the same little boxers and strappy T-shirt as the night he'd made love to her. The night he'd almost told her he thought he was falling in love with her. From the first, he'd known she was trouble with a capital T, but he still wanted her, was aroused just looking at her. Tearing his gaze away, he opened the box and lifted a slice of pizza he really didn't want.

A furball appeared from nowhere, landing next to him. "Meep."

"Hello, Junior. That is your real name, right?" He didn't like how mean he was feeling, but he couldn't seem to help himself.

"Meep."

He took that as a yes, and picked up a clump of sausage and cheese, putting it on the box top. Although he pointedly ignored Sugar, he subtly watched her out of the corner of his eye, and she'd flinched at his jab. She folded into herself, wrapping her arms around her legs, her head hanging like one who was defeated. Feeling like a jerk, he decided he should give her a chance to explain.

"This Rodney Vanders; he's after you, why? Is he just an old boyfriend who doesn't know how to let go, or is there more to it than that? And, Sugar, see if you can manage the truth."

Her head snapped up, fury in her eyes. "Screw you, Jamie. I didn't ask you to follow me. I don't even know why you're here. How did you find me, anyway?"

Well, he had that coming. Her belligerence was welcome though. Better than her beaten-down attitude of a minute ago. As to why he'd come after her, he still hadn't figured that one out. Not wanting to admit he'd put a tracking device in her car, he ignored her second question.

"I'm sorry, that was uncalled for. Come here." He pushed the box aside and scooted over.

"I don't think so. Please, I'd like you to leave."

Not happening. He wasn't going anywhere until he got to the bottom of whatever was going on with her. "Did our time together mean nothing to you then?" Low blow maybe, but a question he needed answered.

She stared hard at him for a moment, then her eyes softened. "It meant everything to me. You'll never know how much, but I can't stay in Pensacola, not if he's found me. So, there's no future for us. There can't be, and I won't drag you into this shit."

"Too late. I'm here, and I'm not leaving, so you might as well tell me what's going on." His gaze zoned in on the bottom lip she chewed on, and he wished she wouldn't do that.

"If I tell you, will you leave?"

No. "Depends on what you say."

Her response was a long sigh, then she pushed up, went to her suitcase, and rummaged around in it. If she realized the view of her bottom she'd given him and where it led his thoughts, she'd probably slap him. He was a bad man to be thinking of making love to her when she was clearly upset and afraid. Pulling a sweater out, she wrapped it around her shoulders and tugged on it until it covered her breasts. The room wasn't cold, so she was hiding herself from him. That only added to his anger.

With the sweater pulled around the top half of her, she sat on the only chair in the room, curling her legs under her. "Rodney stole seven hundred thousand dollars."

"What?"

# CHAPTER TWENTY

That got his attention. God, she didn't want to do this, but Sugar believed him when he said he wasn't leaving until she explained. There were things she wouldn't tell him though, only enough so he'd leave.

"I said Rodney stole seven hundred thousand dollars." From the kindest woman she'd ever known.

Junior, having scarfed up the cheese and sausage treat, hopped onto Jamie's lap and made three turns before curling up and sticking his nose under his tail. Masculine fingers she knew firsthand could make a woman forget her name stroked her cat's fur, the sound of his purrs the loudest she'd ever heard from him. Really stupid to envy a damn cat, but she did.

She'd thought to never see Jamie again, yet there he was sitting on the bed of her motel room waiting for answers, and all she could think about was wanting his hands on her. Wanting him to do those magical things to her and bring her to that wonderful feeling again.

After he heard what she had to say, however, he'd never want to touch her again, a good enough reason to cry an ocean of tears. When he got his answers and walked out for the last time, she'd give herself permission to do just that. She pressed her hand over her heart, wishing it didn't ache so badly.

The blue eyes staring at her hardened. "Sometime today would be good, or are you trying to come up with more lies?"

It was close, but she managed not to flinch. She had that coming, she supposed, but it still hurt. Resentment simmered at the coldness in the gaze he leveled at her. He didn't know what she'd lived through and managed to escape from, so what gave him the right to judge her?

Inhaling a deep breath, she looked him square in the eyes. She'd be damned if she'd cower in front of him. "Fine. You want to know my sad story?" Unable to hold his gaze, she focused on Junior, still asleep on Jamie's lap. "On my tenth birthday, my mother died suddenly, and nothing was the same after that. Unable to cope with her loss, my father went on a downward spiral, drinking heavily, gambling . . . honestly, I probably don't know the half of it. He was a Charleston cop, had been an honorable one up 'til then, but he ended up getting fired. We lost our home, and he moved us into public housing."

God, it was hard remembering that time in her life, watching her daddy turn into a man she didn't recognize. "He rarely came home anymore, and it was too dangerous to leave the apartment so I took refuge in schoolwork. My grades were perfect, but there was no one home to care." Why was she telling him that much? She could've gone straight to the theft, but the part of her that craved his respect wanted him to understand how she came to such lows.

"You're going to pick that sweater apart if you keep pulling on it."

She glanced down to see she was tugging on a loose piece of yarn, and not knowing what else to do with her hands, she clasped them tightly, resting them on her lap.

"Go on. Tell me the rest."

Taking some comfort in the softening of his voice, she eyed the root beers, wishing she had one to soothe her dry throat. As if reading her mind, he reached for one and twisted the cap. Just as she was about to ask if she could have one too, he held it out.

"I'd bring it to you, but then I'd disturb my friend here."

"Thanks." She crossed the room and took the bottle, careful not to touch his fingers. How did one stop loving a man who didn't want to wake up her cat? There must be a way, and she'd have plenty of time to puzzle out the answer in the days ahead.

"Where was I?" she asked after returning to her chair.

"There was no one home to care."

She'd rather his voice didn't sound so gentle, as if he cared. "Right. Well, it went along like that until I turned fifteen. For the first time since my mom died, daddy remembered my birthday and decided to treat me to a night out to dinner at . . ." Unable to resist, she let the moment draw out until Jamie lifted a brow. "Crazy Zollie's Roadside Eats But There's No Seats." Turned out, that had been the only thing funny about that night.

Jamie's lips twitched. "I'll have to put that on my bucket list."

Lips she'd thought would never smile again curved upward. She resisted the urge to touch her fingers to her mouth to know for a fact she was smiling. "That really was the actual name of the place, even had a hand-painted sign saying so. Crazy Zollie had an outdoor grill, and the tables were cement blocks piled atop each other with a wood plank across them. He claimed he tried picnic tables and chairs once, but people kept stealing them."

It hadn't mattered to her. All she'd cared about was that her father had remembered her birthday and was spending time with her. If she'd known the outcome of that night, however, she'd have begged to be taken anywhere else, or nowhere at all.

"So . . ." More than anything, she didn't want to tell him the rest, would rather parade naked in front of a convention of Southern Baptists. "So, there we were, eating our pulled pork and Hoppin'

Johns when this man walked over to our standing-up table and asked if we'd mind if he joined us. There was only me and my daddy there before the man arrived, and there was another table he could've gone to."

She set the root beer on the floor and hugged her knees. "I wish my father had said 'yes, I do mind. It's my daughter's birthday, and I want her all to myself.' But he didn't. The next thing I wish is that I'd left, just started walking down the street and kept going. But I was Hannah Conley then, and Hannah was too dumb to recognize the evil in Rodney Vanders's eyes when he looked at her."

"So he fixated on you, *Hannah?*"

She jerked her gaze to his. "Don't call me that. Hannah's dead. Buried. Never coming back." Hannah was no longer capable of facing the world.

"Good. I've grown used to Sugar, but help me understand why you feel you have to live a lie."

Hearing her name spoken aloud after two years sent rogue-sized waves of regret flowing through her. So many things she could've done differently if she'd only known. Her only excuse was that she'd not understood how very clever the devil was. *I'm sorry, Mrs. Lederman. I'm so Goddamned sorry.*

Stupid, stupid hot tears rolled down her cheeks despite her effort to stop them. Jamie wanted her to explain why she lived a lie, but how did she explain her part in a murder?

"Sugar?"

So she was Sugar again. But not for long. As soon as she got his interrogation over with and sent him on his way, she'd be Nikki Swanson. She decided Nikki would get lost somewhere in Arizona and never look at another man. They just weren't worth it. You either hated them or loved them and either way led to heartbreak.

"Okay. I just need a minute." She soaked in the sight of him, imprinted on her brain how his eyes had softened with the telling of her story so far, knowing that was about to change. He still stroked Junior's chin and neck as if he knew exactly where a cat wanted to be worshiped. *I love you, Jamie Turner, even though you're fixin' to rip my heart out of my chest and stomp it to pieces.* Because he would, this man of honor who hated liars.

"Turned out Rodney took one look at me and decided I belonged to him no matter what I wanted. I didn't understand that until it was too late. He and my father started talking, and before the night was over, Rodney Vanders, chief of police in a town his family had ruled with an iron fist for decades, offered my father a job. Daddy was thrilled to be back as a cop, a job he thought he deserved. Rodney isn't stupid, not then and not now. He eased his way into our life, and when my father thought he hung the moon, Rodney asked for me as payment for all he'd done for us. My father agreed." She waited for Jamie's reaction. Did he think it was okay for a father to give his only daughter to a man who lusted after a girl not yet sixteen?

"Jesus." Junior gave a little growl when Jamie's fingers dug into his neck. "What . . . what kind of father . . ."

He seemed at a loss for words, and she could sympathize. Yeah, what kind of father? That Saint even uttered Jesus's name told her how shocked he was. Well, he'd yet to hear the worst of it.

"Anyway, from then on, Hannah's life was monitored by Rodney. Where she went, who she saw, who she talked to. Mostly, she wasn't allowed to go anywhere, or see or talk to anyone but him. She . . . she was weak and inexperienced and didn't know how to say no to bad cop and bad cop. That's what I call them, and if it had been me, Sugar, I would've told them both to go straight to hell and to drop dead on their way." The tears stilled flowed, both from anger at having to lay herself open to Jamie and the remembering.

If she could somehow manage to curl up and die right then, she would.

Jamie had prepared himself to listen to her lies, and then he thought he would be able to walk away for the last time. Instead, the woman with the tears streaming down her cheeks broke his heart, and he was going nowhere.

He picked up Junior and moved him to the bottom of the bed. "Come here, Sugar."

"But you haven't heard the worst."

"I don't care." And he didn't. Whatever she told him next, he now understood she'd been the victim of a man who preyed on the people he was charged with protecting. Even worse, her own father hadn't kept her safe from a pedophile. Sugar—she'd always be Sugar to him—had been a pawn in a game no young girl could understand, nor stop.

With the wariness of a kitten creeping up to a rottweiler that might eat it, she came to him and crawled onto his lap. Although he wanted to assure her he wouldn't bite, he still wasn't sure how he felt about her, nor what he wanted from her. That she was finally telling the truth, he believed. It was beyond his comprehension how a father could give his young daughter away. When he had a daughter, he'd love and protect her with every fiber of his being. He'd love her the way his parents had loved him.

"Tell me the worst," he said after he had her safely tucked into his arms. He pressed his nose into her hair and inhaled the scent of her, one he'd recognize a hundred years from then. In this world or some other.

"I don't want to."

"Tell me anyway." He didn't imagine she did. If it was beyond what she'd told him so far, something to do with her involvement in stealing seven hundred thousand dollars, it would be a hard thing for her to admit. Had she been forced into it, or had she willingly participated? Afraid of the answer, he wasn't sure he wanted to know. They had come this far though, and he suspected the last part of the story was why she was running. Wrapping his arms around her, he waited for her to speak.

"Are ya sure you'd not just rather leave? Go back to Brown Jill, and forget you ever met me?"

With his lips pressed against the top of her head, he smiled against her hair on hearing her description of poor Jill. "I'm sure."

The sigh she heaved pressed her breasts against his chest, and he willed his erection to go away . . . at least for now. Later? Depended on what she had to say.

"Damn you, Jamie Turner. I was supposed to be rid of you by now."

There was no force to her words, and he didn't take offense. "I got that when you disappeared. But I found you, didn't I? That should tell you something."

She lifted her head, and her eyes searched his as if looking for what he wasn't saying. He wasn't ready for such truths and lowered his gaze to her mouth. The one he was going to kiss if she didn't start talking.

"All right. The worst is that Rodney stole seven hundred thousand from a very nice woman, Mrs. Lederman. I was the one who recommended the attorney when she wanted to change something in her will. The man was indebted to Rodney and would do anything Rodney asked. Hell, half the town owes him this favor or that, and the other half is too afraid to cross him. I suspected he was up to something bad, and I didn't try to stop him. That makes me guilty, right?"

"Let me get this straight. Did Vanders tell you who to recommend?"

"Yes, he made me." She clamped her teeth down on her lower lip, her eyes going distant, to some other time. "You remember I said he tried to drown me? He did it to make sure I understood his power over me and what he could do if I didn't obey. At first . . . well, at first Hannah refused to go along, but she wasn't strong, and when he showed her what he could do to her, she gave up."

Jamie wondered if she understood how much she distanced herself from the girl she'd been, as if she couldn't bear to think of herself capable of doing those things. Not that he blamed her from what he'd heard so far. She'd basically been a child, and a lonely, hurting one at that. If he had one wish, it'd be ten minutes in a room with Rodney Vanders, followed by another ten with her father.

Still, there had to be more to the story for her to feel so guilty. "Why is he so determined to find you, Sugar?" Her gaze fixated on the middle of his chest, and he lifted her chin. "Why?"

"Because I stole the money back. Don't look at me like that. I didn't keep it. She didn't know they'd changed her will, but she told me once where she wanted her money to go. So, I made sure it went to the right places. The Wounded Warriors because her only son died in Viet Nam, and two animal shelters because she loved animals."

From the beginning, he'd judged her and found her lacking without ever giving her a chance to prove otherwise. As for lying about her name, he now understood why she'd changed it. Not that she'd owed it to him to tell him. He'd given her little reason to think she meant anything to him beyond a few hours of mutual enjoyment.

"Does he think you still have the money?"

"I don't know. Probably, but it doesn't matter. He'd want me back with or without it so he could properly punish me. He-he thinks he owns me."

Her voice trembled, and the tears pooling in her eyes had his burning. He blinked them away and did some fast thinking. If the man had near-drowned her and put a whiplash scar on her back, he was clearly dangerous. But—and it was the big but—she couldn't, nor shouldn't, have to run and hide the rest of her life. She had him and K2 to protect her, and a small town chief of police would be no match for them.

That was part of the reason for the decision he came to. The other part: he just couldn't bear the thought of never seeing her again. The beautiful, wounded woman was his, flaws and all.

"Get your stuff ready. We're going home."

# CHAPTER TWENTY-ONE

No. I won't put you and your friends in danger." Sugar scrambled to the end of the bed. "I have a plan and enough money. You don't have to worry about me."

Jamie exhaled a long breath, as if she was trying his patience. "I'm not giving you a choice, sweetheart. And before you get all huffy, consider that you have me and the K2 team on your side. We are badass bad, and your Rodney Vanders, cop or no cop, doesn't stand a chance against us."

"He's not mine." The longing to give in, to stay with Jamie and to have the baddest guys she could think of at her side, almost had her saying yes. She shook her head. "These are my troubles, Jamie, and I won't dump them on you or anyone else."

Never mind that she still hadn't told him everything. Would he be so willing to be her champion if he knew the worst?

He shook his head as if she were an errant child in need of a scolding. "Sugar, don't ask me to walk away. I don't think I can. If you insist on going on to wherever it is you're planning to go, I'm coming with you. We can hide together."

"You don't mean that." Jamie go into hiding? He would wither and die.

"Yes, I do. Which will it be?"

Still dazed by the speed at which she'd been hustled back to Pensacola, Sugar stood in front of Jamie's door waiting to learn why she was at his house instead of her condo. Although the drive back should've given her plenty of time to think, her mind had closed down on her. Jamie had stayed behind her the entire way, and when she'd put on her blinker to turn for home, he'd come up beside her, blown his horn, and motioned her to follow him.

Now what?

"You forgot something," he said, walking up with her suitcase and laptop bag in one hand, and her cat carrier in the other.

So she was staying with him? Her knees almost buckled from relief at not having to spend the night at her place, alone and peeking out the window until daylight, watching for Rodney. He was near. She could feel his evil creeping up on her.

"I didn't know. That I was staying here, I mean." Did her voice sound as pathetic and needy to him as it did to her?

"You are. At least, until this is resolved." He handed her the carrier, then dug his keys out of his pocket. "If nothing else, Junior travels well," he said as he unlocked the door. "Maria's cat yowls like a banshee at the mere picture of a car."

He was trying to cheer her up, and she dutifully chuckled, appreciating that he cared enough to attempt the impossible. She was scared out of her freaking mind and eyed the road they'd just come in on with longing. The smart side of her brain screamed that she should be halfway through Texas by now.

The dumb side wanted to be with Jamie even though she didn't see a future for them; there were just too many unknowns where she was concerned. As for him, he was like some kind of knight of old, out to right a wrong; then he'd be off on his next adventure.

It was stupid of her and unfair to him not to tell him everything. Before much longer he'd find out anyway, and he'd hate her for lying to him. After a good night's sleep, she promised herself she would tell him. At the moment, though, she was dog-assed tired and not thinking straight. Once she was coherent again, she'd give him the whole truth and nothing but. So help her God, and all that.

"The guest bedroom's this way."

Sugar blinked, finding herself standing in the middle of his living room. The guest bedroom? *What'd you expect, Sugar? That he brought you here to play house with him?* As she followed him, she glanced around, taking note of his furnishings. The décor reminded her of the eighties, with the blue-and-white Laura Ashley prints, even a well-worn, blue fabric recliner. Except for the wide-screen TV, it certainly wasn't what she would've expected Saint's home to look like, or any single man's for that matter. It was like . . . it was like he'd re-created a place from his past.

As he led her to the guest room, her gaze roamed over his back, his wide shoulders, then down to his trim waist, and lean hips. Such a contradiction in what he showed the world and what was inside him. For the first time, she thought she understood him. He was stuck in the past, in a time when he'd had it all—loving parents, a bright future, and the homecoming queen for a girlfriend. And she thought she was screwed up. It was good to know, though, that he was human after all, and not the perfect, blue-eyed angel she'd first thought.

Or, a past girlfriend had decorated his home to look girlie, and he just hadn't gotten around to changing it.

"This is pretty," she said when she took in the white dresser, white headboard, the patchwork quilt in blues, greens, and peach.

"Do you think so? My mom kept a room like this for guests."

His question was so serious, as if her answer really mattered to him. "I do." And he hadn't cared enough about some other woman to let her drape his home in Laura Ashley prints.

"I figured she knew better than me how a guest room should be decorated." There was longing in his eyes as he glanced around the room.

Yep, he was messed up. Impulsively, she lifted onto her toes and brushed her mouth over his, drawing back before he could push her away. "It's lovely, Jamie. Really." She'd give anything to be the one to help him put his past to rest, but that had about as much chance of happening as her marrying her secret crush, Prince Harry.

His face lowered toward hers, and she thought he was going to kiss her, thought, yes, please. But he pulled back, stepping away. "You have your own bathroom. Why don't you get settled, then we'll decide what to do about dinner." He caressed her cheek with the back of his hand, then left.

Sugar set the carrier on the bed and opened the door. When her cat strolled out and meeped, she picked him up, and hugged him to her chest. "He's pretty messed up, Junior, but I don't care. Let's take a bath, then we'll go see what he's got to offer for dinner."

There was no bathtub to luxuriate in, but the shower felt almost as good. Surprising her, Junior pawed at the glass door. Opening it a little, he jumped in and chased droplets of water from one end of the tiled floor to the other, not seeming to mind he was getting soaked.

"Silly boy. Don't you know you're a cat, and you're supposed to hate water?" He never had, though. To him water was as fascinating as his toy mouse. "Maybe our new home, wherever that ends up being, will have a shower for you to play in." She laughed when he reared up, his paws high in the air, then pounced on a soap bubble slithering toward the drain.

After drying off, and choosing something to wear from her meager supply, she went looking for Jamie.

"He's wet," Jamie said when she walked into the living room with Junior wrapped in a towel.

"Well, yeah. We just took a shower."

"Okaaay." One corner of his lips twitched. "If you wanted a shower partner, you could've checked with me."

*Oh.* She tried to think of a clever comeback, but the man stole her wits sitting there in the old-fashioned recliner—a root beer dangling from his fingers and his bare feet hanging over the too-short leg rest—and wearing a lazy smile on his face. He wasn't the same unsmiling man who'd showed her to the guest room before briskly walking away. Truthfully, he was wearing her out, hiding behind the walls he'd built around him one minute, flirting with her the next. How was she supposed to know what to expect at any given time, or how to act around him?

Still not sure of his mood, she perched on the edge of the blue-and-white print sofa. It was weird, this feeling she was sitting in some grandmother's living room instead of one belonging to a he-man warrior who faced danger without a blink of his eyes. Talk about contradictions. Her gaze flitted around, settling on a collection of bells, some of them crystal, some porcelain, and a few brass.

"They were my mother's. She loved collecting them. Made it easy to know what to get her for Christmas."

The wistfulness in his voice tugged at her heart, and suddenly, she missed her mother with an ache that brought tears to her eyes. What a sad pair the two of them were. "They're lovely."

He cleared his throat. "Unless you want moldy cheese, potato chips, and a root beer for dinner, we need to make a trip to the grocery store."

Subtly clearing her own throat, Sugar forced a smile. "Sure. Could we make a stop at my condo so I can pick up a few things? I kinda packed lightly. If I still have a job, I'd like to go to work tomorrow. Guess I should call Maria, and see if I can take back the e-mail I sent her."

"I've taken care of it. Called when we were driving back, and she said to tell you she expects to see your smiling face at K2 first thing in the morning."

Well, she wasn't so sure about that. What if she had to run again? Was it fair to expect Maria to spend time training her if she wasn't sure she'd stay? The only way she'd feel right about it would be to lay it all out and let Maria decide. Looked like a day of true confessions ahead. Both Jamie and Maria would get the full story, and more than likely, they would send her on her way, both relieved to be rid of her.

"Let me grab my shoes and purse," she said, setting a sleeping Junior next to her on the couch.

Although she wore leggings and a loose T-shirt, except for the addition of a bra, she decided not to change. Not like she had much to choose from anyway. She pulled her damp hair up into a short ponytail, and other than some lip gloss, skipped applying makeup. Slipping her feet into a pair of flip-flops, she slung her purse over her shoulder. At the bedroom door, she stopped, considered, and then went to her suitcase and retrieved her stash of money, along with her gun and fake identity. After stuffing them in the bottom of her purse, she returned to the living room.

Jamie gave her the once-over, then grinned. "You look like a teenager."

"I'm sorry. I'll go change." What had she been thinking? Like he would want to be seen with a woman dressed like she was fixin' to clean house or something.

"Take it as a compliment, Sugar, the way it was meant."

Then he prowled toward her, his gaze capturing hers, freezing her like the proverbial deer in the headlights. Then he was kissing her, and she dropped her purse to the floor and wrapped her arms around his neck. His fingers grasped her hips, pulling her against him. Their tongues found each other, and hers rejoiced in the taste of him as flavors of lemon and root beer burst through her mouth.

As she slid her hands up, gliding them over the bristles of his short hair, she pressed her body into his, felt the tingles in her breasts, in her oversensitive nipples, felt his erection pushing against her stomach, low and almost right where she wanted to feel him. She trembled from need for him.

A moan filled the air between them, one she realized with gratitude came from Jamie. Desperate to show him she loved him without saying the words, she climbed up his body, and wrapped her legs around his waist. His arousal pressed against the part of her that would only and ever belong to him.

"Store," he gasped, the one word vibrating over her lips.

"Store?" She sucked on his tongue, wanting to crawl under his clothes and put her hands all over his body. She wanted to press her fingers into the muscles she knew existed in his arms, his chest, his abs, his legs. She'd explore him, taste him, love him until he'd never want any woman but her.

He put his hands on her waist and lifted her into the air, then set her on her feet. "If we don't go now, we won't. I hurt for you, Sugar." He took her hand and pressed it against his erection. "See?"

She nodded, too dumbfounded to do anything but nod like some kind of head-bobbing toy. He could remember they needed to go to the store? After the most explosive kiss ever?

"If we don't go now, we won't."

"Ya just said that," she said, proud she was following their conversation, something she considered a miracle when all she wanted was to climb right back up him and finish what he'd started.

His laugh was shaky as his hand blatantly readjusted his jeans. "You'll be the death of me yet. Let's go get our errands out of the way. Then . . ." He winked. "Then we'll have all night for, um, whatever."

No man had ever winked at her before, and Sugar decided it was the sexiest thing a man could do. It seemed such an intimate gesture, something meant just for her. Storing his gift in her treasure box marked *Jamie*, she snatched her purse from the floor, then walked to the couch and picked up Junior.

"You're not taking him with us, Sugar. Close him up in your room. He'll be okay."

No way. If something happened, she needed Junior with her. She had her money and new identity on her, and the last thing she wanted was to have to find her way back to Jamie's house to collect her cat. "I don't want to leave him in a strange place alone. He'll be fine if I hold him."

A roll of his eyes and a manly sigh was his only response before he opened the front door and ushered her out. She gave him a cheeky grin as she walked past him, impulsively adding a wink. Maybe it'd please him as much as it had her.

It occurred to Jamie as he followed Sugar to the car that she was the first woman to ever wink at him. It was kind of cute. The last thing he'd expected when he'd chased after her was to bring her back home with him. As he'd followed her on the return drive, he'd finally accepted that he needed her in his life, and the best way to keep her safe was to keep her with him.

He glanced over at her, sitting with her cat standing on her lap, his paws on the window as they both looked out. She was giving

Junior a running commentary of the sights they were passing, and it appeared the creature was paying close attention.

He shook his head at his whimsy. The woman messed with his mind. Like when she'd walked out after her shower, her hair damp, the leggings and T-shirt hiding none of her curves, her wet cat snuggled in her arms, and all his intentions had gone the way of . . . wherever. They'd just gone, and he'd found himself smiling and flirting with her. And kissing her. He'd meant to keep his distance until they took care of her problems, then they could turn their attention to whatever was going on between them. As soon as she walked into the living room, however, her cheeks pink from the shower, and a shy smile on her face, he'd known keeping his distance wasn't an option. As usual where Sugar was concerned, things didn't go as planned.

"Why are you scowling?" she'd asked.

*Because I think I've had it all wrong the past ten years.* "Sorry, it's been a long day, and I'm just a little tired." The setting sun disappeared over the horizon, making the interior of the car dark. Although he couldn't see her expression, her hesitation hung in the air between them and he knew, just knew what she was going to say.

"I'm sorry. I didn't mean for you to come after me." Her gaze shifted to the window, and she peered out. "I didn't want to involve you in this mess."

Bingo. He held out his hand and waited for Sugar to put hers in it. Instead, he got a handful of fur as Junior scrambled over, arching his back under Jamie's fingers.

"Mowwl."

"Mowwl back atcha." As if he'd just given permission in cat talk, Junior hopped over the console and curled up in Jamie's lap. Amused, he chuckled. The cat was the ugliest thing he'd ever seen, but with his missing ear and bent tail, he had the marks of a warrior and was impossible not to like.

"He likes you."

"And I like his owner." He held out his hand again. She looked at it for a few seconds, then slid her palm over his and entwined their fingers. Such a feeling of rightness flowed from their joined hands that he almost jerked away. What if he truly did fall for her, and she wanted no part of him when everything was over?

"I never thought I'd see this place again," she said when he pulled into her parking spot.

"Where did you plan to end up?"

"New Mexico. Arizona, maybe."

That seemed a world away, and thinking of her on the run and alone sent a wave of relief through him that he'd found her. "You shouldn't have to spend your life looking over your shoulder, sweetheart. Let's get whatever you need, get our grocery shopping done, and not think about any of this tonight. Tomorrow, we'll start planning how to put an end to it."

"Okay. I'll only be a minute."

"I'll come in with you." He wasn't letting her out of his sight.

Taking Junior, she draped him over one shoulder and her purse strap over the other. Once inside her condo, she set Junior on the floor. "Go get your toys," she said.

Jamie watched in amazement as the cat scampered under the sofa, returning a few seconds later with a small ball in his mouth, which he dropped at her feet.

"Go get the rest."

"Are you sure he's not a dog?" he asked when Junior trotted off again.

Her beautiful eyes crinkled at the corners. "One sometimes wonders. If you'd get the cat food from the pantry for me, I'll grab some clothes, and we can be off. You'll see some plastic bags on the same shelf you can put the cans in," she called over her shoulder as she headed down the hall.

The cans were easy to find, and he also added the bag of dry cat food. Noticing a wine rack on the floor, he grabbed a few bottles. Just because he didn't drink didn't mean she couldn't relax with a glass or two. With two plastic bags in hand, he turned toward the living room.

The only warning he had was Junior crouched under the coffee table, his tail twitching, the pupils in his green eyes dilated, and the fur on his back standing straight up as he stared intently down the hallway. His low growl sent a chill down Jamie's spine.

He gently set the bags on the counter and reached for his gun.

# CHAPTER TWENTY-TWO

*S**tupid.***

*S* She was so damn stupid. Hadn't she felt his evil coming closer? Because she'd ignored all the warnings, she'd put Jamie in danger, and she'd rather die than see him hurt.

"Who is he, Hannah?"

The slick-as-oil voice sent a shudder of revulsion through her. It was impossible to answer with Rodney's hand covering her mouth, and the gun poking into her back did nothing to help calm her nerves.

"If you've fucked him, I'll kill you both."

And he would. OhGodOhGodOhGod.

*Snap out of it, Sugar. You're not Hannah. Think!*

Yes, she needed to think, to figure out how to keep Jamie safe. That was all that mattered. Rodney was crazy, but he was crazy like a fox. Somehow, she had to outwit him. Tugging on the hand covering her mouth, she muttered against his fingers, hoping he'd let her talk.

"If you scream, I'll put a bullet through your spine. You won't die, but you'll be paralyzed for life. All the better to make you stay put." His hand loosened, although he still kept it over her mouth.

"He's just a friend," she whispered. "Someone I work with."

"If he's only a friend, why is he here? Where were you last night?"

The unmade bed caught her attention, the one she'd carefully made up for what she'd thought would be the last time. Oh, just gross. He'd slept in it. Her mind trailed off to a vision of burning it. If he were in it, all the better when it went up in flames.

"Where were you, Hannah?"

She snapped back to her current predicament. Where had she been? Think. Where? Somewhere she'd read that when telling a lie, one should keep it as close to the truth as possible. "At a weekend away in New Orleans that the people I work for hold every year. Everyone was there, all twenty-six of them. My car quit on me and had to be left at a repair place. Ja . . ." Sugar almost bit her tongue off when she heard herself about to say Jamie's name. "He gave me a ride back, that's all. He only came in because I have a book he wants to read." Lame, Sugar. So freakin' lame.

"I want to believe you, Hannah. I really do. But you've given me no reason to. Let's go meet this friend of yours."

"I'll come home with you, Rodney, if you'll leave him alone. I was going to anyway. I thought I wanted to be on my own, but it wasn't what I expected. I missed you. Let's just go home, okay?"

The man who'd claimed a fifteen-year-old girl as his—the man who'd beat her, made her steal money from a kind woman, and laughed at her tears when that woman had been murdered—spun her around and lowered his Bradley Cooper handsome face to hers.

"You'll come home with me whether I let him live or not, Hannah. And you'll tell me where my money is."

It took every fiber of her being not to vomit all over him. Swallowing her bile, she nodded. "I will, I promise."

*Please God, keep Jamie safe, and do your God thing, and make him take Junior home with him.*

If the man and cat she loved were together, she could accept her fate. And some day she'd escape again, but when she did, she'd cross some ocean or other and disappear somewhere he'd never find her. Rodney pushed her ahead of him, the gun still digging into her spine.

"Where is he?" Rodney said, pulling her to a stop when they reached the end of the hall.

"Probably left. I told you, he just wanted a book." Where the hell was he?

"I'm right here, behind you."

She'd never heard Jamie's voice sound so cold and deadly. Hope exploded inside her. Jamie had somehow known Rodney was there. If Rodney thought he was a badass, he didn't have a clue. The K2 men expected the worst, trained for the worst, and could show a small-town, bully cop who thought he was a badass the true meaning of the word. She exhaled a slow breath, but tensed again when Rodney pressed the gun hard against her back.

No, Rodney played dirty and she didn't want Jamie involved; she couldn't bear to think of him being hurt.

"Go home, Saint. This isn't your concern." Please, Jamie, go home.

Jamie laughed, but it wasn't really a laugh. It was a sound that would've scared her into handing him her gun, and agreeing to anything he asked.

"Saint?" Rodney echoed. "Who the hell wants to be a saint? I'll put a bullet through her if you don't step in front of us. Like right now."

The air sizzled with determined male testosterone as the two men refused to give way. "Please, Saint. Please."

"I don't think so, Sugar. He won't shoot you cause he knows I'll end his sorry-assed life before his finger's off the trigger. You do know that, don't you, Mr. Vanders."

Rodney's fingers dug into her arm at hearing his name from Jamie. "It warms my heart to know you've talked about me to your *friend,* Hannah." He poked her again with his gun. "Tell him if he doesn't step in front of us right now, I really will shoot you."

What she'd dreaded telling Jamie might be the only thing to make him leave, the only way to keep him safe. She'd just hoped after she explained, he could forgive her, but any chance of that had been stolen by Rodney's appearance. Blinking back tears of regret, she took a deep breath and willed herself to say the one word she'd hoped to never hear pass her lips again.

"Please do as my husband asked, Saint." Rodney's thumb made a slow caress over her skin as if in approval. She really was going to vomit.

Time seemed to stop, the air seemed to leave the room, and her heart seemed to cease its beats. No one moved, no one spoke, yet through the dead air, she could sense Jamie's shock.

Any second, if something didn't happen, she was going to either faint or lose the contents of her stomach. Then Jamie was standing in front of her, his gun pointed at her. Was he going to shoot her? Not that she'd blame him.

Ice-blue eyes lasered onto hers. "Is that true?"

She resisted lowering her eyes in shame. She was still Sugar, still had balls Hannah had never dreamed of possessing. Sugar could look the man she loved in the eyes and do whatever it took to keep him safe.

"Yes, it's true, so you should go now." *Please, go.* "Rodney . . ." She glanced up at her husband, aiming for a softness she would never feel in this life or the next for bad cop, and fearing she'd failed miserably. How the hell was she supposed to go all soft for a man who'd raped Hannah and murdered her only friend? "Um, Rodney's my husband, and I'm going home with him."

Whoever said things got easier with repetition lied. Saying *my husband* made her want to vigorously scrub a Brillo Pad over her tongue. Jamie's hard gaze speared through her, and she gave up trying to pretend anything.

The wood floor at her feet could use a good wax, something she'd meant to get around to doing. Thinking about failing to wax her floors was damn easier than meeting Jamie's gaze and seeing what a disappointment she was to him.

"Go home, Jamie," she whispered, the fight having gone out of her. "Just go home."

Rodney laughed, the absurd sound of it grating over her skin like the feel of fingernails over a blackboard. "You really should listen to my wife, Saint . . . or should I call you Jamie?"

Oh, shit. She'd called him Jamie. She did not want Rodney to know his name, not even his first one.

"You're still hesitating, Saint Jamie," Rodney said. "Maybe it'll make a difference if you knew my wife killed a nice old woman just to steal money that wasn't hers. Smothered her with a pillow and then slept through the night like a baby."

Sugar jerked her gaze up to Jamie's and opened her mouth to deny she could do such a thing, that she'd spent the entire night crying for her friend. *I didn't,* she almost screamed, but the cold-as-glaciers blue eyes stopped any protest she might have uttered. It was better that way. Let him believe she was pond scum so he'd take himself safely away.

"Makes all the difference in the world, Mr. Vanders. I assume you're here to arrest her?"

Never having the brains God gave even a goat, Rodney took an agonizing full minute to consider the excuse Jamie had just given him. Nor did it occur to him to wonder how Jamie knew he was a cop. But Sugar knew her husband. Unfortunately. Knew he'd latch onto the excuse Jamie had handed him to justify his right to her.

What was Jamie up to? During the long seconds she could almost hear Rodney's small brain making an effort to engage, she stared at Jamie. He stared back with an expression devoid of any clue to his feelings, and she wondered if she knew him at all. She'd wanted him to walk away, to not get hurt by anything she or Rodney did. She guessed she was about to get her wish.

Her poor, deluded heart, however, had thought he just might step up and be her hero.

"Arrest her? Exactly. That's why I'm here. To take Hannah back where she can face her crime."

Jamie almost snorted at the blatant lie. How had Sugar's father justified to himself putting his young daughter into the man's hands? Sugar . . . He tried to think of her as Hannah, but it just didn't work. She was Sugar to him and always would be. The woman he'd come to know would chop off her fingers before she'd hold a pillow over an old woman's face.

But she had neglected to mention she had a husband. Stupid him, it hadn't occurred to him to ask if she was married. Biting down his disappointment that she still hadn't trusted him enough to tell him everything, he focused on the situation at hand. Later, when she was safe, they'd have another *little* chat.

With a gun pressed to her spine, his options were limited. If he put a bullet through the middle of the man's forehead as he longed to do, there was too great a risk of Vanders's gun going off. The smartest thing to do would be to convince her bad-cop husband that he couldn't care less about her well-being and make his exit.

Vanders would be anxious to get back home where he felt in control, and Jamie would be waiting for them to walk out of the condo. It wasn't the greatest plan, but it was the best under the circumstances.

"You know what, I knew the minute I met her she was trouble, and as far as I'm concerned, she's all yours." Trusting the man wasn't fool enough to shoot a stranger, Jamie stuck his gun in the back of his waistband. "I'll just leave you two lovebirds with best wishes for a happy life."

"You can go, Saint Jamie, but your gun stays."

Jamie snorted. "Not happening." Forcing himself to ignore the desperation in Sugar's eyes, he backed toward the door, hands held out in front of him.

Then all hell broke loose.

Out of nowhere, a hissing, spitting cat flew through the air, his back feet landing on Vanders's shoulder as his claws dug into the man's face. Vanders screamed and punched at the cat. Jamie reached for Sugar to pull her away.

"Junior," she cried when he pushed her toward the door.

"Damn it, Sugar, just go."

Upon hearing his name, Junior sprinted to Sugar, and she snatched him up.

"Go," Jamie urged.

"He's going to shoot you," she cried, then tossed Junior onto the sofa before stepping in front of Jamie just as Vanders fired.

Jamie had seen the crazed look in the man's eyes and was reaching for his gun even as he knew he'd be shot before he could get to it. He had expected to feel the pain of a bullet slicing into him, and had even had enough time to hope it wouldn't hit a vital organ.

He had not expected Sugar to take a bullet meant for him.

Vanders stared in shock as Sugar crumpled to the floor, then he took off, heading for the back door. Acting on instinct, Jamie fired at the fleeing man. Vanders let out a yell and clutched his arm, but kept going. As much as Jamie wanted to chase him down, Sugar was hurt and needed him.

"Stupid woman," he murmured, swallowing past the lump of fear in his throat. As he searched for where she'd been shot, his heart felt like it had tripled in size and no longer fit in his chest.

"Not . . . not stupid. Ha-have an IQ of over one forty."

"We'll debate that later." Her weak voice worried him. A circle of blood grew on her T-shirt near her stomach, and he lifted the shirt. "Thank God," he said upon seeing the bullet had gone through the skin at the edge of her waist. He gently probed her back, relieved to feel an exit wound.

"H-hurts."

"I need to get some towels, sweetheart. I'll be right back."

She grabbed his hand. "I'm sorry."

"Hush, my love."

*My love.* He backed away from the pain-filled eyes that were welling with tears. He'd never used those two words before with any woman. Hadn't wanted to. Ever. People he loved died. Hadn't he just proved that all over again by almost getting her killed?

Unable to face what was in his heart, he turned his attention to summoning help. Hanging up after calling for an ambulance, he dialed Jake's number as he pulled a bath towel out of her linen closet.

"Sugar's been shot," he said as soon as Jake answered, praying he and Maria had returned from New Orleans.

"Where are you?"

"Her condo. Are you home?"

"Just walked in the door. We're on our way."

Jamie stuck his phone into his pocket as he hurried back to the living room. Curled next to Sugar's neck, Junior blinked green eyes at him as he gave a cry that Jamie fully understood. He could easily curl up on the other side of her neck and cry, too.

"I don't know if you saved her or made things worse, cat, but I don't doubt you love her. She's going to be okay. I promise."

Sugar opened her eyes and pressed her chin against Junior's head. "I love both of you."

*Don't! Don't love me.* Jamie wanted to shake her back to smart, back to that IQ she claimed to have. When she felt better, when she had her brains back and remembered how he'd failed to keep her safe, she'd see he was dangerous to those he loved.

Sirens sounded as he pressed the towel against her wound. "Hold this for a minute, sweetheart, while I go open the door."

"I do love you, Jamie," she said; then her head fell to the side as she lost consciousness.

"What the hell happened here?" Jake asked as he followed two cops and the EMTs in, Maria on his heels.

Jamie pressed the paramedic's hand onto the towel he'd put over her wound and backed away. She'd said she loved him. She had taken a bullet meant for him.

"I almost got her killed," he spat, standing back as the paramedics carried Sugar to the ambulance.

# CHAPTER TWENTY-THREE

Why did she smell medicine? And who was that chattering like a squirrel on speed?

"Wake up, dearie. Is your name really Sugar? Says here on this chart your name's Sugar Darling. Sounds like some kind of porn star to me. If you are, can I have your autograph? Gertie and Frances won't believe it, and they'll have to come meet you in person. I watched a porn movie once. Back when I was young and wild. Can't say I liked it much. Still, if you're a star, then you're the second one I've met. I met Ellen DeGeneres first . . . sorry, dearie, you're my second famous person, and if I'm being honest, I liked Ellen better'n you. She's the tiniest little thing. Looks bigger on TV. She's gay. Did you know that? Doesn't bother me none. I figure God has better things to worry about than who someone loves. You know, like murderers and child molesters. The wars popping up all over. Now them things, God surely worries about. I'm not home to watch her show because I'm here taking care of all my wounded little birdies, but I tape her and watch her at night with a glass of wine. Gertie says drinking spirits is a sin, but . . ."

Sugar cracked open an eye to see a small, thin woman with pink-tinted hair, and wearing a pink pinafore, bustling around the room with the energy of a busy hummingbird. "Who are you?"

The woman gave one last adjustment to a vase of flowers, then came to the bed and leaned her face over Sugar's. "Oh, good, you're awake, dearie." She pressed a button on a little box at Sugar's side. "The nurses will want to know."

"Nurses?" Sugar eyed the plastic bag hanging above her and followed the tube coming from it to the needle in her arm. "Hospital? Why?" Her throat felt like she'd swallowed the contents of a sandbag. "Water?"

"Patience, dearie." The woman patted Sugar's shoulder. "See, here's your nurse now."

The pink woman disappeared from sight, and a young man in a teddy-bear-print scrub shirt came into view. "Water?" Why was she so thirsty?

He handed her a cup of ice. "This to start. If you hold it down, then we'll get you a little water. I'm Mike by the way."

The sliver of ice felt like pure heaven on her tongue, and she sucked on it, letting the melted drops slide down her parched throat. The man went to lift her hospital gown, and she grabbed his hand.

"I just need to look at your wound, Sugar. I'm not going to hurt you."

*Wound.* It all came back then. She'd been shot. Precisely, Rodney had shot her.

"Jamie? Is he . . . is he okay?"

"If you mean the man who sat outside your room all night, guarding you, yes, he's fine. Open your mouth."

A thermometer was stuck under her tongue, keeping her from asking more questions. He'd sat outside all night? Not that he was responsible for her, but why hadn't he stayed in her room?

The door opened, and Maria stepped in, then stopped. "Oh, sorry. We'll just wait outside."

Mike glanced over his shoulder. "No, come on in. I'm done for now." He turned back to Sugar and smiled. "I'll be back in about

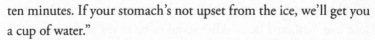 

ten minutes. If your stomach's not upset from the ice, we'll get you a cup of water."

"Thank you."

"Oh, honey, how are you feeling?" Maria said as she rushed to the bed, taking Sugar's hand.

"Pretty good, considering. I think there's some drugs in that bag though, so that must be why I feel like I'm floating away." She yawned, but forced her eyes to stay open. "Jamie?"

Jake stepped up to the bed. "We made him go home to get some sleep. While you're here, one of our men will be stationed in the hall. We've got everyone else out investigating, trying to find out where Vanders might have stayed, who might have seen him. Kincaid's talking to one of our FBI contacts, and he'd like to meet with you."

"Who? The FBI?" Rodney really would kill her if she talked to anyone about him, especially the FBI.

"Maybe, but I mean the boss first."

"I don't know." She couldn't think right then, just wanted to pull the covers over her head and go to sleep. But first, she had to know. "Jamie? Is he mad at me?" Maria and Jake exchanged a glance, confirming her fear. Tears burned her eyes, and she just wanted them to leave before she embarrassed herself and cried.

"Ah, I think it's girl-talk time. I'll be just outside." Jake brushed his lips over his wife's. "Take your time, Chiquita."

Sugar winced as she pushed up against the pillow. Maybe if she sat up she could stay awake. Mike walked in, and she held in her questions while he filled a cup half-full of water.

"If you're not barfing by now, you're good to go," he said with a cute grin that revealed a dimple on the left side of his cheek. He handed her the cup.

"Barfing, Mike? Is that what they taught ya to say in nursing school? You do have a charming bedside manner though." Where was this flirting coming from? Yeah, he was cute, but she'd only ever love one man, and he couldn't stand to be in the same room with her. It must be the drugs.

"Sometimes, Sugar," he leaned over her. "I improvise."

There went that dimpled grin again. She grinned back. "I bet you were a handful for your mama."

Mike gave a burst of laughter. "You don't know the half of it, Sugar, my sweet." He turned to Maria. "She'll probably fall asleep on you. Buzz me if she needs anything."

"Now there's some serious eye candy," Maria said, her gaze following Mike's retreating back.

"Don't let Jake hear ya say that."

Her friend's eyes went soft at the mention of her husband. "He knows he's my man, but it doesn't hurt to keep him on his toes. Why don't you slide down and get some rest? I'll send Jake back to the office and sit here with you."

"Don't wanna be a pest." A question hovered at the edge of her mind, but the fuzz in her head made thinking impossible. She snuggled down under the covers as her eyes insisted on closing. *Jamie. I want Jamie.* Forcing her eyes open, she glanced at the door. "Jamie. He's gone. He hates me."

"Oh, Sugar, wherever did you get that idea? The man loves—"

She tried to stay awake to hear what Maria said, but sleep took her.

Long strides took Jamie to Sugar's room. He wouldn't go in, just needed to make sure Kincaid had stationed a guard like he'd promised. Her husband—every time he thought the word *husband* connected to her, he wanted to put his fist through something—was nowhere to be found. If, as he suspected, the bastard had fled back to the town he believed would protect him, Jamie had news for the

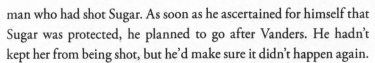 

man who had shot Sugar. As soon as he ascertained for himself that Sugar was protected, he planned to go after Vanders. He hadn't kept her from being shot, but he'd make sure it didn't happen again.

*I'm coming for you, you sorry excuse for a man.*

Ryan O'Connor glanced up from the game he played on his cell phone, gave Jamie a curt nod, then pushed the door to Sugar's room open. "Maria," he said quietly, "he's here."

"Not staying." How could he face her after letting her get shot?

"Not my problem," O'Connor responded from his chair posted outside Sugar's door.

"I meant I didn't want you to tell them I'm here."

"Again, not my problem. Maria said to tell her when you were, so I did." He gave Jamie a smirk, accompanied by a lift of one eyebrow. "She can fire me. You can't."

"Go to hell." The mood Jamie was in, Doc was lucky he didn't get a fist in his face.

Both of Ryan's brows lifted, and his damn mouth curved in amusement. "Saint's still cussing? The apocalypse has arrived."

Before Jamie could knock Doc senseless, Maria poked her head out, grabbed Jamie's wrist, and pulled him inside. He could've pulled away. Should have. But he wanted to see Sugar . . . needed to see her. Then he'd go.

"She's asleep right now, but she's been asking for you."

"I'm not staying, just wanted to check on her, make sure someone was guarding her door." He'd avoided looking at her when entering the room, but his gaze finally strayed to the woman lying in the hospital bed. She was so pale. Guilt surged through him that he hadn't been with her when she'd awakened.

Her beautiful eyes blinked open and instantly locked on him. A smile curved her lips, sending his heart into a tailspin. He fisted his hands to keep from going to her.

"I thought I heard your voice." When he didn't respond, her smile faltered. "Jamie?"

"I have to go," he said, and walked out.

*Coward.* That he was, and it was for Sugar's own good. During the long hours he'd sat outside her hospital room hoping a certain chief of police had the nerve to show his face, Jamie had reached an unwanted conclusion. He loved Sugar Darling, or Hannah Conley, or whatever her name was.

Nevertheless, he was bad news to those he loved.

Once he'd seen to it that Vanders would never bother her again, he'd leave Sugar alone. If he was lucky, she would move away so he'd not have to see her every day, or stand on the sidelines and watch her fall in love with one of his buddies.

He walked out of the hospital to find a thunderstorm had moved in while he was inside. "That's Florida for you," he muttered as he ran to his car. Returning home, he planned to take a quick shower, then go to work. Check in and see if the boss had found out anything. If he learned Vanders had returned to South Carolina, then Jamie planned to take a few personal days and make a little trip to discuss matters with the bastard.

"Meep," Junior said when Jamie walked into his house.

The furball's word for *feed me*, he remembered Sugar saying. "You can't be hungry again." The cat almost tripped him making his figure eights as Jamie headed to the kitchen. Before he fell flat on his face, Jamie picked up Junior.

"A few treats, that's all you're getting." After they'd taken Sugar away and the cops had finally left, he'd spied the cat peeking out from under the couch. Unable to leave him alone, he had brought Junior home with him.

Leaving him to his treats, Jamie wandered into his living room. Standing in the middle of the room, he made a slow circle, seeing it as Sugar must have. He hadn't missed the speculation in her eyes when she'd taken in the décor.

The furniture that once belonged to his parents and had brought him such comfort suddenly seemed old and tired. The books on the shelves belonged to his dad; the knickknacks his mom had collected.

Where was anything of Jamie's? He made another circle, and the only thing he could find belonging to him was the wide-screen TV. A thought bolted its way through his brain like lightning, staggering him.

He was frozen in time.

Sitting heavily on the blue-and-white-print couch, he finally admitted to himself that he'd stopped living the day his parents had died. Yes, he was driving the car. Yes, he was going fast, and the worst part, he'd smoked a couple of joints, along with downing a few beers, prior to getting behind the wheel.

If he had known his father was going to have a heart attack, he'd never have smoked or drank, but how was a kid supposed to predict something like that? He'd been going fast because his father was dying. The black ice he'd hit had been the reason he lost control of the car. If he would have done anything different if he hadn't been half-stoned, there was no way to know.

A memory came to him of the day he learned he had lost his scholarships. He'd hung a tire from a tree in the backyard and was trying to throw a football through the middle, something he'd been able to do to perfection before hurting his shoulder.

Frustrated when he kept missing, he spiked the ball. "Stupid fucking shoulder."

"Don't let your mother hear you say that word. She'll blame herself for raising you wrong."

"It wasn't like I knew you were spying on me," he'd snarled to cover his embarrassment at learning his dad had been watching him. His parents had been so proud of him when he'd received two scholarship offers, one from Ohio State, and one from Stanford. He knew it had been a blessing to them as it would have been a hardship on their part to pay his way through college. Then he had gone and screwed everything up.

"And I didn't raise you to be disrespectful, son. Also, I happen to own this backyard and can come and go as I please." He put his arm around Jamie's shoulder. "I'm a firm believer that things happen for a reason. Maybe God has a different plan in mind for you than playing football and baseball. You still have the rest of the summer for your shoulder to heal, but if it doesn't, then it doesn't. The question then becomes, what will you do with your life?"

Jamie kicked at the freshly mown grass. "I know you can't afford to send me to college."

"If that's what you want, we'll find a way. Just know this, Jamie. Your life will be what you make it, and I for one believe in you."

His parents had believed in him, even when he'd given them reason not to. Looking back, Jamie realized he had been meant for something different than sports, pot, and partying. Instead, he'd joined the SEALs, had done some good in the world, and still did. If not for his injury, he would probably be playing pro ball.

Yet, he was glad he wasn't, and that enlightenment had taken ten years in coming. For that, he had to thank Sugar. She'd crashed into his life—almost literally if he considered the beer truck incident—and had sent him to questioning everything he thought he wanted.

What he wanted was her. What his parents wouldn't have wanted was for him to stay stuck in their lives. He surveyed the furniture that belonged to the past and wondered what kind of style Sugar liked.

Junior jumped onto the sofa and stood on his hind legs, butting Jamie's cheek. A plaintive wail sounded from the cat. Jamie knew just how Junior felt.

"Do you know why I don't cuss, Junior? Well, until recently, anyway. No? I'll tell you why. It's because my mother raised me right. She would've loved Sugar." Both his parents would have loved her feistiness, her quick humor, and the kindness residing at her very core.

"Mowl."

Her cat missed her and so did he.

# CHAPTER TWENTY-FOUR

What just happened?" Sugar asked as the door closed behind Jamie.

Maria rolled her eyes. "Men can be such idiots when they're in love. Believe me, I know."

"He's not in love with me. He can't stand the sight of me." What else explained him stomping off like that? She eased up and leaned back on the pillow. "I need to go home. Junior's there by himself."

"Who's Junior?"

"My cat." Poor baby, he probably thought he'd been abandoned. She pushed off the covers and swung her legs over the side of the bed, then winced. God, moving hurt her side.

"Oh, that's his name. Jamie took him home with him." She put her hands on Sugar's shoulders and pushed her back onto the bed. "You're not going anywhere until the doctor says you can."

Too weak to protest, Sugar let herself be fussed over as Maria put the covers back and tucked her in.

"He hates me."

"Junior? I doubt that." Maria's grin said she knew exactly whom Sugar meant.

Although she wanted to pour her heart out, Sugar never had a best friend, and didn't know how to be one. "When can I get out of here?"

"Do I look like a doctor? Everything's being taken care of, Sugar. You just need to relax and trust us." She pulled the chair close to the bed and sat, tucking her feet under her. "Do you want to talk about it?"

*Trust.* She hadn't trusted anyone since her mother died. But she wanted to, and had thought she trusted Jamie. But she hadn't really, at least not enough to tell him all her secrets. It would probably go down as the biggest mistake of her life.

Maria's warm brown eyes stared back at her, offering friendship and a sympathetic ear. *Accept what she's offering, Sugar. Tell her everything.* "I was fifteen when—"

The door opened, and a woman in a lab coat with a stethoscope draped around her neck walked in. Twenty minutes later, Sugar lay back exhausted from being poked and prodded. Why was she getting tired so easily? Oh, right, she'd been shot. By her bastard of a husband. At least, the doctor had said she could go home the next day if she didn't have a fever. Damned if she would. There were things she needed to do.

She fell asleep as the glimmer of a plan formed in her mind.

The chattering squirrel was back. Sugar floated between sleep and wakefulness, listening to the pink lady.

"You boys remind me of my Henry when he was young and virile. So handsome he was. First time I saw him, he was the best man at my cousin's wedding. Lordie, I couldn't take my eyes off that man in his dress uniform. He was in the marines. Decided right then and there he was going to be mine. You boys marines?"

Boys? Who was there? Sugar slitted her eyes open to see Pink Lady craning her neck to peer up at the boss and Jamie. Both men stared down at the miniscule woman with amusement on their faces.

"No ma'am," Kincaid said. "We're not military."

"Could've fooled me. You both got that look about you."

"They used to be navy SEALs." That came from Maria, curled up in the chair. The boss shot his sister a glare, and Maria responded with a mischievous wink. "Just trying to be helpful."

"I knew it," Pink Lady said with a dainty grunt of satisfaction.

Sugar half listened to the banter, her attention on Jamie. After the way he'd walked out, she hadn't expected to see him again, at least not while she was in the hospital. He was so gorgeous, so damn hot, she could drool like a baby just looking at him. She'd known that body intimately, had felt the rock-hard abs as she'd pressed her fingers over them, had climaxed while he had held her close and whispered in her ear.

And it would never happen again because he hated her. Biting down on her bottom lip to keep from crying, she hungrily soaked in the sight of him while she still could. As soon as he realized she was awake, he'd likely storm out again.

As if sensing her scrutiny, his blue eyes locked onto hers before she could pretend to still be asleep. Caught in his gaze, she waited for him to leave, expected it. His attention on her was so intense that she felt an electrical current of some sort sizzling in the air between them.

He wore his warrior face, and what was going on inside his head, she couldn't fathom, but he didn't leave. The boss stepped into her line of vision, cutting off the connection between her and Jamie. Air swished out of her lungs as she realized she'd been holding her breath.

"I have a few questions if you feel up to it."

"Sure." Surprised when Kincaid sat on the edge of her bed, she pushed up against the pillows. The man made her nervous. There was a dangerous edge to him, and he rarely laughed. Although she'd never seen him with his wife, she'd heard he was putty in the woman's hands. Sugar found that hard to believe.

"We've been busy since the ambulance carried you away, and we now have a background report on you. What that means is we know who you are, who Vanders is, and that your father works for him as a cop."

Not sure how she felt about them digging into her life, she remained silent. He must have sensed her uneasiness as he gave her a rare smile, his eyes softening just a little.

"You were shot, Sugar . . . is that the name you prefer?"

She nodded.

"We take care of our own, and when our own are threatened, we get busy. Information is vital to the success of any operation, and because you were pretty much out of it, we didn't feel we could wait. So we started investigating."

Interesting that he didn't apologize for nosing into her business, but her mind stuck on one word. Were they planning an operation on her behalf? She glanced at Jamie, and he nodded as if he could read her mind. Such a feeling of gratitude for these men of K2 welled up that she couldn't utter a word. If she tried, she'd blubber incoherently.

"Let's give her a few minutes," Maria said.

Sugar shot her friend a look of appreciation for understanding she needed time to collect herself.

"Not you," Maria said, grabbing Jamie's arm when he turned to leave.

Alone with him, she searched for something to say to the man who'd stolen her heart. For his part, Jamie seemed as much at a loss for words as she was.

Sugar sucked in her breath, steeling herself to take a blind leap off a cliff. He'd either catch her or let her crash on the rocks below. Either way, at least she'd know what the future meant for them.

"I love you, you know." There, she'd said it.

He said nothing back. Only stood just out of her reach and gave her nothing from his unreadable blue eyes. Damn and hell and damn. She should've done as Hannah would have and pulled the sheet over her head until he'd gone away.

At her words, ones Jamie had never thought to want from her, the last piece of the block of ice that had frozen him in place for ten long years melted away. Although she'd said it before, she had just been shot, and it could have been her fear talking. But this time she'd said the words while alert and aware. His feet took one step toward her, his heart joining in the march at his second step, his mind giving up the fight the moment he touched her.

"Sugar," he said, and wrapped his arms around her as he pushed his way onto her bed. "My sweet Sugar." He curled around her and pressed her head onto his shoulder. Nothing in his sorry life had felt better than how she trustingly nestled into him and sighed his name.

Still cocooned together when Kincaid and Maria returned to the room, Jamie slid out of the bed. Although no other words had been said between them, he hoped she understood he'd just given her his heart. He'd almost told her he loved her, but as the words reached the tip of his tongue, a way to show her occurred to him, and he stayed quiet. It would be much better than confessing his love in a hospital room. He hoped.

"Are you ready to help us put a stop to your bad cop, sweetheart?"

"He's not mine, and I never wanted him to be."

"Then let's make sure he understands that." If there were any other way, he wouldn't put her through the questions they needed answers to. "We need to know everything there is to know about Rodney Vanders. We've had a chance to dig a little into his personal affairs, and there's some interesting stuff. It would speed things along if you know anything."

Her harsh laugh grated in his ears, and he glanced at Kincaid, who nodded that he, too, understood the implications of her response. She knew enough to take the man down.

At her hesitation, Maria placed her hand on Sugar's blanket-covered foot and squeezed. "We're your friends, Sugar, and we want to help. You can trust us."

"I know," Sugar whispered. "It's just that it's been so long since I could trust anyone, and your stepping up to protect someone you barely know is hard to believe."

Jamie squeezed her hand, and she took a deep breath and started talking. As he listened to her speak of how the Vanders family had ruled the town for generations through intimidation, threats, and blackmail, Jamie's urge to wrap his hands around the man's neck grew with each word. Even if the man had been taught from birth he was entitled to take what he wanted by whatever means he wanted and didn't know any better, Jamie felt no guilt over what they had planned for him. Evil was evil no matter how it got to be evil.

"The first time I met him, I was fifteen. If I . . . if I had known then what he was and that he'd decided the moment he set eyes on me that I belonged to him, I would've run away from home." One shoulder lifted in a small shrug, then her gaze traveled over Kincaid and Maria. "There's personal stuff I'm just not willing to talk about."

Nor did he want the boss to hear intimate details of her time with Vanders. "That's okay, baby, you don't have to." Believing she would respond to him best, they'd decided before entering her room that Jamie would ask the questions. "What we really need to know about is the money he stole, and I'm sorry, sweetheart, but you're going to have to tell us about the woman he claims you killed."

Indignation flared in her eyes. "Is that what you believe, that I'm a murderer?"

There was his Sugar Darling, the woman who'd defied the devil in the disguise of a man by trying to make things right, then had managed to hide herself for two years. "Did you miss the part where I said he *claims* you did it? No, I know you didn't, so you can quit shooting fire at me with those beautiful eyes of yours."

He'd not missed her slight wince when she'd moved too fast, and he put a hand on her shoulder, leaving it there. "Easy. You're going to hurt yourself moving around like that. What happened, Sugar?"

"She was so nice to me, and h-he k-killed her." With that, she burst into tears. He got back on the bed with her and wrapped his arms around her as her cries grew until she was sobbing. Hearing a whimper, he glanced up to see tears streaming down Maria's face. When she pressed her hands over her face, he lifted his chin at Kincaid, who nodded and stood.

"We'll be outside," he said, grabbing Maria's hand and towing her out of the room.

Not caring that she was soaking his shirt with her tears, he held the woman who'd snuck her way into his heart and marveled at how right it felt. When he'd entered the room and stood beside her bed, staring down at her, he'd known then he would never let her go. There was the problem of her having a husband, but she could remedy that with a quick divorce. Once Vanders was behind bars, she'd finally be free of the man.

With her face buried against his chest, she started talking. "Her name was Mrs. Lederman, and she was homebound. Rodney started taking me to her house in the afternoons after I got out of school. I was a senior then. He said she was lonely and needed a friend. I didn't suspect his real reason at first."

"To steal her money?" he asked when she paused.

"Yes, to steal her money. It was only when he gave me the name of an attorney to recommend to her that I got suspicious, but by then I was too afraid of him to refuse. I don't know how they managed to trick her, but somehow, Rodney ended up as her beneficiary. Then one day he arrived to pick me up, and he told me to go to the car. I didn't though. By then, I knew what kind of man he was, and I didn't trust him. So, I tiptoed down the hall and peeked into the room. He-he had a pillow over her face."

She wasn't going to need a divorce because he was going to kill the bastard.

"If I'd been . . ." she took a shuddering breath. "If I'd been Sugar then, I would've run to the kitchen, grabbed a knife, and killed him." As if she couldn't meet his gaze, her eyes lifted to the monitor. "Hannah though, she knew he would kill her, too, if he caught her watching, so she slipped away and obediently waited in the car for him. She was so scared."

Turning back to him, a spark of defiance in her eyes, she said, "It was the day Sugar was born. The day the seed was planted to get revenge for what he had done to my friend, and then disappear."

"Oh, baby," Jamie whispered, and gently rocked her as more tears flowed. She was amazing! Young, alone, and without any of the skills most would need to go up against a man who thought nothing of taking an old woman's life, Sugar had managed to deliver a serious blow to a bully of the worst kind.

She pushed away and turned to face him. Her eyes lowered to his chest, and she touched his damp shirt. "Sorry, I didn't mean to cry and get you all wet."

"You can get me wet anytime you want, Sugar."

"I love it when you talk dirty."

He hadn't intended the double entendre, but when she gave him a wavering smile, light returning to her eyes, he grinned. "If that's what turns you on, I can talk even dirtier, trust me."

"I do trust you, Jamie."

He trailed the back of his knuckles down her damp cheek. "I have things to say to you, Sugar Darling, but not here. When I say them, I want your undivided attention." Unable to resist those lush lips, he kissed her.

"Jamie," she breathed into his mouth.

Even as he mentally thanked Kincaid for arranging for her to be in a private room, he remembered they were in a hospital. "Wicked girl," he said. "Another minute and we're going to set off every alarm on that machine hooked up to you. We keep going, and we're gonna have an audience."

"Can we charge admission?" she asked, merriment dancing in her beautiful eyes.

"No, I'm not a sharing kind of man." He was toast, burned to a crisp by an amazing woman. To keep from taking her in a narrow bed where any one of a dozen people could walk in on them, he let go of her and lowered his feet to the floor. "Sugar, there are some things we need to talk—"

"Did she agree?" Kincaid asked, striding into the room. Maria scooted around him and went straight to Sugar.

Sugar kept her gaze on him, ignoring Kincaid. "Agree to what?"

"To how we can end this," Jamie answered, taking her hand. He'd argued against Kincaid's plan, not wanting to put Sugar anywhere near the monster calling himself her husband. "We have good intel that he's back home, and we could have him arrested today for the assault on you. What we want, and I know you want, however, is for him to go to prison for the rest of his life, and a murder charge will do that. We have a plan, but you—"

"Wait." Her gaze shifted from him, to the boss, then back to him. "I have a plan, too. I want you to show me how to wear a wire, then I'm going to arrange a meeting with my . . . with Rodney."

She'd almost said *my husband*, and he wished she'd just refer to the man how she often did, as *bad cop*.

"That's what we were going to ask you to do, Sugar," Kincaid said. "We need you to get him to admit he killed Mrs. Lederman."

"I still don't agree with this," Jamie said, trying one last time to stop the inevitable.

Kincaid and Sugar ignored him as they settled something between them without words.

"It's the only way," the woman he loved said.

It wasn't. He could always steal her away and take her to a foreign country where no one would ever find them. He had the know-how, the contacts to make it happen. But she'd hate him for taking away her courage to stand up to the man who had stolen her innocence, who had decided a fifteen-year-old girl was fair game for his proclivities.

"It is the only way," he said, ignoring the urge to forbid her getting anywhere near Vanders.

# CHAPTER TWENTY-FIVE

Sugar sat in what Jamie had told her was the war room, ready to hear the details of Operation Free Sugar, a mission name that she really, really liked. She tried not to stare all wide-eyed at the various large screens and digital maps, and especially not at the men sitting at the conference room table—Mr. Kincaid, Jamie, Jake Buchanan, and Ryan O'Connor. They were, for sure, a badass bunch of men, and they were there for her.

Everything was happening so fast that she wouldn't be surprised if Jamie leaned over and whispered into her ear that her head was literally spinning. Instead, he slipped his fingers through hers, the top of the table hiding their joined hands from the others. That settled her like nothing else would have.

"Why did you call the FBI?" she asked, suddenly remembering something Mr. Kincaid had said at the hospital. Rodney would kill her if he knew that, because of her, the Feds now had his name.

"Because they can call off the local cops and let us take care of this for you," Mr. Kincaid—the man who so intimidated her that she couldn't think of him without a Mr. in front of his name—said. "And, Sugar, there is no one you want on your side more than the men at this table. We will take Vanders down, and then we'll turn him over to the FBI where he will be prosecuted to the fullest by federal authorities."

The hard glimmer in his dark eyes that told her he spoke the truth won her over. "Okay, how are we going to do it?"

As Jamie squeezed her hand in what she took as approval, Mr. Kincaid smiled a rare smile. She wasn't quite as afraid of him after that.

"Isn't there some other way than putting her anywhere near that bastard?" Jamie said.

Before anyone else could answer, she shook her head. "No. It has to be me." She lifted her gaze to his. "I know you're worried, but it really is the only way."

At Jamie's resigned nod, Kincaid said, "Then let's get to work."

"I'm going to have to wear a wire, aren't I?" That was what frightened her the most. If Rodney found a wire on her, he would kill her before any of them could get to her, no matter how badass they were.

"He will never find it, sweetheart," Jamie said, as if he understood her greatest fear. He took the watch Mr. Kincaid slid across the table and held it in front of her. "Hold out your arm and let me put it on you. You need to get used to wearing it so that by the time you see him, you'll forget you have it on."

The silver watch Jamie slid over her hand and clasped at her wrist was pretty, and she would never have guessed there was a wire in it.

The screen on the far wall flicked on, startling Sugar. She glanced over to see that Mr. Kincaid had a tablet open in front of him, and he tapped his finger on it. Just like that, the house she had lived in with Rodney was there on the wall. As she watched, she was taken on a tour, starting with a view of the outside and the sidewalk leading up to the front door.

"We have the blueprint of the inside, Sugar, but tell us what we're not seeing. Describe each room, the furniture, the floors," Jamie said. "Are they hardwood or carpet? Is there anything I might trip over?"

It was hard to breathe. That house held her worst memories . . . no, they held Hannah's memories, not hers. She straightened in her chair, and with her hand clutched tightly around Jamie's, she answered all their questions about the place she'd hoped never to see again—where the sofa was, the coffee table, which wall the bed was near, and on and on. By the time they were satisfied with room sizes and where every single piece of furniture was located, she felt numb and in a strange way, removed from the house she'd once called home.

Perhaps that had been intentional, and if so, she didn't have the words to tell the men how much she appreciated it.

"You did good, sweetheart," Jamie said, leaning over and giving her a soft kiss near her eye.

Mr. Kincaid closed his tablet. "Tomorrow, I want you to wear the exact clothes you will have on when you knock on Vanders's door."

That was strange, and she glanced at Jamie, getting only a mysterious smile from him. "You'll see," he said.

For the second day in a row, Sugar was wide-eyed. These people were freakin' scary and just plain amazing. Covered from her neck to below the knee in a long-sleeved, dark blue dress with a white Peter Pan collar, she stood at the entrance of a warehouse in the back of K2 that she hadn't even known existed. Who were these people? Although she understood they were involved in things not to be talked about, she'd not had a clue of what they were capable.

In front of her was a replica of Rodney's house that, as far as she could see, was as real as she remembered. There was even a gouge at the bottom of the door where Rodney had once kicked it in anger. Her stomach rolled, and she turned to leave.

"Easy, sweetheart."

Jamie wrapped his arms around her, and she sank into his protective warmth. "I don't think I can do this."

"Is that Hannah talking or Sugar?"

A hammer to her head wouldn't have gotten through to her any better than Jamie's question. With a renewed sense of determination, she turned and faced the house of her nightmares.

"That was Hannah," Sugar said as she marched toward the door. For the remainder of the day, they had her knocking on that door over and over, and when Mr. Kincaid opened it, playing the role of Rodney, which he did frighteningly well, they acted out different scenarios.

By the time night fell and she was deemed as prepared as possible, she was exhausted and considered kissing every one of them in thankfulness. Mr. Kincaid still intimidated her too much to even try to plant a smack on him, and she figured Jamie wouldn't appreciate her kissing Jake and Ryan, so she settled for sinking into Jamie's arms and letting him hold her.

"Thank you, all of you," she said. The words were inadequate for what they were doing for her, and she tried to blink away her tears of gratitude. Ryan winked at her as he left, Jake saluted her as he followed Ryan out, and Mr. Kincaid came to a stop in front of her.

"I've told you this before, Sugar, but it bears repeating. We take care of our own, and you are one of ours now. This won't be nearly as hard as living with that bastard, so remember that." He dipped his head at her, then strode away.

"I'm almost getting over shakin' in my boots whenever he's around," she said when she and Jamie were alone.

Jamie laughed. "Took me years to accomplish that. Whadda you say we go home, order a pizza, and then snuggle up?"

"Sounds like heaven."

Since she'd been out of the hospital, Jamie had constantly been by her side, whether at K2 or at his place, jumping to take care of her every need. She couldn't go to the bathroom without him breathing down her neck. More than once, she'd bitten her tongue to keep from snapping at him. Like now.

"You know, I really can go pee without you standing outside the door."

"What if you fall or something?"

"Then I'll just get back up." He sighed when she bypassed the bed he wanted her to get into and headed for the living room. If the man and cat didn't stop shadowing her, she'd scare them both when she started screaming for them to give her room to breathe. It was like the two were afraid to let her out of their sight.

It really was sweet the way Jamie worried over her, but he'd also refused to touch her out of fear of hurting her. Installing her in his bed because it was bigger and more comfortable, he'd spent his nights in the guest bedroom. As much as she loved Junior, he wasn't the male she wanted next to her when the sun set.

At the hospital, he'd mentioned he had things to say to her. Apparently, he was in no hurry to have the promised conversation. Although it was driving her crazy not knowing what was on his mind and how he felt about her, she'd managed to be patient. So far.

Her tolerance for his silence was at an end, however. The following day, she and Jamie would travel to South Carolina, and she would walk into a house she had hoped to never enter again. Before confronting Rodney, she wanted . . . needed . . . things settled between her and Jamie. If she had his love, she could face anything, even her snake of a husband. If not, she had plans to make.

As soon as she sat on the couch, Junior jumped onto her lap and bumped her arm with his head. "You," then she glanced up at Jamie, "and you should have a guy's night out, and give me an hour or two of peace." Damn, she'd meant it as a tease but at the flash of hurt in Jamie's eyes, she realized how grouchy she sounded.

"You gave us both a scare," he said from the other side of the sofa.

She really was acting as if she were ungrateful, but she wasn't. Not by a long shot. "I'm sorry, that didn't come out right. It's just that I can't take two steps without you two panicking that something's going to happen. At least Junior's willing to touch me." She glared at Jamie. "But you sit as far away from me as possible because you're afraid you're going to hurt me. I'm fine, really. The stitches are out, and my side doesn't hurt. Not two hours ago, you said we were going to have pizza and then we'd snuggle. We've had the pizza, now I want the snuggling."

"You took a bullet meant for me, Sugar. First, don't do that again. Ever." His eyes glittered an I-mean-business stare at her before his gaze slid away. "I thought I'd lost you," he whispered.

"I'm here forever, if that's what you want." Would he finally tell her how he felt?

He eyed the purring cat curled up on her lap. "When you were crumbled into a heap on the floor, your life bleeding out of you, Junior wrapped himself around your neck and gave the saddest cry I've ever heard. I thought it was a death cry, that somehow he knew you were gone." Beautiful blue eyes that were suspiciously watery lifted to meet hers. "I thought I'd killed another person I loved."

It all tumbled out of him then, the story she'd already pieced together. By the time he finished, tears streamed down both their cheeks. How had he been so broken and yet been able to hide it so well? His SEAL training and discipline, she supposed. But that had also allowed him to lie to himself. The last thing he needed was the kind of women he had dated, the kind who would meekly stand aside while he continued to wallow in his own misery. He needed someone like her, who wouldn't stand for anything but him being the real Jamie, like the boy who had laughed and enjoyed life to its fullest.

She lowered Junior to the floor, slid across the couch, and straddled Jamie. Unsure what to say, she circled her arms around his shoulders, and he pulled her hard against him, burying his face against her neck.

She just held him and cried with him while wondering if this was the first time he'd allowed his grief to surface. "Did you cry for them when it happened," she asked when he quieted.

"No, I got stoned." He wiped a hand over his face. "I-I'm sorry. I don't know what just happened. It's been ten years. I should be over it by now."

"Oh, Jamie. One never gets over losing a parent. Believe me, I know." She leaned away and cradled his cheeks with her palms. "Hush, baby. Your parents are together this very minute, sitting on a fluffy white cloud, looking down at you. And ya know what? They're prouder than a peacock with a tail full of flamboyant feathers. If you really want to honor them, then be happy. That's what they'd want for you."

He sat back against the sofa and blinked moist lashes, then one side of his mouth quirked up. "They're sitting on a cloud this very minute?"

Sugar nodded. "Yep. Looked out the window a few minutes ago and saw them float by." She leaned forward as if to impart a secret. "They were kissing."

Both sides of his mouth lifted. "They did that a lot. Used to disgust me when I was a kid." The smile faded. "I do know they'd want me to be happy. Until you, I didn't think that was possible."

*Oh, well then.* When his hands found their way to her thighs, gliding his palms over the thin material of her lounge pants, she tugged on the waist of his jeans. "Make love to me, Jamie."

With a tenderness that didn't surprise her, he slipped an arm under her knees and one behind her back. Lifting her, he carried her to his bedroom, kicking the door closed before Junior could follow them in.

As he held her over the bed, he peered down at her. "Are you sure you're well enough?"

No longer wishing to talk, she wrapped her fingers around his neck and pulled his mouth to hers.

"Sugar," he hissed, the vibration of her name against her lips sending electrical currents across her skin. The muscles in his arms flexed their strength as he lowered her to the bed, then he stretched his long frame alongside her. "Are you well enough for this?" he asked again.

"Shut up, Jamie." She hid the little wince of pain in her side as she straddled him. So much love for him bubbled up, consuming her to the point she feared she'd bite off her tongue to keep from telling him again.

His gaze lingered on where her legs pressed against his hips, and she waited for him to lift his eyes to hers. When he did, she smiled and grasped the hem of her T-shirt, pulled it over her head, and tossed it behind her.

As she looked down at her beautiful man—a complicated mix of warrior and wounded soul—she wished she had the power to heal, wished she could lay her hand over his heart and bring light to the dark corners of that damaged organ. She didn't have that kind of magic, but she put her hand there anyway.

Maybe it was her imagination, but it seemed his eyes did grow brighter, clearer. As if he understood what she was doing, he placed his hand over her heart, and his heat coursed through her, easing the ache of her father's betrayal and Rodney's treachery.

Time hung suspended between them, and although neither spoke, she sensed it was the moment they truly gifted their hearts to each other. She prayed it was true.

Still holding her gaze, he skimmed his hand over her skin, from her heart to her waist where he spread his fingers across her stomach. From there, he cupped her mound with his palm, his long fingers curling into the material of her pants. His eyes stayed locked on hers.

"Mine, Sugar. Everywhere I just touched is mine."

Her heart, her womb, her feminine core, the most important parts of her he'd just claimed for himself. Earlier, he'd said something about those he loved, and although he'd yet to say he loved her specifically, it was there in his eyes and his touch, in the declaration he'd just made. It was good enough for the moment.

She tugged on his shirt. "Off, please."

His eyes narrowed. "Did you hear what I just said?"

She swallowed a jubilant laugh, loving that he needed confirmation she belonged to him. Silly man. She'd been his since the day she laid eyes on him. "Yes, I heard you, and if you would be so kind as to get naked, I'll give you this . . ." she put her hand over his and pressed down. Then she moved his hand to her stomach. "This." Next, she put his palm against her heart. "And most of all, this."

A low growl rumbled from his throat, and he flipped her so fast, she yelped in surprise. Positioned between her legs, he rose to his knees, and in seconds, his shirt went flying across the room. She watched in anticipation as he unzipped his jeans, pushing them and his briefs down his hips.

Unable to help it, she licked her lips when his erection sprang free. His eyes—darkened to that midnight blue she loved—locked onto her mouth. Liking the hungry look she saw in them, and to drive him a little crazy, she did it again. Slower this time, though, watching his reaction as she inched her tongue across her top lip.

Air hissed past his mouth, and not wasting any time, he pulled her pants down, dropping them over the side of the bed. As he kneeled in front of her, her gaze roamed over his magnificent body. She could spend days doing nothing but admiring him.

His cock jerked when her eyes settled on it, and she reached up and with her finger, spread the drop of moisture around the head. The thrill of willingly wanting to touch a man there brought more tears to her eyes. The hands hanging at his sides fisted, and his thigh muscles tensed. A heady feeling of power surged through her that she had that kind of effect on him. She wanted her hands all over him, wanted to explore him, wanted to learn every contour and plane of his body.

"Don't move." Sitting up, she raised to her knees in front of him. He stared back at her, the only movement a tick in his right jaw. So much heat radiated from him, and she couldn't wait to be covered by it. First though, she had other things in mind.

One corner of his mouth twitched. "Can I at least talk?"

She nodded. "Talk away, just don't move." Scooting around to his back, she decided to start at the top and work her way down his body. His hair, such a lovely golden honey color, was cut military style. She put both hands on his head and closed her eyes, letting her senses take over. The bristly ends tickled her palms as she massaged his scalp with her fingertips. His drawn-out sigh delighted her.

"Are you off on some kind of adventure, Sugar?"

How did he know? "I am. I never thought I'd like touching a man, not after . . ." She didn't want to bring Rodney into their time, but she wanted Jamie to know what it meant to her to want her hands on him.

"I understand."

By the softness of his words, she believed he did. Staying on his knees, he remained still as her exploration moved down the back of his neck and to his shoulders. Broad and muscle hard, she glided her hands over their width, smiling when little goose bumps rose on his skin. From there, she explored his back, running her fingers down his spine, then back up.

"Why did you decide to call yourself Sugar Darling?"

The question took her by surprise, and her hands stilled.

He glanced over his shoulder, his blue eyes shimmering with desire. "Don't stop, baby. I like what you're doing."

"That's good because I like what I'm doing, too."

He smiled and winked, then turned his head forward. Although it seemed a silly idea, she thought maybe her heart had smiled back at him. Back to her examination of his body, she slipped her hands under his armpits and flattened her palms over his skin, then trailed them down to his waist. Muscles rippled under her touch like soft, undulating waves.

"When I was a little girl, my dad's pet name for me was sugar, and my mom called me her little darling. When it came time to pick a new name, I wanted something as different from Hannah Conley as possible. Hannah was meek . . . she-she was scared. I needed to be her polar opposite, and it seemed to me anyone named Sugar Darling would be confident and not afraid of anything."

"Your dad, he didn't try to protect you?"

"He changed after my mom died, but I told you about that. He stopped being my dad, and now he's just the man who fathered me. Once he went to work for Rodney, he let himself be corrupted by the pure evil that was Rodney."

"Did your father know how Vanders treated you?"

A question she'd often pondered. "He had to know life wasn't a bed of roses for me, but I pray that he didn't know the extent of Rodney's abuse. If he had and did nothing, I think that would kill me." Several times, she'd tried to tell her father things, but each time she'd panicked at the possibility of him going straight to Rodney.

"You could say I lost both my parents on that horrible day I found my mom on the kitchen floor. I was ten years old the last time anyone loved me."

"Sugar."

The way he said her name with so much tenderness almost undid her. "I know. Poor me." A lump the size of a small rock lodged in her throat, and she tried to swallow it away.

She hadn't thought she wanted to talk about all that stuff, but now that she'd started, the need to share her heartbreak with him kept the words coming. It was funny how she could tell him her secrets as long as she was touching him, like she was stealing some of his strength for herself.

His butt cheeks flexed when her fingers danced over them, and she pressed her hands down, smoothing her palms across the taut skin. Rodney prided himself on keeping his body in prime shape, but she'd hated touching him with a passion. Why it was so different with Jamie, she didn't know, but she loved having her hands on him.

"How old were you when you married Vanders?"

"I didn't marry him. He married me. I consider that a big difference." Hanging between his legs, the edge of his sacs were visible. Slipping her fingers under him, she lifted them, testing their weight. He let out a long breath, and spread his legs apart. Taking that as a sign he liked her touching him there, she cupped him in her palm.

It was as if there were two of her. The one whose hands were investigating all the parts of Jamie, and the one who had a story to tell. She let her mind separate from her body, let Hannah continue her sad tale while Sugar shut out the words as she held a man's balls in her hand and glorified in doing so.

"He married me the day after I graduated high school. He stood on one side of me, my father on the other, and poof, I was a wife to a man I'd already learned to hate. You're probably wondering why I let that happen, so I'll tell ya. Rodney made sure I understood he had the power, that he could make me or my father disappear without anyone wondering where we'd gone."

Letting go of his balls, she lowered her face and kissed the dimple on Jamie's lower spine. Although she was tempted to linger on the area of his ass, she still had his legs and feet to explore. The hairs on his thighs and legs were golden—like him. That's how she saw him, golden and beautiful. She trailed her fingers over his skin, down to the backs of his calves. Touching him sent liquid fire to the deepest part of her, and she felt the wet between her legs, felt the ache of wanting him.

"Can I kill him for you?"

Sugar froze. As she stared down at the soles of his long, elegant feet, she fought the urge to cover her eyes and weep. Jamie might be kidding, but she didn't think so. Not even her father had cared enough to protect her from Rodney. She curled her hand around the high arch of his right foot.

"He's not worth going to prison for, so no. Let's just do what it takes to make sure he's the one who goes away." The sparse hairs on his legs were honey colored, and she combed her fingers through the springy curls, up the back of his knees, returning to his amazing ass.

"I'm not going to be able to take much more of this, sweetheart."

The low huskiness of his voice vibrated though her, drawing her around to face him. She sucked in a steadying breath at the hunger in his eyes.

Jamie's gaze roamed over Sugar's breasts, her narrow waist, and then to the flare of her hips. He leaned toward her, fully intending to kiss her until they both forgot their names.

"On your back," she said with a sneaky smile, as if she had plans for him he just might like.

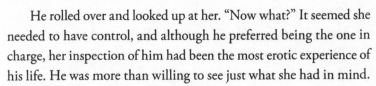 

He rolled over and looked up at her. "Now what?" It seemed she needed to have control, and although he preferred being the one in charge, her inspection of him had been the most erotic experience of his life. He was more than willing to see just what she had in mind.

"Now I get to learn the front of you."

Already hard, he gritted his teeth at the thought of what she might do. He expected her to start at his top, but after a lingering glance on his erection, she turned her back and leaned over his toes. Mother Mary, the view! Nothing but her rounded bottom and the back of her thighs were visible, and he fisted his hands into the sheet to keep from grabbing her and pulling her down on him.

"So I knew I had to get away before he killed me . . . before the day came when I did something that sent him over the edge. I researched how to disappear, and here I am." She lifted her head from her inspection of his feet, glanced over her shoulder and smiled, as if she'd just told him something as trivial as the day was a nice one.

She'd made him forget she was telling him her story—one that was breaking his heart—with her exploration of his body, with the soft touch of her hands as they glided over him. He wished they could save this conversation for later as one second he was in a wonderful place with her touches, and then she'd say something that made him want to don his warrior gear and go kill a man. It was disconcerting. But if this was the only way she could speak of her life, then somehow he would bear it.

When she pivoted, he lost the lovely view of her backside, but the front of her was just as beautiful. Her hands skimmed up his legs to his knees, stopping there and tracing his kneecap with the tips of her fingers. The woman was seriously messing with his head.

Finally, she reached his erection, licking her lips as she eyed his raging hard-on. He about lost it then. "Sugar?"

A mischievous smile lifted her lips. "What?"

"Touch me, damnit!"

Her eyes narrowed in disapproval. "You cursed."

"Because you're driving me crazy."

"Is that what you want? For me to touch you?"

Was she kidding? "Yes, that is what I want."

"I plan on doing just that," she said as her hand wrapped around him.

Even though it was obvious she didn't quite know what to do with him, her experimental licks and sucks were sending him to the edge. When her exploring fingers found his balls and squeezed at the same time her tongue trailed a wet line from the base of his shaft to the sensitive F-spot, he squeezed his eyes shut. Somehow, she had instinctively found that little knob of flesh under the head, sending an electrical bolt throughout his body. Jamie clenched his stomach muscles to keep from coming in her mouth.

"Enough." Flipping her, grinning when her eyes widened and she giggled at finding herself suddenly under him, he lowered his face and brushed his lips over hers. "My turn," he murmured before trailing a path of kisses down to her breasts. While his fingers played with one rose-colored nipple, he sucked the other into his mouth and gently bit down.

"Ahhhh."

The drawn-out word brought a smile to his lips. "Like that, do you?"

"Uh-huh."

He chuckled, pleased he'd robbed her of speech. It was fair payback. She tasted like sweet, summer strawberries, and he knew he'd never get tired of loving her. With his mouth still sucking on her breast, he trailed his hand over her stomach, down to her folds, and slipped a finger inside her. A sigh escaped at how wet she was, at how her desire drenched his finger. She was so incredibly ready for him, but he wanted her begging. He slid another finger inside and found her clit with his thumb.

"Jamie." A shiver passed through her, and she brought her knees up, spreading her legs open for him.

"Yes," he said in approval. As soon as he felt the muscles in her sheath clench around his fingers signaling she was close to climaxing, he pushed down and pressed his face against her mound. The musky scent of her drove him wild, and he drank her in as she came. He almost did, too, barely managing to hold back.

Although she didn't yet know it, she owned him heart, body, and soul.

When the last of her convulsions faded, he made one last lick with his tongue through her curls, then rose to his knees. "Condom." At the puzzlement on her face, he laid over her and opened the drawer, snatching the box.

Ripping the foil package open with his teeth, he rolled the condom over him when it was the last thing he wanted to do. He wanted to feel her, skin to skin, no barrier. Once he was fully encased in rubber, he gripped her hips with his hands, and because she was so wet, he easily slid into her. Stilling when he was buried to the hilt, he stared into the dilated, violet eyes trained on him, and for the second time, he almost blurted that he loved her. But he wanted it to be special when he said them, so he swallowed the words and concentrated on their physical connection. He moved, leaving her, then sinking back in.

She was heaven. *She was his home.* He'd not had a true home since his parents had died, and he suddenly didn't know what to do with the intense longing raging inside him. All he knew was that he needed to claim the woman who'd decided Sugar Darling was a good name.

He dug his fingers into her hips, marking her and not caring if he left his prints. He hoped he did. She was his. As if she returned his need, she gripped his arms, scraping his skin with her fingernails.

"Jamie." She rolled her head to the right. "Jamie," she whispered, rising up to meet his thrusts. "Jamie, please."

"All right, love." He gave up on being gentle. As he thrust into the velvety heat of her, he leaned down and captured her mouth. She sucked his bottom lip into her mouth, then bit down on it.

The wildness that had once been a part of him returned full force, and he pulled out and flipped her over. "Damn you, Sugar. Get on your knees." As the command left his mouth, he had a moment to worry that he'd scared her. But she obeyed with a too-pleased-with-herself smirk tossed over her shoulder.

"If I'm going to be bad, I want to be bad with you, Jamie."

"Then let's be bad together." He eyed her sweet bottom and gritted his teeth to keep from coming just from looking. Leaning over her back, he put his face an inch from her shoulder. "When a stallion covers his lady love, he clamps his teeth onto her shoulder so she knows she can't get away. Like this." Opening his mouth, he pressed his lips on her soft skin. "You're not getting away from me, Sugar. Ever." He bit down, ready to enter her.

A needy moan sounded low in her throat when he ground against her, and she wiggled her bottom, trying to capture him.

"Like that, sweetheart?" he whispered, rubbing harder.

She laughed. "Stupid question, hot guy."

"I'd take insult at being called stupid if you didn't think I was hot," he said, giving her bottom a light slap as the last of the heavy weight he'd carried around in his heart for what seemed like forever floated away. It had been years—over ten of them—since he'd played during sex. He'd never been with such a responsive woman before, one who knelt in front of him, looking back at him with a challenge in her eyes.

"Do that again, or I'll take it back."

"This?" He gave the opposite cheek a light tap. "Or this?" he asked, gilding his erection through her slick folds again. Her body trembled, and she came, hard and fast. As the last shudder passed through her, he slid inside her, closing his eyes at the rightness of loving her.

"Oh, God." She lowered her face to the pillow. "Oh God, Jamie."

The huskiness of her words, combined with the heat of her, was almost too much. Gripping her waist with his hands, he pressed his fingers into her skin and rocked his hips. She pushed back against him as if she couldn't get enough. Already on the edge, but wanting her to come again, he slid his hand down her stomach and into her curls. When he flicked his thumb over her clit, she exhaled a rush of breath, then screamed his name as an orgasm shook her body.

That was all it took. The force of his climax, the way he kept coming and coming, was like nothing he'd ever experienced. When the last shudder ripped through him, he fell onto her back, squashing her into the mattress.

"Jesus, Sugar," he gasped, unable to find the strength to move away.

She twisted her head and found his mouth. Her tongue swiped across his bottom lip. "I love you, Jamie."

He felt reborn. He was reborn, and it was amazing that a violet-eyed—worst driver in the world—woman named Sugar Darling had brought him to his senses. "I . . ." Remembering his plan on how to tell her he loved her, he changed his words midstream. "I'm crazy about you, sweetheart."

The hurt in her eyes almost had him telling her, but he kissed her senseless instead.

# CHAPTER TWENTY-SIX

Sugar pressed her hand over her heart and willed it to beat normally. The collar on the demure dress she wore suddenly felt too tight, making it hard to breathe. It helped that Mr. Kincaid had had the foresight to have her wear the dress when they'd put her through all that training, but she hated wearing Hannah's clothes.

Rodney had only allowed Hannah to wear modest dresses, and the one time he'd caught her wearing a pair of shorts, he'd called her a slut. Even though she'd been inside the house where no one else would see her, he'd used a belt on her to teach her a lesson, resulting in the scar on her shoulder.

He'd fled for home after shooting her, believing he would be safe where he ruled his little kingdom. She could only hope he still believed he was the king, and his arrogance would be his downfall. If only her damn heart would stop its incessant pounding in her ears. Rodney would search her for a wire, but she didn't see how he could find it. Those K2 guys had the kinds of toys that made her think of James Bond movies. Knowing that Jamie could hear everything happening inside the house on his headset calmed her a little.

The guys had debated the merits of sending a team with her and Jamie, but feared Rodney would have people watching for strangers arriving in town. A carload of scary-looking men would have been suspicious, so the guys were staged at a private airport in a nearby town. She did have to admit that the helicopter ride they'd taken out of Pensacola had been thrilling. After landing, she and Jamie had rented a car, slipping into Vanders just before dawn and hiding the car in a stand of woods a mile from Rodney's house. The plan was for Jamie to break into a back bedroom window while she had her husband occupied.

It had done wonders to her battered heart that Jamie would just as soon have put a bullet between Rodney's eyes than put her though what she was about to do. If only he'd said he loved her. What if he didn't want her when this was over?

The door swung open, and she almost bolted at the sight of her husband.

"I-I've come home." The words tasted sour and vile on her tongue.

He grabbed her wrist and pulled her inside. The deadbolt clicked with a solid thunk, sounding like something out of a Stephen King novel. Before she could speak, he pushed her against the wall and grabbed her breasts so hard it brought tears to her eyes. He thrust his thumbs over the vee of her bra, digging them into her skin. When she tried to pull away, he wrapped hard fingers around her neck and forced her chin up.

"You wearing a wire, Hannah?"

"No. No, I'm not." It was difficult to talk with the pressure of his hand against her throat.

"Forgive me if I don't believe you."

With that, he spun her around and began a thorough frisk of her body. She tasted bile at the back of her throat from his touch on her skin. It took every ounce of her willpower not to cringe. He had to believe she had returned willingly and was prepared to stay. Seeing his face badly scratched by Junior gave her some satisfaction. She eased air out of her lungs, and did her best to stay calm.

"What are you up to, Hannah?"

Because Rodney's mouth was inches from her ear, his hot breath crawled over her cheek. She smelled the cologne he always wore, hating the heavy sweet scent with a passion. Her face pressed to the wall, she squeezed her eyes shut against the tears burning in them. She could stand a little roughness if it meant putting an end to the nightmare named Rodney Vanders, but his closeness, his touching her, made her feel sick.

"I told you. I want to come home."

Blunt fingers dug into her shoulders and jerked her around. "Bitch. You're lying through your teeth, Hannah. I can always tell."

He was right. Hannah didn't know how to lie, especially to Rodney, and from the minute he'd opened the door, she'd been Hannah. No way Hannah could manage what needed to be done. Sugar mentally wrapped her arms around Hannah and led her away to a safe place, tucking her into a quiet corner.

Then she thought of Jamie and how strong and self-assured he was, visualized his strength and courage flowing through her veins, and thought of all the training the team had put her through. She raised her eyes to Rodney, reminding herself not to overplay her role. The last thing she needed was his suspicion . . . rather more suspicion.

"I'm not lying, Rodney, I swear. No argument I'm not the same girl who ran away, but it was a stupid thing to do. I thought . . ." she looked away. She had to do this right or he wouldn't believe a word she said. Settling her gaze back onto him, she let her expression go shy and uncertain, and a little fearful. It was what he'd expect from Hannah.

"I thought you killed Mrs. Lederman for her money. But you killed her for me. It took me a while to realize that." She commanded her hand to lift and cup his cheek. "You'd do anything for me, wouldn't you?"

Uncertainty flashed in his eyes before he hid it. Damn, she'd almost screwed up. Hannah would never have been so confident. "You don't need to answer." She let her hand fall from his cheek, sliding her fingers just under his throat—where she'd like nothing better than to squeeze the life out of him.

"I'm sorry, Rodney. I just . . ." She lowered her gaze, hoping he'd think she was too afraid to look at him. That was what he wanted, for her to be in fear of him. "I just forgot you knew what was best for me."

*Let him be in control, Sugar, or at least let him think he was.* The cruel mouth that had abused every part of her curved into a smug smile, and she fisted her hands to keep from adding her own scratches to Junior's.

"You forgot a lot of things, Hannah, but I'll take great pleasure in reminding you."

Still digging his fingers into her shoulders, he marched her into the kitchen. Dirty dishes were piled up in the sink, and burnt food was crusted on the stovetop. No surprise as Rodney considered housework beneath him.

What did surprise her was seeing her father sitting at the foot of the kitchen table, a bottle of beer in his hand, and several empty ones pushed to the side. Her knees buckled, and she grabbed the back of a chair to steady herself. How had they not considered he'd be there? The two men were drinking buddies, partners in crime, and thick as thieves.

"Daddy." The word—one she hadn't used in years—slipped out, and she hated how she sounded like a little girl begging for her father's attention. Rodney pushed her down on a chair and then sat at the end of the table. He'd positioned himself so she was sandwiched between him and a father she no longer trusted.

The urge to jump up and run almost had her doing it. Instead, she gripped the seat of her chair and stayed put, stayed quiet, stayed still. They had things to say to her, and if she were lucky, it would involve the things they had done. If not, somehow, she had to lead the conversation toward admitting they had committed a murder.

"We need to know where you've been the last two years, and what information you shared that wasn't anyone's business," Rodney said. "And I want to know where my damn money is."

*Here goes.* What would Hannah do right now? A no-brainer. She'd stare a hole through the wood of the table as she struggled to answer. Sugar focused on the pine, narrowing her gaze on a darker knot of wood. If she didn't play this just right, someone would get hurt. If it came to that, she prayed it would be her and not Jamie.

"I-I've been in Pensacola the whole time. I-I . . ." she lifted her eyes in embarrassment. "I don't have any friends to tell anything to." She glanced away, hoping her guilty expression was believable. "That's not really true." Returning her attention to Rodney, she shrugged in defeat. "I told Junior everything."

"What did you tell him, Hannah?"

"What I just said, everything." Sugar hated how he kept saying her name, like he could control her by reminding her of who she used to be. Rodney's jaw was going to break if he clamped it any tighter. She sincerely hoped it would. A darted glance at her father to see how he'd reacted to this news didn't give her encouragement, nor did his shuttered look warm her heart.

Rodney snaked his fingers around her throat. "Everything? Just what is everything?"

Swallowing past Rodney's iron grip, she tried to jerk away, but his hold was firm. "I can't talk," she managed to gasp out, inhaling deeply when he loosened his hold. "Everything means everything. I told him how I was forced to marry you. You remember that part, right?"

One blunt finger pressed hard against her skin. "That's not the way I remember it at all."

Damn, she was making him mad, not a good thing to do if she wanted to get a confession out of him.

"Actually, we did force her to marry you, Chief."

Shocked, Sugar stared at her father. He hadn't stood up for her since the day her mother died. *Oh, God, please let my watch be recording this.* It would be something she'd listen to over and over. If she managed to get out of this alive. The man she'd once called *daddy* with affection refused to look back, instead keeping his attention on the bottle of beer he twirled on the table.

"A minor detail and long past," her husband said.

Being forced to marry a man one hated was far from a minor detail. But her father had spoken up for her, and her heart—the one that remembered having parents who loved her—forgave him, just a little.

"I'm waiting, Hannah."

*Well, screw your waiting, Rodney, dearest.* Since that wouldn't be a wise thing to say, she lowered her chin to her chest in what she hoped he would take as defeat.

"I told Junior how you put a pillow over Mrs. Lederman's face." When all five of his fingers bored their way into her neck, she commanded herself not to show how much it hurt. "'Cause that's what you did."

Rage flickered in his cold brown eyes, and she wondered if she'd gone too far. But the only way to get Rodney to admit to anything was to force him to lose his cool. The belief he owed no one an explanation for his actions had been ingrained in him, and the only time she had seen him lose control had been the night he'd tried to drown her. Each time he'd dragged her—coughing and spitting—out of the water, he'd yelled all the reasons she should be afraid of him, chilling her to the bones with his confession of two previous murders. There hadn't been the slightest doubt he could kill her and get away with it.

If he was to be believed, he'd gotten away with murder three times if she included Mrs. Lederman. She had believed him then and did now. Back at K2, they had agreed that to get a confession, she had to anger him so badly that he spoke before he thought.

"You're trying my patience, Hannah. You know what happens when you do that."

She couldn't argue with that. She probably knew what he was capable of better than anyone who'd survived Rodney's displeasure. As she tried to think of the best response that would spur him on to that coveted confession, Sugar caught her father's intent focus on her watch.

*Shit*. Did he realize everything said was being recorded? His blue eyes—a shade lighter than hers—lifted and for a few heartbeats she imagined she saw her daddy. The one who had once loved and protected her, but that was only wishful thinking. He'd forgotten he had a daughter long ago.

"Give her a break," her father said, darting a quick glance at the watch again. "She came back, didn't she? Why piss her off and send her running again? It's just the three of us sitting here, and all of us know you did smother the old woman, Chief."

Sugar sucked in a breath, not quite believing her ears. It was almost as if her dad did know they were being recorded and was making sure the facts were clear. It was almost like the father who'd once loved her was back. Across the span of a kitchen table, her eyes met her father's and for a moment too soon over, she saw her beloved daddy again.

"Daddy?" she whispered.

"So I fucking killed the bitch," Rodney said, drawing her attention, his mouth thinned into a harsh slash. "She was too old to live anyway." He turned an enraged glare on Sugar. "This Junior person. Was that the man with you the other night?"

As much as she wanted to look back at her father to see if what she'd seen in his eyes was true and not her imagination, she kept her attention on Rodney. Wasn't wise to turn one's back on a venomous snake. "Why, so you can kill him, too? What, you find cats a threat now?" She snorted. "Junior's my cat, Rodney. The one who did that to your face."

She'd finally gone too far. She knew it the minute he grabbed her hair and yanked her out of the chair. The blood rushed to her head, the pounding in her ears so loud, she felt faint.

"Where's the fucking money you stole from me?" he snarled, then backhanded her, knocking her to the floor.

Gray tinged her vision when her head hit the tile.

At Vanders's words, Jamie eased down the hall. Breaking in had been easy, and now he wanted Sugar out of there. With the man's admission, they had what they needed, and it was time to get her out of danger. Wearing soft-soled shoes, he followed the sound of their voices. His intention to slip up on them ended when the crack of a hand on skin resonated in his earpiece.

Sprinting toward the kitchen, he pressed against the wall and peered around the corner. His heart took a nosedive at the sight in front of him. Sugar was sprawled faceup on the floor, gasping for breath. Vanders stood over her, his shoe pressed down on her neck.

The only reason he'd finally agreed to allow Sugar to get the cop on tape admitting to murder was because she'd sworn the first thing Vanders did on arriving home was put his gun on his night table. But there was the unexpected problem of her father, who was still in uniform, thus still armed. That hadn't been part of the plan.

As he'd listened to the conversation through his headset, it appeared the man was trying to help his daughter, but Jamie still didn't trust him. He aimed the barrel of his Glock between Vanders's eyes, ignoring the weapon aimed at him by the second cop.

"I assume you're Jeb Conley, her father?" At the affirmative nod, he gave a grunt of disgust. "You should be ashamed of yourself for not protecting your daughter from this man. You can shoot me," he said, then turned his gaze on Vanders, "but your chief will die first."

Vanders pushed harder on Sugar's throat and glared at her father. "Shoot the fucker," he said.

Jamie kept his gaze focused on the man he wanted to kill more than anything, hoping the bastard would give him reason to. "Mr. Vanders, you have exactly two seconds to remove your foot. Less if your friend here tries something stupid."

Vanders turned a murderous glare on Sugar's father. "Pull the Goddamned trigger, Conley."

Sugar, obviously still trying to inhale air, beat on Vanders's legs.

"Time's up," Jamie said, lowering his gun and aiming it at Vander's leg. As much as he longed to kill the man, he didn't want Sugar to witness such a thing. But he had no problem putting a bullet through the wife-beating, murdering, sorry excuse of a man's kneecap.

Suddenly, Conley swung his arm, pointing his gun at Vanders. The ear-splitting crack of a gunshot sounded a split second before a hole appeared between the police chief's eyes.

"Jesus," Jamie whispered as a line of dark red blood flowed down Vanders's nose. The cop who'd forced a girl closer to childhood than adulthood to marry him crumpled to the floor as if in slow motion.

"He did tell me to pull the trigger," Sugar's father said, almost sounding as if he couldn't believe what he'd just done.

Ignoring the distress in her father's voice, Jamie rushed to Sugar.

He slid his arm under her back and pulled her against his chest, hiding the sight of her husband, dead on the floor beside her.

"Are you all right?" Nothing. "Damnit, Sugar, talk to me."

"You cursed." Her chest heaved up as she took a deep breath. "Jamie, I'm so sorry."

He'd never again be a man who cussed freely, but the damn woman just might be the only one he'd do it for. "Jesus, Sugar, why the hell are you sorry?"

Her eyes blinked up at him in confusion. "Stop saying bad words, Jamie. They just don't sound right coming from you." She crawled onto his lap, straddling his thighs. "I don't know why I'm sorry," she said, then lowered her mouth to his lips.

"Do you love her?" The gruff voice of her father penetrated Jamie's brain.

Jamie wrapped his arms around Sugar, and with his hand at the back of her head, he pressed her face against the side of his neck. He then met the gaze of the man standing over him and nodded.

"You'll take care of her?"

"Always."

Conley nodded back as if satisfied, then walked toward the back door. Before leaving, he turned and looked at his daughter. "I'm sorry, Hannah, for everything." He scrubbed a hand over his face, then opened the door and stared into the dark. "You know what they do to cops in prison. I can't . . . I can't go to prison," he said without looking back at them. Then he disappeared into the night.

Sugar reached a hand out. "Daddy?"

Knowing he wouldn't get far, Jamie didn't go after him. The team had been listening in and by then would have taken to the air. They would find the man, and soon enough, Jeb Conley would be behind bars.

The crack of a gunshot sounded, startling both of them. It was stupid of him not to realize what Conley meant when he said he couldn't go to prison, but Jamie had been so focused on Sugar that he hadn't thought of anything past her.

She put her hands on his shoulders and tried to push away. Shocked eyes met his, then she twisted her head toward the back door. Jamie wrapped his arms around her waist to keep her in place, his heart breaking at the tears rolling down her face.

"Daddy!"

It was the very word he'd once screamed upon realizing he'd killed his father. "Oh, baby, I know. I know." He gently rocked her, doing his best to absorb her pain even though he knew better than anyone it was an impossible endeavor.

"Daddy," she whispered with her mouth pressed against his neck, her hot tears burning his skin. Because he could remember as if it were just yesterday how it felt to lose a father, he cried with her.

# CHAPTER TWENTY-SEVEN

Sugar. Hold on to me, sweetheart. You can't help him now."
Jamie's soft voice sounded a hundred miles away. Needing to find her father, she fought the dizziness and struggled to get away. "Please, Jamie . . ." Swallowing against the hurt in her throat from Rodney's attempt to suffocate her, she tried again. "We have to find him. I-I have to see him. Please."

With ease, he lifted from the floor with her still wrapped around him, keeping his hand on the back of her head so her face stayed pressed to his neck. It took a few seconds before she realized he was shielding her from seeing Rodney's body. She didn't give a damn about her husband—dead or alive—she just needed to see her father.

He walked them to the back door and then stopped. "Are you sure, sweetheart? Maybe it's enough to know that in the end he did right by you."

"What if he's still alive?" When Jamie didn't answer, she knew he believed her father was dead. The regret settling heavy in her heart surprised her. She'd thought she had banished any love for the man who had fathered her. A memory, long buried, surfaced. It had been the Christmas before her mother died. His present to his little family had been a trip to Disney World. In Hannah's gift-wrapped box was a Mickey Mouse hat, and she'd worn it all day, loving the little ears. In her mom's box was the receipt for their room at a Disney hotel. They would go during Hannah's spring break. They'd been so happy then, the three of them.

They never went. Only weeks before the family vacation her mother had died, alone in the kitchen. Sugar still had the Mickey Mouse hat, tucked deep in a corner of her closet at her dad's house. Unless he'd cleaned all her stuff out.

Even with her eyes squeezed shut, she couldn't stop other images of those happy days from playing though her head like a movie reel. Nights around the dinner table, their shared laughter filling the air. Small Hannah bent over the table after it was cleared of the dishes, her father leaning over her shoulder, helping her with her homework.

Even years later, she could still recall his scent. English Leather had been his favored cologne, and she'd given him a bottle that Christmas, her last gift to him. Her mom had helped her pick it out. Although he'd acted surprised at the time, he'd probably not been surprised at all. He had smiled and told her it was his favorite gift of all. He'd still loved her then. A sob tore through her for Hannah, the little girl who'd lost everything she held dear.

The hand Jamie slid up and down her back in a gentle caress was warm and comforting, and she wished she could stay attached to him forever. But her father was out there in the dark, alone, and he needed her. She forced her legs to let go of Jamie's waist, and when her feet reached the floor, she turned for the door. A wave of dizziness washed over her, and she swayed, her head pounding out a throbbing beat from hitting the tiled floor.

Before she could take a step, strong arms slipped under her knees, and Jamie lifted her. She wrapped her arms around his neck and rested her aching head on his shoulder as he carried her to the backyard.

"Wait, back up to the door." Without questioning her, he stepped back, and she reached around the doorframe and flipped on the outside lights. At the edge of the patio surrounding the pool, he turned them in a full circle, but she didn't see her father.

"Where is he? Oh God, we have to find him." She tried to see past the rim of light. "Daddy?"

Halfway through another turn, Jamie stopped, then gently pressed her face back against his neck. A few seconds later, he placed her on a pool chair. "Don't move, Sugar."

Confused, she watched him remove his shoes, then two guns and a knife appeared from the pockets of his cargo pants. A neat little stack grew next to him: shoes, weapons, cell phone, wallet, then his shirt. It wasn't until he dived into the pool that she understood.

"No, Daddy, no!"

Rearing up, she took a step, then crumbled into a heap as intense dizziness struck her. On her hands and knees—ignoring the scrape of the patio's cement on her legs and hands—she crawled to the edge of the pool.

Jamie burst though the surface of the water, his arm wrapped around her father's lifeless body. Giving her a sympathetic look, Jamie carried him up the pool's steps and laid him on the patio.

"Nooo, Daddy, nooo. Please God, no."

Why did her voice sound like ten-year-old Hannah's? The memory of seeing paramedics bent over her mother's body on the kitchen floor merged with the sight of Jamie trying to find a pulse on her father.

Suddenly the backyard was lit up and she felt like she was in a windstorm. She looked up at the night sky, then squeezed her eyes shut against the brilliant light shining down on her. The thump-thump sound she heard must be her heart breaking.

"Mommy?" she whispered, then her world turned to black.

Jamie had once prayed for the lives of the people he loved, but it hadn't done any good. As he sat next to Sugar's hospital bed, he held her hands, bowed his head, and begged God to please listen this time. He just wished she'd wake up.

"I got here as fast as I could. The Feds are going through his house, and before I left, they'd found all kinds of incriminating evidence. Not that it matters now. How is she?"

He glanced up at Kincaid, then turned a watchful eye back to Sugar. "She has a grade three concussion. Concerning in itself, but what has the doctors worried is it's the second one she's experienced in the last three years. There's a record of her being brought to the emergency room by Vanders a little over two years ago. Must have happened shortly before she ran away." And who was to say there hadn't been other unreported times she'd been knocked around, hitting her head?

"Bastard," the boss growled.

Even *bastard* was a too kind word for the man. "According to the hospital's records, he claimed she hit her head diving into the pool, but that's a damn lie. She couldn't swim and wouldn't have willingly dived into anything with water in it."

Kincaid squeezed his shoulder before pulling over a second chair. "Did she back up his story?"

"There's nothing in the records that she said anything. I'm guessing she was too afraid to dispute him." Restless, he stood and leaned over her, caressing her cheek. "Sugar, sweetheart, wake up."

Nothing.

If she never woke up, he was going to dig up Vanders's body after he was buried and tear him apart, limb by limb. Jamie hissed out a frustrated breath. Why hadn't he told her he loved her? If he had, then maybe she'd have something to live for. Why had he thought it would be better if he waited until all the mess with her husband was over? Even thinking of the man as her husband turned his stomach sour. What had she lived through married to the bastard of all bastards, with no one to turn to for help?

If she awoke, he'd stop cursing again. *Did you hear that, God?* But looking at her pale face, wondering if he'd ever be able to hold her in his arms again, if he'd ever hear her throaty laugh again, he needed the curse words.

"Why don't you take a break, Saint? I got a couple of hotel rooms for us. Go take a shower, get a few minutes' rest. I'll stay with her."

He turned an incredulous stare at Kincaid. No way was he leaving Sugar. Not an option. What if she woke up and he wasn't here? "So you'd leave Dani to go get rest when she needed you?"

The boss glanced from the woman lying lifeless in the bed to him. "No. I'll go get you a cup of coffee and something to eat."

"Thanks."

Jamie leaned forward in his chair, keeping Sugar's hand in his.

"I can't do this again, sweetheart. I just can't. You have to wake up." Somehow he'd managed to go on living after killing his parents, but if Sugar died, too, he wouldn't be able to bear it.

Hot tears trailed down his cheeks, but he didn't care. Nothing mattered but seeing her smile at him again with mischief in the blue eyes that sometimes turned violet.

# CHAPTER TWENTY-EIGHT

Several doctors had appeared and kicked him out of the room for a while, and he'd lost track of how many hours had passed since they'd allowed him back in. Enough time to debrief the boss, give a statement to the FBI, and more time to think than a man on the brink of losing it should be granted.

She was so pale and still. If only she'd move, even if just a finger. He picked up her hand, cold to the touch, and rubbed both his palms over her skin in an attempt to warm her.

What if she just slept on forever like Sleeping Beauty? Never knowing he was with her, never hearing him tell her he loved her? He leaned his mouth to her ear. "Sugar, sweetheart, wake up."

Still nothing.

"I love you, Sugar Darling. I don't care if you're the worst driver in the world, or if you butcher your metaphors, I still love you." He kissed her icy lips. "Wake up, damn it." When there was no response, he buried his face against her neck and inhaled her scent deep into his lungs.

"Don't . . . don't curse."

At first, he didn't know who'd spoken. The voice was too raspy to recognize as Sugar's. He jerked his gaze to her face, and blue eyes stared unblinkingly back at him.

"Sugar! Christ, you scared the life out of me."

Her beautiful lips curved upward. "Hi."

Profound relief—the likes of which he'd never felt before—morphed into laughter. When she stared at him as if he'd lost his mind, he shrugged. "If angels ever sang in heaven, they should be singing this minute." So he was spouting nonsense now?

Her eyebrows scrunched together. "Why?"

"Why are angels singing? Because, sweetheart, I love you. Don't you think that's something they should sing about?"

"You do?"

"Do I think angels should sing?" An irritated look sparkled in her eyes, and he wanted to sink to his knees and thank God for it. She was alive—awake and ready to take him on—and he fought against, then failed to stop the tears rolling down his face.

"Yeah, I do. Love you, that is. God, Sugar, you scared me. That's twice now, and I'm begging you, please, never again."

She frowned as she surveyed the room, her gaze stopping on the monitor. "Why am I in the hospital?"

"You don't remember?"

Ecstatic to be out of the hospital and home with Jamie, Sugar curled up next to him. The only thing marring her happiness was the blank space in her mind. Whenever she asked about that night, Jamie would change the subject.

"When you're ready, I'll tell you," was all he'd say.

The only reason she'd not insisted on hearing the details was because she couldn't honestly say, even to herself, that she was ready. Something at the back of her mind nagged at her, and deep in her soul, she knew whatever it was, it would hurt. Unable to put her finger on what was troubling her, she kept her thoughts to herself.

Junior jumped onto Jamie's lap and sat, staring at the man with unblinking green eyes. "Meep."

Sugar stifled a giggle. Her cat had learned he was an easy mark. "He's going to end up fat," she said when Jamie pulled a few treats out of his shirt pocket.

"Fat and happy," Jamie replied, unrepentant. "Watch this." He held one of the treats high, just out of reach of Junior's nose. "You want it, say meow."

"Eooul."

"Not quite there, my boy, but close enough for now." Jamie held out his hand with the treat resting on his palm, and her damn cat took it with a daintiness he'd never shown her when giving him something.

"Son of a bitch," she grumbled. "He bites my fingers if I do that."

The man she loved—heart, body, and soul—laid his head back on the couch and laughed so hard that all she could do was stare at him in wonder. That was the Jamie she'd seen pictures of in the newsprints she'd pored over. The always-happy boy—the one with a grin on his face who seemed ready to take on the world—had finally come home.

He was whole again, and before she could say the same, she'd have to face whatever it was he was keeping from her. It would be so easy to let it go and pretend there was nothing left to hurt her, but she was Sugar and Sugar was brave. She'd had to be to survive the attentions of Rodney. It was time to learn the truth.

Once his laughter faded, she took Jamie's hand. "I'm ready to know everything."

His eyes searched hers, and as if understanding it was time, he nodded. "Get dressed. Let's take my boat out."

"Are you warm enough?" Jamie glanced at Sugar, bundled up against the early-November chill. The gulf was calm, allowing the Sea Ray to cut smoothly through the water.

She grinned, lifting her face to the afternoon sun. "I'm as snug as a slug in a rug."

"Bug. It's a bug in a rug." Her eyes, the first thing about her he'd noticed, danced with mischief, and it finally dawned on him that she'd always intentionally misquoted her little sayings.

"What?" she asked when he laughed.

"Just thinking I should've caught on to you sooner. My bad." He put his arm around her shoulders and pulled her tight against him, where she belonged.

A week had passed since she'd been released from the hospital and he'd brought her back home to Pensacola. Seven days of avoiding her questions, insisting she needed to heal before she dealt with anything but getting better. Her headaches had ceased three days ago, along with the frequent naps.

Although knowing she was right and it was time to tell her, he was concerned with how she'd take the news. Wanting a peaceful place where they wouldn't be interrupted, he was taking her back to the spot he'd tried to teach her to swim.

After he dropped anchor, he went below and poured her a glass of wine. "What's the last thing you remember?" he asked once they were settled on the rear bench seat, Sugar sitting between his legs and leaning back against his chest. She took a sip of her wine, then reached for his hand and pulled it around her waist as if she needed his touch. Jamie spread his fingers over her side, wishing it were a warmer day so she didn't need the sweatshirt and fleece-lined jacket. He wanted to feel her skin to skin.

She lifted her face and peered up at him. "I remember ringing Rodney's doorbell, then nothing."

That was good and not good. The beating Vanders had given her wouldn't plague her dreams. He was sorry though that she didn't remember her father had finally done the right thing by her.

Although Jamie considered her father a coward for not facing his punishment like a man, he would never tell her that. Minimizing her treatment at the hands of Vanders, he told her of the events leading up to her father standing up for her. He dreaded telling her the end result.

When he finished, she was so still and quiet, he leaned forward and peered down at her, wondering if she'd fallen asleep. For the first few days after her head injury, she'd be awake one minute, then dead to the world the next with no warning. Her eyes were open though, her gaze fixed on the horizon. He took the empty wineglass from her, setting it on the floor of the boat.

"Are they in jail then?" she finally asked.

Jamie kissed the top of her head, wrapped both arms around her, and held her tight. "No, baby. They're both dead. In the end, your father came through for you. He saved you, sweetheart, and that's what matters."

He held her while she cried.

When her tears dried, she turned and plastered herself over him as if needing the shelter of his body. Her mouth found his, a hunger seeming to rage through her. He'd never been kissed so desperately before. Jamie understood. The day he'd killed his parents, he'd felt the same but there had been no one there to hold him, no one to share his grief. He was there for her though, always would be.

"Hold on," he said, and stood with her in his arms, carrying her below to the cabin. A profound sense of peace he hadn't felt in far too many years settled over him as she nestled her face against his neck. After easing her down to the bunk, he closed the door to keep the chill out, then reached up to the control panel and flipped on the heat.

Light coming in from the overhead hatch shone down on her, making her seem radiant, as if she glowed just for him. He set a knee on the bed beside her and placed his hands on either side of her head, capturing her gaze.

"I don't care what your name is. Sugar Darling, Hannah Conley, Janie Turner, doesn't matter. Whoever you choose to be, know this. I love you. You're not what I thought I wanted, but I was wrong. You're everything I need, all I'll ever want, and the only woman I will ever love." Blue eyes darkened to violet, his new favorite color.

"Show me, Jamie. Show me how much you love me."

"That I can do, sweetheart." Although he wanted to free the man he'd buried so deeply and rip off her clothes so he could make wild, dirty love to her, he knew how much she was hurting. She needed soft and tender, needed him to check his urges and just be there for her.

It was all right. He was no longer afraid of that man, but he could wait just a little longer to return. There was no doubt in his mind Sugar could take on that part of him without a blink of those beautiful eyes.

Heart surging with joy, Jamie unzipped her jacket and pulled her up so he could slip it off. Slowly peeling away each layer of her clothing—torture at its best—he finally had her naked. His eyes raked her body, and if asked what was his favorite part of her, he'd be at a loss to answer. No, he did know. All of her. Every lovely, exquisite inch of her.

He flattened his palm over her stomach and spread his fingers where someday his child would begin its life. What he'd long dreamed of was finally coming true. If the woman who would be his wife was as different from his mother as humanly possible, it no longer mattered. Somehow he knew his parents would have loved her.

"If you're just going to spend the night looking at me, then take off your clothes so I have something to stare at."

A wide grin split his face at the irritation glittering in her eyes, something not too many days ago he'd feared never seeing again. "Yes ma'am."

With her gaze following him in obvious interest, he decided to give her a show, and with teasing slowness, he stripped off jacket, shirt, shoes, and socks. Down to his jeans, he stepped next to the bunk and raised a brow.

His woman, being the smart lady she was, gave him a sultry smile and sat up, wiggling into place in front of him. Staying with his game of going slow, she inched the tip of one finger down the arrow of hair pointing to his groin. She paused, a hair's breadth from the button on his jeans. His cock jerked, demanding freedom from its confines.

"Not yet, big boy," she said, her gaze locked on the movement in his pants. She stroked his stomach, her fingers dancing over his skin. The sweet, familiar scent of her made his mouth water, and his breathing increased its pace. Desire sent a burning need through his blood when she tongued his navel.

"I warned you once about playing with fire, sweetheart."

Sugar lifted her face, grinning up at him. God, she loved the man. "Your growling doesn't scare me. You're my very own saint, and you love me. You said so yourself."

"So I did. Now take off my blasted pants."

She'd watched in awe the day he had—without any visible effort—planted a jack-assed jerk who'd dared to bother her facedown on the airport floor. He'd shown up at the Booby Palace and lifted Kyle off her as if the man weighed no more than a sack of potatoes, then dared him to bother her again. When she'd tried to run, he came for her and brought her back home, promising to protect her.

Although he'd held endless fascination for her, she'd never allowed herself to dream he would one day say he loved her. Only minutes ago, he'd held her while she cried for a father she'd lost the day her mother died. It would take time to deal with losing her daddy before they had a chance to reconcile, and she wasn't ready to talk about it. When she was, though, Jamie would be there for her, to listen and hold her if she cried again, and she was sure she would.

At the moment, the man she loved had a hungry look in his eyes, and it was for her. She was no longer alone, and that was all that mattered. That and loving her man back. She pressed her cheek against the hard length of him, needing to feel his desire for her for a few seconds.

"Sugar."

She turned her face into his jeans, hiding her smile. The man did love to growl. Knowing she was milliseconds away from being tossed on her back—which she really wouldn't mind at all—she lifted her head. After she'd unzipped his jeans, he pushed them and his briefs down his legs and stepped out of them.

"Now what?" she asked, eyeing the appendage jutting out at her, already a bead of moisture on the tip. Without waiting for an answer, she leaned forward and licked the pearly drop. His taste made her think of the sea, and with his hands fisted at his sides, he let her explore him with her tongue. He grew thicker and harder as her mouth devoured him, and when she wrapped her hand around the base of his shaft, he dug his fingers into her hair.

"Enough."

It took only one blink of her eyes before she was flat on her back, and Jamie was between her legs. There was an intensity in his expression she'd never seen from him before, as if he was fighting some kind of internal battle. As he stared at her, the taut lines around his eyes smoothed out, and his lips softened.

"Tender," he murmured. "You need tender from me today."

She wasn't sure she could bear tender without turning into an emotional mess of more tears. No, it wasn't what she needed. Not then. Grabbing his hands with hers, she pulled herself up so that she knelt in front of him. His erection brushed against her already slick folds, and she pressed her thighs together, capturing the hard length of him.

"Not tender," she growled, surprised she could even make such a sound. "I want you, Jamie, the real you. That's what I need from you today."

Blue eyes bored into hers. "You don't know what you're asking."

She clamped her teeth down on his shoulder and bit him. A hiss of air escaped his lungs as she rubbed her breasts over him, the springy dusting of his chest hair teasing her nipples. Other than the quickening cadence of his breathing, he didn't so much as twitch a single muscle. The man was entirely too self-contained, and she wanted him so lost in her that he couldn't remember his name.

"Damn it, Jamie, I want—"

"What? What do you want, sweetheart," he whispered, his mouth near her ear.

"You. The real you, the one you've tried to bury so deep that you almost forgot he existed." To put an exclamation point on her demand, she sucked his bottom lip into her mouth, nipping at it with her teeth. His arousal, held tightly between her legs, throbbed in time to her little bites. He grew harder, heating the sensitive skin of her inner thighs. She rocked her hips and discovered if she moved just right, she could slide her clit across the top of his erection. *Oh, God.* At her moan, he fisted her hair and took control of her mouth. He licked at her inner cheeks, then scraped across her teeth to tangle his tongue with hers.

Blood heated her veins and pulsated through her, making her breasts ache and her groin throb in a primitive beat as if drums pounded out a mating call ages old. One she had to answer, or she just might lose her mind. While he was busy devouring her mouth, she reached down and circled his shaft with her fingers.

With a grunt, he grabbed her hand and pulled it away. "No. Wrap your arms around my neck and hold on."

She did, and he slid a finger into her curls, then two fingers. They moved over her as if sliding through oil. Drenched already from desire more intense than she'd ever known, she felt almost embarrassed at how damp he'd made her.

"You're so damn wet for me, Sugar," he said, his voice sounding strangled.

"Don't cuss or I'll think I've corrupted my very own special saint."

He buried his face into her hair, his chuckle vibrating though her. "If I'm corrupted, I come to it willingly. Speaking of coming . . ."

Holding on to him for dear life, she closed her eyes and buried her face against his shoulder. Pressure built in the very core of her, a place she'd never known existed before Jamie. Little dots of bright white lights flashed on her eyelids, disappeared, then flashed again.

Suddenly, his thumb stayed on her clit—teasing it, toying with it—and the flashing stars grew in brightness and intensity, then exploded, looking as if someone waved a thousand sparklers in front of her eyes. The breath left her lungs as she tightened her muscles around the fingers still moving inside her, the feel of them now almost unbearably exquisite, a kind of pleasure-pain.

"Jamie, oh God, Jamie."

He rocked her as she floated back down to earth, safe in his arms. When her breathing returned to some semblance of normal, his mouth found hers. He gripped the cheeks of her bottom and pulled her against him, trapping his erection between their lower stomachs. His kiss was hot, hungry, and demanding.

"I love you, Jamie Turner," she said when he lowered her back onto the bed. He sat back on his legs and stared down at her with an intensity that should have unnerved her but didn't.

As he knelt over her, he studied her, seeming to be unsure of something. As if coming to a decision, he gave a slight nod. "There's a part of me I've done my best to crush, thinking it was part of the reason my life had gone so wrong. It may have been true at the time, but with you, I feel like I can let go and just be me. That part I'm talking about, Sugar, sometimes likes his sex a little rough and dirty. If that scares you, tell me now."

A thrill—much like cresting the top of a roller coaster and plunging downhill—shot through her at his admission. "Hmm. A little rough and dirty? That sounds interesting." Actually, it sounded beyond interesting. That he felt free to be who he really was with her, after years of pretending otherwise, sent her heart into ecstasy.

She lifted her hands, palms up, and waved her fingers in a come-hither motion. "Bring it on, tough guy."

# CHAPTER TWENTY-NINE

A rush of adrenaline shot through Jamie's veins, followed by doubt. Sugar had been grieving the loss of her father and he'd sworn to himself he would be gentle with her. But inside, it felt like a dark and hungry panther resided deep down in a cage, prowling as he impatiently demanded the gate be opened. If he didn't free the creature, he'd soon be eaten from the inside out.

"I won't hurt you, baby, but if you're the slightest bit uncomfortable, say my name. Say *Saint*." It would be the one word that would penetrate a brain he knew would soon be filled wall-to-wall with nothing but Sugar and his need for her.

"Okay," she said, her eyes full of trust.

He was so hot and bothered, so turned on that it took every ounce of his willpower not to just bury himself inside her and pound her into the mattress. Her legs were spread around his knees and her sex, glistening in the aftermath of her orgasm, beckoned him. What he craved right now was a taste of her.

Along with that taste, he wanted her at his mercy. Jamie reached up, opened an overhead cabinet, and pulled out a soft cashmere scarf. Although he kept it aboard for days when the weather turned chilly, it was about to serve an even better purpose.

"Give me your hands." She eyed the strip of material with a mix of uncertainty and interest. "I've already promised I won't hurt you.

This," he let the scarf dangle from his hand, "involves trust. Do you trust me, Sugar?"

That she held such faith in him, willingly offering her hands without questioning his intentions, humbled him. With eyes burning from unshed tears, he wrapped the cashmere in a figure eight around her wrists, then realized there was no place on the bunk to tie the ends.

"This is going to have to be a two-way trust issue, sweetheart." He lifted her arms over her head and tucked the ends between the mattress and cabin wall. "You're going to have to believe they're tied to the headboard, and as much as you might want to, you can't get loose."

Her eyes never leaving his, she nodded, then pretended to tug on the scarf. "You're right, I can't get loose."

Love—hot, profound, soul-searing love—filled him, almost overwhelming him. "I love you, baby," he whispered past the lump in his throat. Then he kissed her lush, inviting mouth. She tasted of berries and exotic spices from her earlier wine, and he knew he'd never get enough of her. Not now, not ever.

He reluctantly pulled away, and trailed his lips down her throat, down to one breast, tasting her all the way. Her low moan, when he caught the peaked tip of her nipple between his teeth, sent blood rushing south, leaving him aching to be inside her. But not yet.

After minutes spent worshipping each breast, he trailed a path down her stomach to the juncture of a vee of curls. He paused to inhale the earthy, rich scent of her, giving way to a moan of his own. Pushing onto his knees, he placed his hands on her inner thighs and spread her legs, and was momentarily caught by the erotic sight of pink skin glistening with dewdrop wetness.

"Beautiful." A flush of red colored her cheeks, but she didn't try to close her legs. No longer able to resist, he lowered his face and feasted on her, lapping his tongue over her sex. She tasted of salted honey, uniquely Sugar. He would never get enough of that either. In fifty years, he would still be begging her to allow him to taste her.

When she began to squirm underneath him, he swirled his tongue over her clit, then nipped at it with his teeth. Her pelvis lifted from the bed, pushing against his mouth. She was a quiet one in bed, but highly responsive to his any touch. Still keeping her hands above her as if truly bound, she lifted her head and watched him eat away at her. His gaze rose to hers, and he watched as her eyes turned to an even darker shade of violet, and her irises dilated. Dark pools of desire, he thought as he looked at her.

Her head fell back onto the pillow, and she called out his name as shivers traveled from her breasts down to her legs. Her heaving chest and roughened panting almost had him climaxing.

Amazing. If he lasted through this bout of lovemaking still knowing his name, it would be a miracle. He reached inside the open cabinet and grabbed a condom. Tearing the foil with his teeth, he rolled it on. Someday in the not-too-distant future, he wanted to see her belly rounded with his child. First though, they needed time for just the two of them. And a wedding needed to happen.

As her watchful gaze followed his movements, one side of her mouth quirked up. "Next time, you get tied up and I get to be the boss."

That sounded like more fun than he'd had in years. "Deal. Remember, if anything I do is too much, all you have to do is say *Saint*."

"Okay, but you won't be hearing me say it."

That sounded like a challenge.

An hour later, he had the front of her plastered against the cabin wall, penned in by his body, and her hands held captive above her head by one of his.

"Say it," he demanded.

She shook her head.

Four times he'd made her come, and he was well on his way to his second release. She had to be sore and tired, but his woman apparently had her pride. He slid out almost to his tip, then back in, all the while massaging her clit with his finger. When he felt her inner muscles tighten around him, he stilled. She tried to rock back into him, but he had her pressed too tight to the wall.

"Say it."

"No."

God, he loved this crazy, stubborn woman. "Have it your way then." He brought her to the peak again, stopping just before her point of no return. "You ready to say it, baby?" He nibbled on her ear, then swirled his tongue around the little pink shell.

"Saint! There, I said it, damn you. Saint. Saint. Saint."

A roaring noise in his ears deafened him as she clenched down on him and screamed his name. He came so hard and fast that his knees gave out, and he brought them both to the floor with her back pressed to his chest.

"Jesus H. Christ," he muttered between gasps for breath.

She swiveled in his hold until they were face-to-face. "Don't cuss. I'll do all our cursing for us. It's just not right when you do it."

Fascinating that it bothered her, a woman who let naughty words slip past her lips without the blink of an eye. "It's that important to you?"

Her eyes had returned to their lovely blue color. "It is."

"Then I'll leave all the cursing to my lady." He pulled her damp, sweaty hair away from her face and kissed the corner of her eye. Now that his body had its strength back, he lifted them off the floor and returned to the bunk. Pulling the cover aside, he lowered her to the bed and crawled in beside her.

"I love you, Sugar." He lifted onto an elbow and peered down at her, this woman he needed by his side. He pulled the covers over them. "Go to sleep, sweetheart."

Sugar put her hand in Jamie's as he helped her onto the dock. The boat had rocked lazily the night before, and she'd slept like a baby. Or, the reason could have been because Jamie had loved her so hard and so deeply, that her mind was filled with nothing but him. Whatever the reason, she was happy in a way she'd never expected to be again.

"Come here," he said, pulling her to the back of the boat. "I want to show you something."

When he let go of her hand and looked expectantly at her, she was at a loss as to what she was supposed to see. There was a pelican standing at the end of the dock, but that wouldn't put the kind of light in his eyes that said her reaction was important to him. She turned in a slow circle and almost missed it.

*Oh, wow.* She froze and stared at the name painted on the back of his boat. When had he done it, and how had she missed it? Although when they'd come aboard the day before, he'd not let her near the back where she could see her name scripted across the . . . what the hell did one call the back end of a boat? Not that it mattered, just that *Sweet Sugar* was there in a beautiful violet-colored script.

"Well, I think I'm fixin' to cry," she said, then turned to Jamie and buried her face into his chest.

He circled his arms around her waist, the flat of his palms resting on her lower back. "There's just one more thing I need you to do, baby."

It took a minute for his words to penetrate, but once they did, she nodded. "Whatever you need from me, I'll give you. Today, tomorrow, and forever. I love you, Jamie Turner. You haven't asked me to marry you but when you do, the answer's yes. A resounding yes."

His lighthearted laugh rolled over her. "Impatient little thing, aren't you?"

They'd both been crippled by events beyond their control, but they'd come through still kicking and screaming. Oh, how she loved the man who'd not all that long ago tried to resist her. Eyes she'd always thought of as angel eyes glanced away as if afraid she wouldn't understand whatever he was about to ask of her.

"What, Jamie?"

He flicked an uncertain glance at her. "Will you go shopping with me tomorrow, help me pick out new furniture? New stuff just for us?"

This incredible man thought she wouldn't want any of his parents' leftovers. Silly, silly man. "No." He blinked, and she bit down on her smile. "No. Tomorrow, we'll decide together which items of your parents that we want to keep, and then the next day we'll go shopping." Although he'd lived in the past too long, she wasn't about to help him forget the people he'd loved so deeply.

An instant later, she was held against his chest as his warm breath caressed her ear. "Sugar, the first thing I'll do every morning when I get up, and then every night before I go to sleep, is to thank God that you found me."

Well, she did kind of pick him before he even knew he wanted to be picked, but she had her own blessings to count where he was concerned.

"I love you, Jamie, but the next time you dare me to cry uncle . . . rather, Saint, so not happening."

He gave her a wicked grin. "Bet I can make you."

She bet he could, too.

# Acknowledgments

Where to start? With you the reader, I think. I would write even if no one read my books, but turns out they do. Because of my books, I have made so many friends all over the world. For that I am deeply, sincerely thankful. Your posts on social media begging for the next story keep me motivated to write the best possible book for you. Your e-mails telling me that you loved a particular book, or which hero is your favorite, or how you related to the heroine, are so special to me, and I save them all. So, thank you from the bottom of my heart. If you took the time to leave a review for one of my books, or any book for that matter, you have every author's gratitude.

Like most authors, I have a support group, a tight circle of friends who are there for me, be it to discuss a plot issue, read/ critique for each other, or whatever. Some I have met and some I haven't, but each and every one is almost as important to me as the air I breathe. They keep me sane; they often make me laugh; they tell me when I've gone astray with my story. Jenny Holiday, we've been together from the beginning and have shared our disappointments and celebrated our successes (looking forward to sending the champagne glass tiara back to you). You know I love you! Lindsey Ross (super-duper beta reader) and Felice Stevens (super-duper author), don't either one of you ever break up with me. I'd just pull the covers over my head and never get out of bed if you did. Our late-night chats, sharing our secrets, laughing at our dumb typos—for all that and more, I love you both. Miranda Liasson, Lucky 13 Golden Heart® sister and now one of my Montlake Romance sisters, my life is better for knowing you. Truthfully, my life is better for knowing all of my amazingly talented Golden Heart® and Montlake Romance sisters. With every book the circle of people important to me grows wider, and that is such a wonderful thing.

This is the third book of the K2 Special Services series, and I want to say a big thank-you to my Montlake Romance editor, Maria Gomez. You're the greatest! And, Maria, however do I thank you for assigning Melody Guy as my developmental editor for each book? She totally gets me and her suggestions for improving my stories are spot on. My copy editor, Scott Calamar, is the best, and he's even learning to grin and bear my fragmented sentences. To everyone at Montlake Romance who plays a part in seeing my books published, thank you! You have my sincere appreciation.

Then there is my agent, Courtney Miller-Callihan of Sanford J. Greenburger Associates. You are awesome, Courtney! There are too many reasons to list, so I'll just say thank you for everything, because you know what all those everythings are. xoxoxo

# About the Author

*Photo © 2015 Catherine Ford-Coates*

A native of Florida, Sandra now lives in the beautiful Blue Ridge Mountains of North Carolina. Before achieving her dream of writing books, Sandra managed a Harley-Davidson dealership (and yes, she rode a Harley), and was once the manager of a private airport where she had the opportunity to fly in a stunt plane while the pilot performed aerobatic maneuvers. She thought that was great fun, as was the thrilling time she skydived.

These days, Sandra spends her time writing. In addition to *Crazy for Her*—a 2013 Golden Heart® finalist for Romantic Suspense—her works include *Someone Like Her*, book two in the K2 Special Services series, and the Regency Romance novels, *The Training of a Marquess*, winner of the 2013 Golden Claddagh Award, and *The Letter*, winner of the 2014 Golden Quill Award for published authors.

Sandra is a member of Romance Writers of America. Connect with Sandra:

Website: www.sandra-owens.com

Facebook: www.facebook.com/SandraOwensAuthor

Twitter: @SandyOwens1